Unsurprisingly, Rodney appeared at my feet. He wound around my calves, letting his tail touch me, even as he settled at my ankles. If I wasn't mistaken, he jingled his collar more than necessary and scratched at it, looking me straight in the eyes.

Not a light was on. Only moonlight through the stained-glass cupola three floors above gave the slightest illumination.

"Books," I said. "Tell me. Which one?"

To my right, a faint glow, barely perceptible, came from fiction. I followed the light and found a volume buzzing with energy on a shelf close to the fireplace. I pulled the book from the shelf. It was warm in my hands.

A slender volume, a horror novella, I noted and had the sudden desire to cram it back into the shelf and leave. No. I'd asked for help, and this is what the books provided. It was my duty to follow up.

As my grandmother had taught me, I closed my eyes and prepared to let my fingers shuffle through the book's pages. The book wouldn't open. My finger stopped at its title.

I took the book, my finger still lying on its cover, to a table lamp and clicked it on.

"*The Man in the Picture*," it read.

I opened to the title page. Although the novella had been written recently, it was set in the nineteenth century, the Wilfred family's world when they first came to the region.

The man in the picture.

This was my clue . . .

Books by Angela M. Sanders

BAIT AND WITCH

SEVEN-YEAR WITCH

Published by Kensington Publishing Corp.

Seven-Year Witch

Angela M. Sanders

KENSINGTON
PUBLISHING CORP.

www.kensingtonbooks.com

KENSINGTON BOOKS are published by

Kensington Publishing Corp.
119 West 40th Street
New York, NY 10018

All Kensington titles, imprints, and distributed lines are available at special quantity discounts for bulk purchases for sales promotion, premiums, fund-raising, educational, or institutional use.

Special book excerpts or customized printings can also be created to fit specific needs. For details, write or phone the office of the Kensington Sales Manager: Attn.: Sales Department. Kensington Publishing Corp., 119 West 40th Street, New York, NY 10018. Phone: 1-800-221-2647.

The K logo is a trademark of Kensington Publishing Corp.

First Printing: September 2021
ISBN-13: 978-1-4967-2876-0
ISBN-10: 1-4967-2876-9

ISBN-13: 978-1-4967-2877-7 (ebook)
ISBN-10: 1-4967-2877-7 (ebook)

10 9 8 7 6 5 4 3 2 1

Printed in the United States of America

CHAPTER ONE

Still catching her breath, Mrs. Garlington plopped herself at a stool at the counter of Darla's Café. She unsnapped the plastic rain bonnet from her blue-tinted hair. "I can see that none of you believe me."

"Of course we believe you," Darla said in a placating tone. "Soft-boiled egg?"

"I'm telling you, it's why the retreat center hasn't broken ground yet," she said. "The land is cursed. That awful man I just saw is proof."

The envelope I'd randomly selected from Grandma's box that morning for my witchcraft lesson was on curses. I'd learned that these lessons had a way of reflecting real life. So, my ears perked up at Mrs. Garlington's pronouncement.

"Cursed? Tell us again," I said, earning a reproachful glance from Darla.

Mrs. Garlington faced me from a few stools down. "It was like this. I was taking a walk and letting the muse wash over me—feeding the muse is a vital part of being a poet—when a black SUV roared in, kicking up gravel."

"You were at the old mill site, right?" I asked.

"Yes. The cursed site. The muse had demanded an especially long walk today. You see, I'm working on an epic poem, and—"

"What did the black SUV do?" I knew better than to let Mrs. Garlington be distracted.

She flinched at the memory. "The windows were tinted, and I couldn't see inside. Then, the driver's side window slid down. I jumped into the brush and hid behind a tree."

"Maybe he was lost," Duke said. Duke used to drive a forklift at the mill. When it closed, he'd repaired coin-operated telephones, which turned out to be a shortsighted career move. Lately, he was a jack-of-all-trades, and, contrary to the old saying, had mastered them all.

"Oh, but you should have seen him. Dark glasses, black jacket, tall and skinny, from what I could tell. And he had a shoulder holster."

We all gasped. Our town, Wilfred, was rural, and guns weren't unheard of, but holstered handguns were things of crime movies.

"One thing I appreciate about you, Helen, is your imagination," Darla said. "Soft-boiled egg and an extra-large pot of tea on the house. You've had a rough morning."

"I bet it was the retreat's contractor," Duke said. "He set up an office trailer beyond the millpond."

Unwilling to let the drama go, Mrs. Garlington reluctantly sighed. "I suppose it's possible. But I still insist the site is cursed. Everything on it is doomed to fail. I wrote a poem about it once."

The few people at the counter near her, including Darla, chose that moment to busy themselves elsewhere. Mrs. Garlington's poems tended to be long affairs larded with nineteenth-century turns of phrase and metaphors involving shipwrecks and orphans.

She'd closed her eyes and was about to launch into the first stanza, when the café's front door opened, letting in spring air thick with Pacific Northwest drizzle. A man stood, door ajar, surveying the room.

"Or maybe this is him," I whispered to Mrs. Garlington.

She glanced at the door. "Not him."

"In or out," Darla said to the man in the doorway. "Pick one."

The man let the door close behind him. Judging from his meticulously crafted sideburns and angular glasses, he was from a big city hipster neighborhood.

"Charming," he said and ambled to the counter, taking the seat next to Mrs. Garlington that we locals avoided. Aside from regular outbursts of her own poetry, Mrs. Garlington taught organ lessons and liked to hum snatches between bites, sometimes shooting sprays of egg yolk or toast crumbs.

"Coffee, please," the stranger said, and Darla served him with the coffee pot that seemed to be permanently affixed to her hand. After a sip, he set his mug down in surprise. "This is good."

"Uh-huh," Darla said.

"I don't suppose you have anything that isn't, um, made from a mix?"

"We mix everything that needs it," she said.

Darla didn't go for being condescended to. Someone passing through Wilfred—although most people didn't make it this far off the main highway unless they had a reason—might have mistaken Darla for your typical middle-aged, no-nonsense waitress with a taste for animal prints and snappy comebacks. In fact, she was Wilfred's de facto mayor.

"Try the shrimp and grits," I said. Despite being a native Oregonian, Darla had a way with Southern food.

"Thank you." His gaze took me in, clogs to mess of red curls, and he must have decided I was okay. "Lewis Cruikshank. Architect for the new retreat center."

"Josie Way, librarian." We shook hands.

He set a leather bag by his feet, and I heard his copy of *Finnegan's Wake* grumbling inside. Books talked to me. The novel was unhappy being lugged around and only having a page or two read every few weeks to impress onlookers. Thomas Pynchon's work often had similar complaints.

"Architect, you say?" Mrs. Garlington asked. "We were just talking about the retreat center. When are you going to break ground?"

"It's been a wet spring, but soon."

"What's planned?" I asked. "Anything you can show us?"

"Not much. I have a few ideas jotted down."

Just then, the door opened again, and Thor and Buffy burst in, Thor wearing a cape and Buffy carrying a sparkly pink purse. They must have been watching from across the street, and when they saw a stranger's car in the lot, they made a beeline.

Thor stopped in front of the architect. At eight years

old, he was barely taller than the counter. "I am Thor the Fluoridator, and—"

"Fluoridator?" Cruikshank said.

"Yes," he said firmly.

I'd tried to convince Thor he might want to give "magnificent" or "mighty" or even "the all-seeing" a try, but he liked the sound of "fluoridator," and there was no changing his mind.

Thor threw his cape over his shoulders. "For a small fee, I will mystify you with my magical skill. Buffy?"

Buffy extracted from her purse a worn deck of cards with the Taj Mahal printed on the back. Buffy was a few years younger than her brother. Despite her wide-eyed resemblance to a doll, reinforced by her love of pink and purple, she was the brains of the operation.

"Thor," Darla said. "You're interrupting. Besides, I've already told you not to bother my customers with your magic tricks."

"But I—"

"Do I have to call your grandma?"

"Come on, Thor," Buffy said. "Mrs. Esperanza just went into the PO Grocery. She hasn't seen our trick yet." They scrambled from the café almost as quickly as they'd come in.

"Use the door handle, not the glass," Darla yelled after them. She turned to the architect. "Sorry. My sister's grandchildren. I'd love to see the drawings."

"I don't have much yet—just sketches. The only solid plans so far are for preparing the site." He reached into his bag, earning a groan from the novel, and flattened a sketch pad on the counter. "I'm here for inspiration and to meet with the owners and contractor." He tapped a page.

"Here's one idea. Notice the reference to tribal dwellings."

We crowded around him. The drawings showed a building with conical protrusions that made it look like a ceramic hedgehog.

"Tribal?" Mrs. Garlington said, squinting. "What tribe is that?"

The architect rolled up his sleeves, revealing the edge of a blue-black tattoo. "In this one, the main hall has a thirty-foot ceiling with skylights." He pointed to a long, lower building in the rear. "Those would be the residences for people who come for longer retreats. In this sketch, the center faces the river and the millpond."

"It's damp out there," Duke said.

"Oh, I know. Wilfred is on a flood plain," Lewis Cruikshank said. "We're going to rebuild the levee. First step."

His shrimp and grits arrived, and after replacing the sketch pad in his satchel, he tucked in. We slowly returned to our seats. Between bites, he examined the diner, casting a glance toward the attached tavern, then the parking lot.

My specialty was folk history, but I tried to keep up on national news, and Cruikshank's name sounded familiar. A museum in Baltimore, that was it. Cruikshank had designed it. Plus an airport in Amsterdam. Wilfred was so small it wasn't even a proper town. It had lost its incorporation years ago. Why had he even taken a job here?

The architect cleared his throat.

"Pardon?" Mrs. Garlington said.

"Great layout. You ever think about adding a patio?"

"Where?" Darla said.

"You could punch in a door there," he said, pointing

his fork toward the café's northern wall, "and orient the patio away from the road. It would be a fairly inexpensive job and would double your seating in the summer." He set down his fork and flipped over the paper place mat next to him. "Do you mind?"

"Go ahead," Darla said, elbows on the counter.

He sketched an aerial view of the café, including the gravel parking lot out front, then, more slowly, outlined a patio that connected with the corner of the café closest to the kitchen. "That way you can run food straight outside." He finished the drawing with a striped awning and a potted tree.

"Not bad," Darla said. "May I keep it?"

He slid the place mat to her. "With my compliments."

"How long will you be in Wilfred?" she asked.

"A few days. Just long enough for the meeting and to get a good sense of the area. Maybe do some hiking. In fact, can you recommend a place to stay? I didn't realize Wilfred was so far from Portland."

"No hotel here," I said. Besides Darla's diner-slash-tavern, Wilfred boasted only the library, a church, the PO Grocery, and Patty's This-N-That, which was getting a lot of attention thanks to the karaoke lounge she'd recently installed in the basement.

"I'll tell you what. I've got an empty home at the Magnolia," Darla said. Behind the diner was the Magnolia Rolling Estates, the modest trailer court where Duke and a handful of others lived. "I'll make you a good price. Or we could talk design for a patio."

"Sold," he said, cleaning his plate. He turned to me. "Maybe you could point me toward some resources on local history."

"I'd be happy to show you our collection," I said.

"Stop by anytime. The library's up the hill. You can't miss it."

"If we do this right, it will be a spectacular retreat center," he said. "Artistically engaging, useful—something people will come from all over to see."

"Just watch out for gangsters driving black SUVs," Darla said with a wink.

Mrs. Garlington rapped her knife against the shell of her soft-boiled egg, and it gave with a crack. "Don't say I didn't warn you. That land is cursed."

As I walked back up the hill, I pondered Mrs. Garlington's warning. Somehow, I wasn't surprised that the morning's witchcraft lesson was about curses. This kind of synchronicity didn't even raise an eyebrow anymore. I planned to read the lesson tonight.

I took the bridge up the sleepy two-lane highway over the Kirby River and cut right toward the old Thurston Wilfred mansion, now the library. I couldn't help but cast a wistful glance at Big House as I approached. It had been six months since Sam had left, but my memory of him was too sticky to shed. Now the house stood empty.

As I rounded the corner, I stopped short. Parked in front of Big House was a moving van. Was it taking things in or out? In, I noted. Two men hustled boxes, one marked "stereo" and the other "books."

"Hey," I shouted to one of the movers. "Someone's moving in?"

The older mover, the one who looked like he was in charge, paused with his hand truck and grunted. "Yeah, I'd say someone is moving in."

When Sam had left town, he'd told me he wanted to return to Wilfred. He'd also mentioned a wife and had shown no particular interest in me besides brotherly affection. However, Wilfred's grapevine had said he was in the middle of a divorce. Despite myself, I felt my hopes rise.

"Who?" I said.

"Don't know," the man said, resuming the push of his hand truck. "We move, we don't interview."

"Sam," the books told me as they jostled in their crate. "Sam Wilfred."

Well, well, I thought. *He's come home.*

CHAPTER TWO

I opened the library for the day and tried not to dwell on Sam's return. After all, I had plenty to take care of here. The library was in a Victorian mansion built by Wilfred's founder and converted into a library by his youngest daughter, Marilyn Wilfred. At best, the library was unconventional. At worst, alarmingly eccentric. The pipe organ in the former dressing room on the mansion's second floor was home to Mrs. Garlington's music lessons and impromptu concerts. The old house's kitchen was an informal town gathering spot, dispensing nearly as much coffee as Darla's Café down the hill. The conservatory was a classroom space, as well as Roz's—the assistant librarian—office, where she wrote romance novels when she wasn't on duty.

And, of course, my cat, Rodney, wandered the stacks. He looked tough with his black coat and torn ear, but he was a softie and demanded nightly brushing to maintain his silky fur. When I call him "my cat," I might be going too far. Locals said he'd showed up only a few days before I'd arrived, but he'd attached himself to me right away. He now lived in my apartment on the library's top floor.

"Your boyfriend's back. Sam," Roz said, appearing from nowhere. Personality-wise, she was a middle-aged Eeyore, but she was built of mounded surfaces—curvy figure, round face, big round eyes. She rarely took the optimistic view, but I knew her heart was as warm as a basket of puppies.

"I see." I busied myself with labeling the new releases.

"Don't you want to know why?"

I shrugged, not because I didn't want to know, but because I wasn't sure if I wanted to know just then. I needed to absorb his return at my own pace.

"Why are you being so coy?" Roz rested a hand on a plump hip. Thanks to her romance novels, written as Eliza Chatterly Windsor, she professed herself an expert in love.

"What? I'm not being coy. Yes, I saw the moving van."

"Uh-huh," she said. "Word is, he's back for good. He's applying for the vacant sheriff's position. Plans to settle here."

My face warmed. "You must have dropped by Darla's after I left."

"Dylan's dad came in. He'd talked to Jimmy from the gas station in Gaston, who'd heard it from one of the moving guys."

"Interesting," I said in my most blasé tone. "You know he's married, right?"

"Last fall he was getting a divorce. Timing's right for him to be single about now." When I didn't respond, she said, "All right. I give up. If you need me, I'll be working in Natural History."

When I'd arrived, Wilfred's entire collection was indexed in a card catalog. I'd convinced the library's trustees to wire the library for the Internet, and now Roz and I—with the occasional help of Dylan, our high school intern—were putting the collection into an online database.

Mostly ignoring the moving van next door, I engrossed myself in the day's work. I kept busy helping patrons, shelving returns, and taking care of the minutiae that filled a librarian's day, with only a few peeks out the window to monitor the progress next door. Midafternoon, Duke ambled into the front parlor, now Circulation. Duke's manners might be crude sometimes, but he was meticulous about his ironed Western shirts and the Brylcreemed curl in his hair.

"I'm talking with the contractor about taking on the role of foreman on the retreat center project," he said, clearly too proud to keep it in.

"No kidding, Duke. That's great."

He seemed to stand a few inches taller. "Said he wanted someone to be his go-between with the locals. I know this town. I know how to get him the crew he needs. Plus, we're both Navy veterans."

Which reminded me. I pulled two heavy tomes from the hold shelf. One of them emitted faint sounds of explosions and the whirring of plane engines. The other dryly recited battle dates.

"Here are the World War II books you requested. Does this have to do with that tank out back of the trailer court?"

"That's no tank. It's my M29 Weasel, an amphibious vehicle I bought from a fellow out at the coast. I'm getting it running again. Studebaker engine, and a devil to get parts for."

"What are you going to do with it?"

"World War Two military vehicle club," he said. "We should never forget our history."

"I couldn't agree more." I'd be willing to bet it was more the quirks of the vehicle's engine than the battles it had been in that interested Duke.

He bundled the books under an arm. "Say, did you hear Sam Wilfred is back?"

"No kidding?" I said.

"Josie, I'm glad you're here." It was Ruth Littlewood, bird-watcher and inheritor of a vegetable canning operation in the valley that she ran with an iron fist. She was built on the no-frills concept—short gray hair, nondescript clothing—and usually had a pair of binoculars at hand's reach. "It's about that cat." She was never one to mince words.

"Rodney?"

"Letting cats roam outdoors is irresponsible. Cats are the number-one predator of songbirds."

Rodney wasn't a normal cat. All I had to do was relax for a moment and place my hand on his head to know he wasn't a hunter. He liked chasing bugs and sleeping in the blackberry bushes, but birds were something to watch, not attack. I couldn't tell that to Ruth. No one knew I was a witch or that Rodney and I had a special bond.

"But I—"

Ruth held up a palm. "No. I know what you're going to say. He's used to going outdoors and can't possibly stay inside or he'll go nuts."

She was right. That was exactly what I would have said.

"So I'm proposing a compromise. A collar." She dangled a blue collar with a bell. "This way birds will hear him coming. It's not ideal, but it's a step in the right direction. Eventually we'll be able to transition him indoors."

"He's not a hunter."

"How do you know? Do you follow him everywhere he goes? Cats are biologically programmed to kill. They can't help it. Look, I'm not asking you to lock him inside. Yet. Simply make him wear this collar." She dropped it on the circulation desk.

"Okay," I said. Rodney and I could work it out later, but I wasn't feeling optimistic. "Thank you."

"Happy to help." Ruth Littlewood turned for the front door. She pivoted just before entering the foyer. "Sam Wilfred's back. Have you heard?"

I managed a weak smile. "Yes."

CHAPTER THREE

That night, I sautéed a chicken breast on the tiny mid-century stove upstairs, in my apartment. Ever since my grandmother's spell had been broken and my magic released, my senses were on overdrive—including taste. In the old days, when I'd lived in D.C. and worked at the Library of Congress, I was happy with takeout and microwaved frozen meals. Not any longer.

I was trying something new: blending the recipe for a classic chicken paillard with another recipe for a curry. Two books lay open on the counter next to me.

"*Oh là*. Too much spice," the French cookbook said. "Just butter and a hint of garlic. Maybe parsley. Or, if you can get chervil—"

"No, I say," the Indian cookbook replied. "Perhaps cardamom. Did you roast the spices yourself?"

"Hush," I told them. "This is my party."

"Very well," the Indian cookbook said. "But don't blame me when it has no pizzazz."

"Pizzazz! Because she has added no cream," the French cookbook said.

I shut both books, planning to place them in their new home on the second floor. For years, the cookbooks had been shelved in the library's bathroom, and generations of Wilfredians dropping in for a bath in the extra-large tub had warped their pages.

Dinner in hand, I settled at the kitchen table and set my grandmother's lesson next to me. Before she'd died, Grandma had written me more than a hundred letters about magic. My mother, forced to admit I'd inherited my dead grandmother's magical powers, had sent me the letters about six months ago, soon after I'd moved to Wilfred. My instructions were to choose a letter at random and absorb its lesson before moving on to the next. This morning over coffee, I'd slit one open. The top of the yellowed page had read simply "Curse."

I was tempted to take the lesson to the living room, which, like my bedroom, faced Big House, but I resisted the impulse to try to glimpse Sam through a lit window. I needed to focus. Besides, this infatuation was ridiculous. I concentrated on the matter at hand.

Some of my grandmother's lessons I'd swallowed whole and immediately put into practice. For instance, the lesson on bibliomancy was fun, front to back. I learned I could open a book, eyes closed, and point to a sentence, and it had a lesson for me. Sometimes the result was opaquer than others—or more mundane. For instance, one effort at bibliomancy landed on a scrap of dialogue. "Philip," the character said, "remember your umbrella." Sure enough, a thunderstorm had kicked in just as I made my way up the hill with a bag of groceries. The umbrella had saved me from a complete soaking.

As I did with each letter, I approached this one slowly, first acknowledging the subject, then reading it. Later, I'd put the lesson to the test with my magic.

Rodney leapt to the chair next to me, his purring soothing. The birthmark on my shoulder tingled. Although I followed the words with my eyes, I heard Grandma's voice, soft and sure, as I read.

"Dear Josie," she began. I smoothed it onto the table. It had been folded in its envelope since before she'd died, more than a decade earlier.

> *Dear Josie,*
> *I am so sorry this lesson has come up for you.*

Rodney's purr melted into a faint growl for a few seconds as I caught my breath.

> *I hope you selected this lesson several years into your apprenticeship. A curse is complex, not easy to understand. It can be something almost accidentally created and just as easily dissolved, or something nearly as firm and permanent as the earth itself. I'll give you an overview of what curses are about, but I'm afraid I can't help you as completely as I'd like to. If I were there . . . but if you're reading this letter, I'm not. I'm so sorry, my darling.*

As I read, I ate a few bites of dinner—better than either of the cookbooks would have wagered. The lesson on curses had come up for a reason. All of my lessons did. I was coming into a situation where I'd benefit from knowing how to deal with them.

Tonight, though . . . I wasn't ready to read on. My mind was somewhere else. I folded the lesson and returned it to its envelope to study later. Then I gave in to the impulse to look out the window overlooking Big House.

"I'll just have a peek," I told Rodney. He followed me into the living room and leapt into the empty kindling box next to the carved walnut fireplace. Rodney never could resist a box.

I paused before nudging the curtain aside. Why did I torture myself? I knew Sam was married. I'd let the rumors that he was in the middle of a divorce influence my feelings. Just because he'd snuck into my dreams, I'd let my infatuation simmer. It was simply a silly hope, I reminded myself. A disappointment waiting to happen.

Outside, a soft spring rain melted the view into a cloudy gray. In Sam's old room, the one he'd slept in as a boy, and the room he'd favored when he was last in Wilfred, his figure was easy to make out. My pulse leapt, and I moved out of view. It was Sam, all right.

Last fall, he'd sometimes play opera on the stereo, and the music had drifted over the stretch of garden between our houses. I unlatched my window and pushed it up. No music tonight, just the soothing patter of rain on the shingles.

He was home. He might be single now. We had a connection, I knew we did. My heart lightened and began to warm. After all these months, he'd returned. Now we might see where that connection would lead.

Then I heard it, a baby's wail, sharp and clear.

I let the curtain drop. Maybe the curse wasn't on the old mill site. Maybe it was on my love life.

CHAPTER FOUR

The next morning, coffee cake in hand and a determined smile on my face, I braced myself and stepped into the damp grass.

When I'd gone to bed the night before, Emily Post's etiquette book—a print from the 1960s, judging from its cover—was on my bedside table. The books I needed had a way of turning up there. I didn't even have to crack its pages. I knew what it wanted me to do, so I'd risen early and put on an apron. A cookbook was already open to the pull-apart coffee cake recipe.

I knocked on Big House's front door. Sam answered. He held a baby over one shoulder, its head on a burping towel.

"Josie. I was planning on coming to see you as soon as Nicky was fed. How have you been?"

Sam's lips turned down slightly—he frowned when he

was happy—and watch out when he smiled. His eyes relaxed into a sleepy squint. Except for the curly-headed infant in his arms, he looked just as he had last fall: barely receding hairline, firm chin and full mouth, and a deceptively lazy expression.

There were a few things I'd like to have said, such as "I thought you were getting a divorce," and "Why didn't you stay in touch?" but, instead, I held out the cake tin. "I made this for you." My smile was beginning to ache now. I nodded toward the baby. "Looks like you've been busy."

"This is Nicky," he said. "Thurston Wilfred the sixth, of course, but we call him Nicky."

A laughing brunette bounded up behind him. She was petite and as beautifully formed as a Dresden figurine with a heart-shaped face, but she wore a contemporary black dress in an avant-garde cut you couldn't get at the mall. Her face broke into a wide smile when she saw me.

"Hello," she said and thrust a cool hand into mine. "Fiona Wilfred."

I forced my lips into an answering smile. "Josie Way. I live next door. I'm the librarian."

She was serious for a moment while she took me in, head to toe, then a smile flashed across her face. "Such lovely hair. Sam, you always liked redheads, didn't you?"

Sam was too busy with Nicky to respond. He shifted the baby to his other shoulder and patted his back. Fiona made no move to take him.

"For us?" Fiona took the coffee cake. "Thank you so much." She stepped onto the porch to better see the library. "That's your great-grandfather's house, isn't it, Sam?"

"Great-great-grandfather," he said.

22 *Angela M. Sanders*

The baby stiffened. Thanks to my niece Letty, I knew that look. He was going to burp up a big one. I didn't feel the need to warn Sam.

"Such a picturesque town." Fiona rubbed her black-clad arms. The morning was still fresh. "Maybe I'll do a show on it."

"Fiona's an artist," Sam said.

The baby reared his head. I figured Sam had five seconds, tops.

"It's time I did more landscape work," Fiona said.

At that moment, the baby expelled a stream of creamy spittle down Sam's back and relaxed, eyes closed, against his shoulder.

"I'll let you go," I said. "I just wanted to welcome you back."

"See you soon." Sam wiped his neck.

"Thanks for the cake," Fiona added.

"That's a super cute baby," I said.

As I sorted new arrivals at the library, I couldn't help replaying the morning's scene at Big House. At least our reintroduction was over, and I knew where things stood. Nothing Fiona had said could be construed as mean or wrong, but something about her didn't sit well with me. And Sam—damn it. I wasn't happy about it, but seeing him still brought butterflies to my stomach.

"Josie. I'm here, as promised." Lewis Cruikshank, the architect from the day before, stood in the doorway craning his neck to take in the atrium. He wore a leather jacket that had never seen a motorcyclist's back and carried his satchel. "This building is a period piece."

The atrium rose three floors, capped by a cupola with a

stained-glass window. At each floor, an open walkway circled the hall. Once, the rooms leading off of it had been bedrooms. Now they were full of books. Above us, Marilyn Wilfred's life-sized portrait stared down in a cloche and ruby-hued flapper dress, a black cat at her feet.

The architect couldn't take his eyes off the library's interior. "Classic. Stuffy and aspirational." He shook his head. "Nineteenth-century Italianate, if I'm not mistaken. That bell tower is astonishing. And the stained glass in the cupola. I feel like I'm in a Vincent Price film."

I laughed. "I felt that way at first, too. I'm doing my best to bring it up to date, but, yes, we definitely have one foot set a century ago. Would you like a tour?"

He smiled, and all his pretension melted away. He seemed almost boyish. "Please. You said you might have some local history I could look at, too?"

"Follow me."

I showed Lewis the old kitchen and pantry—now my office—and he insisted on going up the service staircase. "More authentic," he said. He ran his hands over the marble chimneypieces and exclaimed at the old-growth fir molding. "Marvelous. Simply marvelous. The original owner—Thurston Wilfred, right?"

"Right," I said. "We call him old man Thurston since every firstborn male in the family is christened Thurston, too."

"Well, Thurston had an eye for what the well-to-do classes were doing." He knelt to knock on a baseboard. "At least twenty years prior, that is. I bet he found the floor plan in a pattern book."

Hmm, a book whispered from somewhere below.

"Why did you take on the retreat?" I asked. "You

could be working anywhere—Dubai, Amsterdam. I love the hotel you did in Bangkok." That morning, I'd done a few minutes of research on Cruikshank's background. Wilfredians would be asking.

"I needed a break from the big projects." He hesitated, then seemed to decide it was okay to speak. "I used to know someone named Wilfred. I guess I took it as a sign."

"Here it's a last name. Let's look at the tower." The floorboards creaked under our feet as we set down the hall to the tower. I felt for the key above the door frame and unlocked the door. "I hope you'll like it in Wilfred. I haven't lived here long, but it's a special town."

The tower was dusty, and Lewis crossed the room right away to open the casement window. He leaned out, inhaling the fir-tinged air. "I can see that. A building is so much more than wood and stone. People give it soul." He turned to face me. "That's what I want for the retreat center. I want it to be a structure that elevates the people who use it."

If Lewis were a witch, his power would come from buildings, like mine came from books. He loved the structures people inhabited, and it showed. "Your designs might be more contemporary than Wilfredians are used to."

"Over time, they'll love it. You'll see," he said. "We're meeting later on today—the contractor, me, and Ruff and Sita. You know the Waterses?"

I did. Ruff and Sita Waters were the new owners of the mill site and the visionaries behind the retreat center. They were definitely outsiders with their New Age habits, but Wilfred had embraced them as financial saviors.

"We're looking forward to the retreat center, and the Waterses seem to really love Wilfred. The town has had some setbacks in the past few decades—"

Cruikshank nodded. "I get it." Wilfred's financial struggle wasn't hard to see in its abandoned storefronts.

"The retreat center could really turn things around," I said.

"I'll do what I can to help."

We filed out of the tower room. "Let me show you to Local History." I led Lewis Cruikshank downstairs. "Why don't you have a seat here, by the fireplace?" The fire wasn't lit, but a chintz-covered armchair and roomy side table with a lamp made it a comfortable study area, especially if he planned to settle in for a few hours.

He twirled the end of his mustache, like he wasn't used to having one. I caught a whiff of patchouli, probably from his beard oil, although he only had a modest soul patch above his cleft chin. He dropped his leather satchel, and *Finnegan's Wake* grumbled from inside.

"Feel free to look around. Meanwhile, I'll pull some books for you," I said.

It would be a cinch to find what the architect needed. All I had to do was relax, and the titles and their locations on our shelves would slide to mind as neatly as if I'd had the Olympic Library Research team riffling the card catalog. Before long, I had a good collection of books for him to peruse.

"Here you go. I hope they inspire a lot of good ideas," I said.

"I'm already inspired. Thank you, Josie."

I remembered the sketch he'd shown us yesterday and bit my tongue from suggesting that a retreat center wasn't the same as a Swedish airport terminal. Ruth Littlewood passed by, binoculars swinging on her neck. I waved.

"One more thing." He lowered his eyeglasses. "Who was the lady talking about a curse?"

"Mrs. Garlington?" I said. "She saw a stranger at the mill site yesterday morning. She loves drama—must be the poet in her—and an old curse would be catnip to her. That's all." The thought of the coincidence of my lesson on curses upstairs made me less sure than I wanted to let on.

"Well, if there's anything to it, I guess I'll find out this afternoon."

On my way downstairs, I was surprised to pass Ruff and Sita Waters. Ruff—Rafael on his birth certificate—might have been Lewis Cruikshank's hippie brother. He was dark and bearded and wore a denim jacket over a Mexican cotton shirt. Sita had the air of an Indian princess, complete with glass bangles and flowing silk skirt. However, she'd been raised in an affluent suburb on the East Coast, likely on a steady diet of Kahlil Gibran and nag champa incense.

"It's nice to see you again," I said.

"Big meeting at the mill site this afternoon," Ruff said. "Our kickoff."

"At last, I feel like the retreat center is coming to life," Sita added.

"By chance, your architect is here. He's upstairs in the corner room," I said, "gathering ideas for the retreat center design."

"Oh, good," Sita said, clapping her hands like a little

girl. "We haven't met in person yet. I was hoping he was here."

I continued on to Circulation to sort through bids on wiring the library for Internet. I liked knowing that as I worked, upstairs Wilfred's future was being determined. Maybe we'd even make the cover of *Architectural Digest*. Visitors would stream into Wilfred, and the library would surely become a part of their tour. I made a note to ask Lyndon, the caretaker, if our facilities could take the extra business.

Less than half an hour later, shouting roused me from my chair.

"Absolutely not!" a woman's voice said. After unintelligible murmuring, I heard, "I don't care what you say."

We didn't hold with a "whispering only" rule, but this was ridiculous.

In five steps I was in the atrium, where I found Roz and Ruth Littlewood staring upstairs. "What's going on?"

"It's the Waterses and the architect," Roz said.

"Duking it out," Ruth added.

"You're kidding," I said. "This was their big face-to-face meeting."

"Not kidding."

"Maybe it'll stop," I said hopefully.

"We will not!" came Sita's shout.

Ruth looked from Roz to me. "Who's going to take them on?"

"I'll do it," I said.

I was a good twenty-five years younger than Roz, my assistant librarian, and I felt I had something to prove. Thanks to her other life as a romance novelist, Roz hadn't wanted the responsibility of running the library. I sus-

pected she saw me as overeducated and underexperi-
enced, and she might have been right.

I took the stairs and lifted my chin as I strode toward
where they gathered. Sita stood by the window, hands on
her hips. Ruff huddled in a wingback chair, and Lewis
paced in front of them.

"No," Sita said firmly.

"Why not?" Lewis replied.

"It's our retreat center, and it's not going to look like a
pile of bleached bones."

"Is everything okay here?" I asked in my most firm
but indifferent voice.

Lewis gripped the marble fireplace mantel. Sita's head
leaned forward like a goose getting ready to spit. Ruff
pulled at his beard.

"Josie," Lewis said, his voice softening. "Just the person we need to see."

"Yes," Sita said. "In fact, she is."

Uh-oh. "What seems to be the problem?" The cover
for an old business classic, *Getting to Yes*, flashed through
my mind with *How to Win Friends and Influence People*
on its heels.

"The retreat center—"

"Happy Trails," Ruff said quietly. "That's its name."

The architect shot him a look. "Well, we'll see about
that. As I was saying, the retreat center is poised to be an
example of artistic excellence."

I waited. Sita stared, tapping a foot.

"Ruff and Sita's ideas are"—he searched the air as if
the word he wanted was carved into the wallpaper—"old-
fashioned. Frankly, in some circles they'd be laughed at."

"'Laughed at'?" Sita said.

"That's surely too harsh," I said, knowing that where Lewis Cruikshank came from, he was probably right.

"You don't want to build a complex that will outlast all of us, then find you've outgrown it, do you?" he said.

"I don't want to build a complex that's the latest thing and then hate it in five years. Hate it now, actually," Sita said.

Time to bring on the peacemaker. "You've just talked about ideas, right?" I said. "Maybe you need to see the actual drawings, then decide. I've collected lots of good history on the area. I could look for more about tribal structures. You'll surely find common ground."

No one responded immediately, but I sensed none of them really wanted to argue further.

Ruff's hand dropped from worrying his beard. "Josie's right. We'll go look at the site together this afternoon and see what the land wants. Besides, we need to talk practicalities, like the levee and road."

Sita still stared at the floor, but she nodded. "I'll be patient. We'll see what you create. After all, you're the artist. Besides, 'Holding on to anger is like grasping a hot coal with the intent of throwing it at someone else; you are the one who gets burned.'"

A book on spirituality with a lotus on its cover whispered, *Buddha*, to me from across the atrium. As long as I held my power with books, I'd never need a reference on quotations.

Lewis Cruikshank's voice was low and serious. "You hired me to give you a stellar retreat center."

We all looked at him. His face was red, but his flared nostrils were white. At any second, he might pick up the

Oregon Historical Society quarterly at his elbow and throw it.

"That's right." Buddha forgotten, Sita's voice was equally deadly. "We hired you, and we can fire you."

"Sure, you can fire me. But I have a contract. My retainer is mine to keep."

Ruff's beard would be straightened flat if he kept pulling at it. "Let's wait. No decisions right away. Let's wait until this afternoon and take it from there."

CHAPTER FIVE

The day had already been one tumult after another, and Fiona's appearance was a sign that it wasn't about to end.

"How can I help you? Things comfortable next door?" I said.

"Fine, thank you." Although she was talking to me, she was gawking at the library. It was impressive, I had to admit. Afternoon sun filtered through the French doors, splashing light on the Turkish carpet.

"I'm surprised you haven't been here before," I said. I wasn't sure how long she and Sam had been married, or if they'd ever made the trip here, to his hometown.

Fiona absently twisted her wedding ring, a thin platinum band with three diamonds arranged in a perfect triangle. Delicate and unusual. It suited her.

"You're her, aren't you?" she said. "The woman from Sam's job last fall?"

Her words drove home just what I'd been to him. A job. "That's me," I said with all the cheerfulness I could muster.

"He liked you," she said, keeping her gaze on me. "Said you had guts." She smiled suddenly and sat at the chair we kept near the circulation desk for antsy children and husbands waiting for wives to collect their holds. She took a notebook and a black pencil from her tote bag. "From Sam, that's a compliment."

"That's nice of you to say," I said. Fiona was more than beautiful; she was charming. That smile she just flashed—who could resist it? The second it vanished, I sensed sadness. Or was it simply indifference?

"Hmm." She was sketching something while her mind was clearly elsewhere. She drew a long curve, then a few shorter lines, then started to fill it in. "Sam doesn't own this building, does he?"

"No. It was willed to the town years ago by his aunt." What did she want? "Can I help you find a novel, maybe?"

"No. I'm not much of a reader. Images, not words, are my thing." She set down her pencil. "This is a sweet little town. I wonder what might have happened if—"

"There you are, Fiona."

Standing in the doorway was, to put it mildly, a looker. Roz passed by on her way to Thurston Wilfred's old office—now the children's collection—and she stopped short to stare. He was that handsome, but not conventionally. He had wavy black hair, straight nose, and pale hazel eyes with a slight almond shape that hinted at Eurasian roots somewhere in his family tree.

"Brett," Fiona said with surprise. Despite the change in her tone of voice, she smiled. "Josie, this is Brett Thornsby. Brett, Josie, the librarian."

"From Fiona's gallery." He extended a hand to me, but he spoke to Fiona. "I'm here to help out with the art project."

"Wilfred's a great subject for a show." I made a mental note to tell Ruff and Sita they should consider a plein air workshop when the retreat center was up and running. "The countryside is gorgeous around here."

He looked to Fiona, who seemed to wake up. "Right. Josie," she said, "I hoped you might be able to tell us how to get to the mill site. They say it has a nice view of town. Brett, you and I can catch up on the walk there."

Roz still watched us, not caring that she was baldly listening to everything we said. This would go down well in a few hours at Darla's Café.

"Some of the best views of Wilfred are from Big House," I pointed out.

"Oh, I know. I want something farther west. We could get a few angles with the setting sun."

Not that the sun would show much of itself with the gathering cloud cover, I thought. "Well, the old mill site is on this side of the Kirby River. The river curves around the back of Wilfred, and the site is on the western bank. You can't miss it. Take the trail along the river, right in front of the library. It's about a fifteen-minute walk through the woods."

I knew the trail—and the old mill site—well. It was far enough from town to be private, but close enough that I could use its abandoned stacking house to carry out my grandmother's rituals without attracting attention. Graffiti adorned its concrete walls, and trees sprouted from cracks and stretched up to the no-longer-existent ceiling.

Rodney sauntered in and, from the doorway, fixed his gaze at me. I did a double take. Someone—Ruth Little-wood, no doubt—had buckled a collar around his neck with a bell dangling from it. He bent his head to lick a paw, and the bell jingled, earning a pained look. He let out a mournful mew. He pointedly directed his rear end toward me and returned to the atrium.

"That sounds perfect." Fiona slipped her sketch pad and pencil into her bag. "Shall we go, Brett?"

As I heard the front door close, I wondered why Sam hadn't told them about the mill site. Surely he'd have been more than happy to give directions.

Rodney ambled back into the parlor and plopped on his side. I absently scratched his belly. "Something is up," I told him. "I don't know what it is, but I don't feel good about it."

Fiona had left her sketch on the desk. I picked it up, and my breath caught in my throat. It was a jawless skull, and from one eye socket twisted a thorny rose. Below it, in gothic letters, read "*memento mori*."

That night, I returned to my lesson on curses. The evening was chilly and damp, so I built a fire in my living room's fireplace. I deliberately settled into the armchair facing away from the window looking out to Big House. The fire popped and wafted cedar-scented heat. With a jingle, Rodney leapt into the empty kindling box on the hearth.

Earlier, I'd fed him dinner. Or tried, anyway. "You've got to eat, Rodney." I'd heaped both of his bowls with kibble—the bowl in the big kitchen downstairs and his satellite bowl up here—and he'd turned up his nose. The message was clear: not a pellet would cross his lips until I removed the collar. "Sorry, kitten. I'll find some way to convince Ruth you don't need that collar, but until then you'll have to wear it. So you might as well eat."

Rodney had given me a skeptical look with, perhaps, a hint of accusation, and curled up for a nap.

Read . . . read us, said the collection of novels by the couch. I'd always loved books, but it wasn't until my magic opened up that I understood how much books loved us. Their pages craved touch, and they were happiest in a person's hands as they poured out their stories. The books on my nightstand almost purred as I walked by them. When I pulled a volume from the library's shelves, it sighed in delight.

"I'll get to you," I told them. "First things first."

Once again, I unfolded my grandmother's letter and took in her loving voice:

> *At its core, a curse is simply a spell, a fabric woven of energy that causes harm. Sometimes curses are set to protect something—to keep people away from objects, say. Think of the Hope Diamond. More often, a curse is directed at a person. It's designed to punish. These are the deadliest curses, and usually the person hurt the most deeply is the person who set the curse. You see, just like a spell, a curse binds the witch with the object she has cursed. Someone who curses creates a twin curse that doubles back and attaches itself to them. It may take years for this shadow curse to show itself, but it will.*

*When I've mentioned curses here, I've assumed
witches cast them. In fact, most curses are cast by
average people through poisonous thoughts or
even by something as minute as spitting. Countless
minor curses are set by drivers cut off in traffic, for
instance. Remember Maggie Mortensen? She had
a hen who'd go to roost just about anywhere but in
the chicken coop. Maggie would curse that hen
every night at dusk, telling her she was a good-for-
nothing chicken. That's exactly what the hen became. I don't think she ever did lay.*

*Sometimes people even curse themselves. They
call themselves fat or lazy, then they're surprised
when they can't be bothered to pick up a broom or
bypass the ice cream. We can be grateful they don't
have the gift to sustain powerful energy.*

*Josie, honey, I pray you will never be the victim
of a witch's curse or have reason to cast one. But
you may be called upon to lift a curse. If so, you'll
need these tools.*

Grandma's voice was full of concern. Anxiety sparked
in my stomach. There was more—the lesson on curses
was one of the longest I'd read so far—but I couldn't absorb it all right now. I refolded the letter, slipped it into its
envelope, and took a few steadying breaths.

How could a curse relate to the old mill site? The mill
itself was long gone, so the curse had to be on the land.
Maybe it was a tribal curse. This bore some looking into.

The fire popped, and Rodney stepped from the basket
and stretched his legs.

"Come here, Rodney-cat."

He fastened his whiskey-tinted eyes on me and leapt

into my lap. His black fur had absorbed the fire's heat, and I soaked its warmth as I petted him.

I scratched his chin and stared into his eyes, and, for a moment, I slipped into his body and saw myself as he saw me, fuzzy up close, but a comforting presence with a mass of long, curly red hair it was fun to bat from time to time. I vibrated with his purrs. A whirlwind rehash of Rodney's day whisked through my mind, from chasing a dragonfly to sleeping in the brambles to dragging a sheet of Mrs. Garlington's music behind the organ. I'd have to fetch it for her tomorrow. And, of course, of Ruth Little-wood snatching him unawares by the nape of his neck and fastening on the collar.

Then I was back in my own body again.

"Time for bed, Rodster."

I stirred the fire's ashes, turned off the lights, and wandered to the hall to look down on bedrooms full of shelves of books, all humming with stories and voices and information.

"Good night, Marilyn," I told her portrait. As usual, she radiated a kind but impenetrable stare. "Good night, books."

Rodney wound through my legs as I rested my fore-arms on the polished banister.

Good night, Josie, the books whispered in a shushing of voices only I could hear. *Good night*.

Slipping among the good nights came another book's voice, low and penetrating. *Watch out*, it said.

I was in the middle of a dream about the mill site and pouring rain and Indian drums when a pounding on my apartment door woke me. My apartment was sealed off from the rest of the library by a locked door—fitted with a cat flap, of course—at the top of the servants' staircase. Someone had made it past the ground floor's dead bolts.

I caught my breath and looked at my phone. Midnight. Who could it be?

The door rapped again, this time accompanied by a baby's squall.

I slipped into my robe. Rodney had already jumped off the bed and padded to the hall, collar jingling. Whoever it was, it hadn't scared him.

I unbolted the door and cracked it open. "Hello?" I opened the door all the way to see Sam, dressed in a thick wool jacket with a shearling collar, carrying a diaper bag. Nicky was slung into a front pack.

"Could you take care of Nicky for a while?" he said.

"Why?"

"Fiona hasn't come home. I need to find her."

CHAPTER SIX

"Wait here." I left Rodney to rub against Sam's legs while I dressed as fast as a showgirl between sets. I was back in the hall within two minutes, with a thick coat and a flashlight. "I'm coming with you."

"You can't," Sam said. "What about Nicky? He'll be asleep in minutes, once he has his bottle. All I ask is that you keep an eye on him. I won't be long."

"I insist. You need me."

"Why? I know the mill site inside and out."

"You might have known it years ago. I know it now."

Sam's family had fled Wilfred in the middle of the night when he was just a kid. He'd rarely returned since. Meanwhile, I'd spent hours on the trail between the library and the mill site, and my feet knew every exposed tree root and pothole.

"Then what do we do with the baby?" Sam shifted the diaper bag to his other shoulder.

"Follow me."

Lyndon, the grounds' caretaker, might have looked like an extra from an *Addams Family* episode, but he loved children. It was hard to see him now as I'd first seen him: creepy, quiet, and startling me by popping up where I'd least expected him. Now I knew him as a sensitive guy who wouldn't eat "anything that feels pain." Plus, he was a night owl. Odds were good that about now he'd be putting the final touches on an Ikebana masterpiece or finishing mixing a batch of cashew cheese.

We exited the side door, and I locked up behind us. The light of a gibbous moon—I'd been tuned in much more tightly to the moon's phases since I'd come into my magic—forced through clouds and iced the lawn.

I knocked at the caretaker's cottage door.

"Lyndon?" Sam said. "You've got to be kidding."

"Just you wait."

Lyndon poked his head out of the door. He wore a red flannel robe over pajamas and eyed us suspiciously. The inside of his cottage was a mystery to Wilfredians and had engendered a lot of speculation. He wasn't about to satisfy us on that point tonight.

"What?" he said in his typical man-of-few-words manner.

"Give him the baby," I told Sam.

"I don't know—"

At that moment, Lyndon's expression melted. "Well, hello, little fellow."

I looked at Sam with an "I told you so" in my eyes.

"This wouldn't be Thurston Wilfred the sixth, would it?" Lyndon said.

"We call him Nicky," Sam said, warming to his tone.

"Lyndon, would you mind keeping an eye on him for an hour or so? You weren't just going to bed, were you?" I asked.

"No, in fact, it would be no trouble at all." Lyndon pulled the baby close. Rodney slipped through the door, too.

"Diapers and a bottle are in the bag," Sam said as Lyndon tickled Nicky's chin.

"We'll be back soon," I told him.

Lyndon's door shut behind us, and we were alone. My drowsiness was gone. The fresh night air—not to mention the sight of Sam—had woken me completely. We set off for the river path, me all too aware of him by my side. "You haven't heard from Fiona at all?"

"The last I saw of her was this afternoon. The gallery staffer had shown up—"

"Brett," I said.

"—and I told him Fiona was at the library. She said she planned to visit the mill site after that."

Other than Sam's SUV, no cars were parked at Big House. "Brett's rental car is gone."

"He left this afternoon," Sam said as I opened my mouth to ask. "One minute the car was there, and the next time I checked, it was gone."

"Where's he staying? Maybe Fiona went with him." I remembered Brett's smooth manner and movie-star looks.

"I'm not sure, but she wouldn't have left town without telling me."

We continued over the trail, with only the sound of the wind in the trees. Somehow, dark made both silence and sound more profound.

"Are you still with the FBI?" I asked.

Sam's expertise had been in "ghosting," or tracking people. It suited him. He was introspective and hard to read until you got to know him. He'd look at me, and I felt he was examining my thoughts. It wasn't just me, though. He turned his penetrating gaze on everyone.

"No. I had to travel too much, and I didn't want to be away from Nicky. It was time to come home, and Washington County advertised a sheriff's position. I want Nicky to grow up here, not in LA."

We were among the fir trees now. An owl hooted somewhere nearby. The flashlight's beam, so strong when I tested it earlier, faltered against the forest's pressing dark.

"All I can tell you," I said, "is that this afternoon around two, Fiona dropped by the library and asked how to get to the old mill site. Brett stopped by soon after. I told them to take this path. You really haven't heard a thing?"

He walked in step beside me. "Fiona's like that," he said finally. "She's a free spirit. Goes off sometimes. She might have wandered off the path or sprained her ankle or something."

"I see," I said, although I didn't see. She had a baby. And Sam. Normal people didn't disappear like that.

"We're divorcing. Josie—" He stopped and lowered his voice. "I didn't know she was pregnant when I was here last. We'd seen an attorney just before I'd left town. Then I came home, and she told me."

"But you're still splitting up? Despite Nicky."

"Yes." We continued down the trail. He had something to add, I felt it, but he stayed silent. "He needs a happy home. We tried working on it, but our marriage is no example for him."

"Sounds complicated," I said, more because it seemed something was required than that I had any idea how to respond.

The path through the woods followed the curve of the Kirby River another ten minutes. At last we came to the clearing where the mill had once stood. Moonlight deepened shadows from the mill's cracked foundation—all that was left of the central building. A small construction trailer sat on higher ground a stone's throw from the millpond, which lay still and heavy.

Beyond the millpond loomed the concrete stacking house. Despite the construction trailer and a few pieces of wood tied with plastic ribbon as markers, the area was quiet. Empty. Even so, a chill prickled my neck and went down my arms. The curse. The land hummed with an uneasy energy. Why hadn't I ever felt it before? Maybe something had triggered it. The retreat center.

"Fiona!" Sam's shout echoed against the stacking house walls.

We listened but heard only a faraway dog barking, probably from the trailer park.

"No one's here but us," I said.

"There." Sam pointed the flashlight to two sets of footprints along the millpond. "Those are hers, the set on the right. Her boots. I know the size and the tread."

We followed the footprints in the soft earth to the stacking house, where they disappeared on the hardened dirt floor. I ran my flashlight over the concrete wall, illuminating decades-old graffiti and disturbing a possum that had been shuffling toward an exit.

"Well, she's not here now," I said. "You say she's a free spirit." Could she have gone somewhere? "You've called her, right?"

"It goes straight to voice mail."

Beyond the millpond, the meadow became the Magnolia Rolling Estates, then Darla's Café and the two-lane highway into Gaston. To the right, the river curved, and the light I'd left on upstairs in my apartment glimmered from the bluff in the distance.

It was easy to imagine the mill in the old days, busy with trucks and mill hands and thousands of board feet of timber moving in and out to the roar of saws. Then there was the fire. Then, nothing.

Mrs. Garlington had talked of a curse. I remembered the SUV she claimed to have seen, and its driver with his shoulder holster.

My breath quickened. As if sensing my thoughts, the ground beneath us seemed to vibrate with anger. I doubted Sam could feel it, but he snapped his head toward me.

"Something's wrong," he said. "I don't know what it is, but I feel it."

That intuition had no doubt helped him in his work. "Let's go back," I said suddenly. "Maybe she's home now."

"Maybe," Sam said. He didn't sound convinced. Somehow, neither was I.

CHAPTER SEVEN

The next day, the sun rose to blue skies, and Fiona still had not returned. I was at Darla's Café when Sam, baby Nicky in hand, arrived. He exchanged a few words with Darla, then turned to the crowd.

"I'm looking for a search party. My wife has gone missing at the old mill site."

Within half an hour, Sam, Lyndon, Duke, and I stood on the old mill's cement foundation. The baby was in Mrs. Garlington's care, with Buffy cooing at him and Thor demonstrating card tricks.

In the morning light, the mill site was simply another derelict building site, scented by fir trees and noisy with birdsong. A breeze rippled over the millpond. Despite its pastoral appearance, from deep in the earth, I sensed the uneasiness I'd felt the night before. Quieter now, but present.

"The ground's soft," Sam said. "We'll be able to see if she went off the trail."

Duke wandered toward him, squinting against the morning sun. He held binoculars in one hand and a steaming travel mug of coffee in the other. "Weren't you two getting a divorce?" he asked. Duke would never enter the diplomatic corps.

I was close enough to listen and faked surveying the landscape.

"Yes," Sam said. "We still are."

"So, she might be off somewhere on her own."

"She might." He wouldn't say more, not in front of everyone.

"Hmm," Duke said, taking an audible slurp from his travel mug. "I suppose she wouldn't wander off when alimony is at stake. You got a bundle for this land, didn't you?"

The mill had been in the Wilfred family since the late 1890s. Last autumn, Sam had sold it to Ruff and Sita for the retreat center. He'd seemed more concerned with the town's future than his own pocketbook at the time, and I wouldn't have been surprised if he'd given Ruff and Sita a good deal.

"Duke, we're looking for my wife. You can save your speculation for spaghetti night at Darla's."

The rumble of a diesel motor drew nearer. A large white Ford rounded the back road to the mill site and killed its engine next to the construction trailer.

"Tommy!" Duke said and hurried to the truck. For such a large man, Duke was surprisingly graceful. I'd heard he was an accomplished ballroom dancer, but this was as close to a foxtrot as I'd seem him perform.

A man with an athletic build and sandy hair stepped

down from the truck. He wore a baseball cap backward and a Portland Blazers T-shirt, and despite the cool morning, shorts and sandals. "What's going on?"

"Search party," Duke said. "Sam here lost his wife."

This seemed like a good time for me to step in. "She came out here yesterday afternoon to sketch, maybe take a few photos. I gave her directions."

"You must be the contractor for the retreat center," Sam said and extended a hand. "You were here yesterday afternoon, right?"

"Sure. Tommy Daniels."

"Did you see a brunette wearing a black wool jacket?" Sam said.

"I was here yesterday afternoon meeting with the architect and owners. A man and a woman came by. We waved. That's it. I was busy."

"Nothing else?" Sam asked.

Tommy looked at him with surprise and seemed about to say something, but thought better of it. "We spent most of the time in there, though," he said, turning to the tiny construction trailer. "She didn't make it home?"

Sam shook his head.

"I'll help search. Why don't I take the path toward the library?"

"Look for trampled brush, broken branches, anything that shows that she might have gone off the trail," Sam said.

"I'll check the stacking house and the meadow on the other side of the millpond," I said.

Because of my time there practicing rituals, I felt proprietary about the stacking house. I walked along the millpond until I reached its entrance. At one time, the stacking house had been a warehouse for storing logs that came off the millpond until a truck could haul them off. Now the roof was long gone, and kids from Gaston had spray-painted murals in it over the years. The effect was at once urban and wild, like a destitute cathedral left to raccoons and birds.

The footprints Sam and I had seen the night before had melted into the soft ground. Inside the stacking house, all was quiet but for the shush of the wind through the gaping holes that had once been doors and windows, and the bowing of the alder saplings that had taken root in its crevices.

I walked the building's perimeter. At the far corner was a nook I had taken shelter in when it drizzled. Enough of the roof remained that it was protected from rain, and here the floor was mossy, not hard-packed dirt as it was elsewhere. A few niches in the foundation were good spots to tuck a candle and matches.

Something charcoal-tinted caught my eye. An artist's pencil like the one Fiona had used yesterday. It had likely rolled down from the protected corner and was now lodged against a dandelion.

Fiona had been here.

I tucked the pencil in my pocket and hurried back toward the construction trailer, where Sam and Tommy Daniels were pointing toward the woods and talking.

"Sam!" I said breathlessly. I held out the pencil. "Was this hers?"

"Might be. Fiona has pencils like this. You found it in the stacking house?"

"She must have been sketching," I said.

"She and Brett," he said. I couldn't read his expression. "I left a message at the gallery this morning. They should be able to give me Brett's number. Maybe he knows something."

"Maybe she got lost on the way back." The woods were thick, but the trail was well marked. Then again, Brett was with her, and he obviously made it back, since his car was gone. "Do you think he left Fiona behind?"

"Sam. Tommy. Back here," Duke shouted from the brush beyond the construction trailer. I'd heard Duke angry, and I'd heard him scared, but I'd never heard such urgency from him.

I hurried after Sam and Tommy Daniels into the woods' edge.

Duke pointed to a clump of brush. "Look. I didn't want to touch it until the police can check it out."

I stepped forward, but Tommy Daniels blocked my way. "Is—is it her?"

"Nope," Duke said.

Daniels stepped aside, opening the view. Protruding from the brush was the sharp end of a tire iron. At first, I thought it was rusted thickly over. Then I knew it was blood.

CHAPTER EIGHT

Back at the library, I didn't have the presence of mind to deal with the patrons who'd soon be streaming in not to ask about books, but to get the scoop on Fiona Wilfred and the tire iron. Roz took over and let me retreat to my office to do paperwork while she ran interference.

Within two minutes of finding the tire iron, Duke had called the sheriff's office. Sam, with his background as an FBI agent, secured the scene. In half an hour, a team had arrived from the sheriff's office. A deputy had taken my name and said I could return to work for the moment. Someone would follow up with me.

So, here I was, absently moving papers on my desk and staring blankly at my computer screen. Fiona was gone. Murdered. Less than a day earlier, she'd strolled in for a chat. She had been beautiful and full of life. With a finger, I traced the edge of the skull she'd drawn before I returned the sketch to a drawer. "*Memento mori*." How appropriate. Sam would want it, but not immediately. Not as gruesome as the drawing was.

Rodney jumped to the desk and curled up in my inbox. I reached out to pet the silky fur between his ears.

"Am I interrupting you?" Sam stood at my office door.

"No, please come in." I pulled my old cardigan off the office's armchair and gestured toward it, trying to look casual, but I couldn't help smoothing my too-often out-of-control hair.

For a former pantry, my office was wonderfully comfortable. I had a scarred oak desk against the wall with casement windows. Bookshelves and a filing cabinet filled the wall opposite the windows, ending at an old coatrack next to the door to the kitchen. Under the angled ceiling—the library's main staircase ran above me—was a slip-covered armchair in clean but stained ecru linen, where Sam took a seat.

"How are you?" I asked.

"I'm all right. I mean, I'm not all right, but . . ."

"I get it," I said.

"How about you? Are you okay?"

"Me?" I shrugged. "Could be better."

He raked his hair with his fingers and looked at me with a vague smile. Meaning: not happy. "I'm here to ask you a favor. I'm worried about Nicky."

"You can take care of him on your own, right?"

"Oh, that's not a problem. He's on formula—Fiona never had the schedule to allow for, um—"

"Nursing," I supplied.

"Yes. So I've been his main caretaker while I've been on paternity leave. No, that's not it."

Sam had come to see me for some reason. I waited

until he was ready to get to the point. Or maybe he simply needed a friend to talk to.

"I worry I won't be around for him," he said.

"What?" I said before he'd even finished the sentence.

"Look, Josie, my whole career has been in law enforcement. I know I'm the chief suspect. Fiona and I were in the middle of a divorce. They'll look to me first. I need someone to take care of Nicky if I'm jailed. Just until I post bail."

"You said 'were,'" I pointed out. "We don't know for sure that she's dead." The last word fell flat. *Dead*. Not a word you wanted to mention to a husband about his wife.

"It's not looking good," Sam said calmly. "A murder weapon was found. The only thing they don't have is a body."

"Oh, Sam—"

He held up a palm. "I've been here. I know what the procedure is. Who has the motive to kill her? I do. Not just because we're divorcing, but because of the money that goes with it. If she died before the divorce was final, I'd be off the hook for alimony and child support. Fiona had hired an attorney with a reputation for flaying spouses financially."

I tapped the arm of my wooden desk chair, and Rodney took it as an invitation to leap into my lap. "What about Brett? He was with her, then took off. He's got to be the sheriff's primary suspect."

"Why would he kill her?"

We stared at each other. I didn't know what was going through Sam's mind, but I had ideas, and they didn't have to do with holy matrimony. "Let the sheriff figure it out. As for Nicky, there's no reason to panic about that yet. You haven't even been interviewed."

He laughed once. "Yeah, the sheriff. I sent in my application for a job in her department last week."

In an unusual move, Rodney leapt from the desk to the arm of Sam's chair and gingerly felt for his lap. Sam pulled him over, and Rodney erupted into a rumbling purr. Sam sneezed. It was a comfort to me. At least he wasn't perfect; he was allergic to cats.

A knock as sharp as a woodpecker's call came once again at my office door. Rodney sprang from Sam's lap and hid under my desk.

"Yes?" I said as I answered the door.

A woman I'd never seen before stood in the doorway. She was petite and polished and about my mother's age, and she wore the khaki uniform of the Washington County Sheriff's Department. Her expression might have been etched on a marble statue entitled "Woman Nonplussed."

"Meg Beattie," she said and offered a hand. "Interim sheriff for this part of the county. You must be Josephine Way?"

"That's me." I glanced at Sam. "Is it time for my interview?"

Her expression didn't change, but I knew she was taking in my flushed face and neck. "No. Not yet. Right now I want to talk with Sam."

I stood at the same time as Sam and placed a hand on his arm. "Don't worry about the baby." *Right now, he's the least of your trouble*, I thought.

Later that day, Sheriff Beattie returned to the library and found me, once again, in my office. She had timed things right. The library was closing, and we wouldn't be disturbed—at least, not until the English as a Second Language class met in the conservatory. She made herself at home at the kitchen's long oak table outside my office door.

"Do you have a few minutes? I'd like to get your take on what happened this morning."

I pulled out the chair opposite hers. "How can I help you?"

"I understand you gave Fiona Wilfred directions to the old mill site yesterday." Sheriff Beattie's expression was completely unreadable.

The cat door popped open, and Rodney strutted in, tail high, collar jingling. I watched to see how he'd treat her. He glided underneath the table and headbutted her khaki-clad pant leg. She absently reached down and scratched him. She'd passed the test. After receiving his due, he continued to his food dish, then froze. He looked straight at me and pointedly walked away from the dish.

"I did give her directions. She stopped by yesterday afternoon. While we talked, someone from her gallery came by—"

"—Brett Thornsby."

"Right. Fiona wanted to know how to get to the old mill site. She was looking for scenic spots to sketch. The view across the millpond and the river is gorgeous."

Sheriff Beattie leaned back and crossed a leg. "How did you suggest she get there?"

"By the trail along the river, through the woods. It's about a fifteen-minute walk."

"Not by car, then?"

"From the library, it's much easier to walk." It was possible to reach the mill site from a road north of town. "I didn't see tire tracks this morning. Other than the contractor's, that is. The big white truck. I did find a pencil in the stacking house. Sam said he thought it was Fiona's."

She nodded. "We have it, thank you. Tell me about last night."

"Last night?" I must have sounded like an idiot, repeating her.

"When Sam showed up."

I remembered my lesson on curses, my uneasy preparation for bed, Sam's knock on the door.

"Sam came by at about midnight. I was asleep. His knock woke me."

"You could hear his knock all the way from the third floor?"

How she knew I lived upstairs, I had no idea. I shook my head. "You get to my apartment from the service stairwell on the side facing Big House. There's another door at the top. He was knocking on that door—the door on the third floor."

"So, he has a key to the library." Sheriff Beattie's tone was emotionless, impartial, but I had the feeling she was implying something.

"Yes. He's a Wilfred. He used to come here as a kid. I imagine there's still a key at Big House."

"How long have you known Sam?"

"Not long at all. I met him when I first came to town six months ago. He was here on an FBI assignment. He left when it was over."

"I'm familiar with the case. You haven't been in touch since then?" Her gaze was steady.

"No."

"You're sure?"

"Absolutely." What was she getting at?

"Continue about last night, please."

I shifted on the chair. In the hall, Dylan was letting in the ESL class, mostly farmworkers looking to improve their language skills. Even though it was beyond his hours, Dylan liked to stick around. It gave him the chance to use his high school Spanish. Patty from the This-N-That shop tag-teamed with Kevin from the PO Grocery in teaching.

"Sam wanted someone to look after the baby while he searched for Fiona, so he came here. I guess I was closest."

"But you didn't look after the baby."

"No." I remembered hurrying into my clothes and a jacket and meeting Sam in the hall. "I know the mill site well, and Sam hadn't been there in a while. I offered to go with him. We left Nicky with Lyndon Forster, the caretaker in the cottage between here and Big House. We walked over together."

"The mill site belonged to Sam's family, didn't it? I imagine he'd be familiar with it."

"He was when he was a kid. Wilfreds haven't lived in Wilfred for more than twenty years, including Sam. They left when the mill burned down in the late 1990s. Since then, Big House has been mostly sitting empty. Lyndon keeps it up for him."

"I see."

These were such straightforward questions, yet I was on the defensive.

Sheriff Beattie raised and lowered her head in a low nod. "So you walked over."

"We took the trail along the river. The same one I recommended to Fiona. Have you seen it?"

"Oh yes." Her tone left no doubt that she'd walked the trail and examined every step of the way.

"We went as far as the mill, but we didn't find her or any sign she'd been there." It had been so quiet. Nothing but the dark construction trailer, the cracked mill foundation, and the cold, still stretch of millpond, and the earth's rumbling warning. Was the tire iron in the brush even then?

"What were you looking for?"

A good question. "I guess Sam just wanted to see if . . ."

She didn't even prompt with an "if what?"

"If she was still there?" That sounded stupid. I quieted my voice. "He was feeling helpless. He had to do something, and I guess going to the mill site was it. I'm sure he told you all about it." Even as the words left my mouth, I knew how dumb they sounded. Sam was a professional. Why would he think Fiona would be gallivanting in the woods in the middle of the night? Then again, she was his wife. Different rules, different emotions applied.

"You say you haven't been in touch with Sam all these months? No calls? No emails?"

"No. As I told you."

She stared at me as if daring me to change my answer.

"No," I repeated. "You think Sam and I went to the mill site to . . . to kill Fiona? That's ridiculous."

"Maybe." She snapped her pad shut. "Maybe not."

"What about Brett Thornsby? Shouldn't you be looking for him?"

"We are looking for him. We're also searching the woods and having the weapon tested for DNA." She stood and softened her voice. "I know these questions might feel insulting, but you have to understand that we need to explore every possible avenue. Sam and Fiona were divorcing. Money and jealousy can drive a person to extremes."

"One more thing," I said and told her about Mrs. Garlington's sighting of a stranger in an SUV the day earlier. The sheriff didn't seem overly impressed, but she took notes.

"You don't even know for sure that Fiona was killed," I pointed out.

Sheriff Beattie raised her eyebrows. "Somebody was."

CHAPTER NINE

After the sheriff left, I found Roz on the second floor, surrounded by books. A few volumes on wildlife sprawled at her side, and a stack of papers on local tribes leaned against the shelf next to her. They were surprisingly quiet, accepting whatever she needed to do to add them to our inventory. I caught a lion's roar from one book, but it felt more like an exercise of privilege than a need to sound the alarm.

"Aren't you going home?" I asked. "It's late."

She clicked a few more notes into the laptop, then shut it. "I guess it's about time. I was hoping to finish up the collection here today. Mrs. Garlington has a music lesson tonight, by the way."

Natural History was in one of the mansion's bedrooms upstairs. Besides a few rows of shelves, a marble fireplace fronted one wall flanked by two windows draped in blue brocade with bobble trim. The sweet-dusty scent of old books filled my nostrils. Heaven.

"How was the talk with the sheriff?" she asked.

"Oh." I laughed once. "You wouldn't believe it. She thought Sam and I had a thing, and we might have knocked off Fiona together."

"Did she, really?" Roz said it as more of a fact than a question.

"Yes. Why are you saying it that way?"

"Well, are you glad?"

"Glad about what?"

"That Fiona's dead."

My breath vanished. "What?" Roz was known for speaking her mind, but this was ridiculous. "Of course not. What makes you say that?"

"Fiona's out of the way now."

"Roz, you're nuts. I don't know what you're talking about." Stunned, I plopped into a nearby Victorian armchair.

She reshelved the last book and slipped off her reading glasses. "Yeah, I guess that was extreme, although I can't say I was wild about her. Seemed kind of flighty to me."

I made a noncommittal noise.

"I just wanted you to come clean that you have a thing for Sam."

"What are you talking about? I barely know him. I didn't hear from him once after he left Wilfred." Not that I hadn't checked my spam file nearly daily to make sure his messages weren't bypassing my inbox.

"Unrequited love is the worst."

"Hello, ladies," Mrs. Garlington said on her way to the dressing-room-slash-music-room.

We both waved.

"I should know," Roz said. "For thirty-three years I pined for Lyndon."

"'Unrequited love' is kind of dramatic. I mean, I barely know Sam."

"What do you call it, then, when you blush when you're around him—a real tell with redheads—and keep finding excuses to look out the windows on the Big House side? I mean, even the sheriff guessed."

Ouch. "You're getting overdramatic."

She shrugged.

"Besides, it worked out with Lyndon," I pointed out.

"Thirty-three years," she repeated. "Since high school. I don't recommend it. That's a lot of nights feeling sorry for yourself, a lot of days looking at what other people have and wondering why you don't have it yourself. Buckets of tears. Sure, it worked out in the end, but it didn't come cheap, and I want something better for you."

Fittingly, "Please Release Me" drifted across the atrium from the organ. I'd be dining by musical scales this evening.

"You got some good romance novels out of it," I said, remembering her many heroes, usually endowed with some form of Lyndon's name. Forster, Duke of Lyndon was one of my favorites, and I occasionally imagined Lyndon in breeches and a powdered wig as he turned the compost. "Anyway, don't worry about my romantic life."

Roz looked me squarely in the eyes. "You do have a thing for him, then."

I lowered my gaze. "Just a crush. That's all." Just a crush that hadn't been fed for months, yet instead of vanishing had, like wine, grown more complex as it aged.

"That's good, because nothing's going to come of it."

"Roz!"

"Oh, Josie, I'm sorry to be so blunt, but it's easier to feel a little bit of pain now than to string it out. Sam's fond of you. That's easy to see. But he doesn't think of you that way." She softened her voice. "He's simply not available right now. I want to make sure you protect yourself."

"You're not telling me anything I don't know. He has a wife and a baby," I said mechanically. Another time, I might have shrugged off her comments as more of her pessimism. This time, I knew she was right.

"Well, he may not have the wife anymore," Roz said, and we let that hang in the air, buffeted by Mrs. Garlington's melodramatic flourish on the organ. "Even if she were alive, he'd be dealing with a messy divorce and a baby. I doubt he's thinking much beyond diaper changes and attorney's fees at this point."

"Or tire irons." I winced at the thought.

"Don't take it personally. It's not you. He doesn't have the emotional bandwidth right now. Think about it. If he'd kept up with you—flirting, sending notes, whatever—he'd be a creep."

I didn't like it, but I had to admit Roz was right. Mrs. Garlington punctuated the thought with a long vibrato.

Roz tucked the laptop under her arm. "I'd better be going. Lyndon ordered a jigsaw puzzle of cigar labels. It's going to be a long night."

I touched her arm. "Roz, thank you for caring enough to talk truth to me."

"Anytime. I consider you a good friend, and I know you'd do the same for me." She was nearly out the door when she stopped at the side table and picked up a fat novel. "What's this doing here? It should be downstairs in fiction."

An alert chimed in my head. "I'll take it." Bibliomancy. The novel had advice for me.

As Roz took the stairs to leave, I turned the novel over. *The Eustace Diamonds* by Trollope, a nineteenth-century potboiler and one of my favorite comfort reads.

I closed my eyes and let my fingers riffle the pages until one tingled. There it was. I ran my hand down the page until the words seemed to grasp a finger.

It was an early chapter about Lucy Morris's unrequited love for Frank Greystone. I sighed. First Roz, now this.

> *In herself she regarded this passion of hers as a healthy man regards the loss of a leg or an arm. It is a great nuisance, a loss that maims the whole life, a misfortune to be regretted. But because a leg is gone, everything is not gone. A man with a wooden leg may stump about through much action, and may enjoy the keenest pleasures of humanity.*

With that, my metaphorical wooden leg and I stumped upstairs.

After dinner, I slipped my grandmother's lesson on curses from its envelope. Roz had gone home, Mrs. Garlington had finished with her student, and the mansion was quiet once again. This time I was determined to read the letter on curses to its end.

As was his habit, Rodney appeared out of nowhere to sit by me while I absorbed my grandmother's words. He seemed to be getting used to his collar, but he wasn't above the occasional gratuitous jingle to let me know he'd prefer to roam commando.

After a quick review of the beginning, I picked up where I'd left off:

> *Removing a curse is more difficult than casting one. When a person is cursed, the curse will vanish with the witch who placed it. The witch dies, and the curse dies with her. However, when an object or place is cursed, the curse will persist until it's lifted. Lifting the curse requires either neutralizing it with good energy, or dispelling the curse by meeting its intention. Let me give you an example. Say a witch cursed someone who was persecuting her. If the person stopped persecuting her or if the witch died, the curse would unbind itself.*
>
> *It's not always possible to remove a curse. To counteract its effects, you must untangle the knot that produced the curse and do what you can to dissolve the original conflict. This might be impossible. A curse can linger for decades, still destroying, with little obvious waning of its powers. You may never find the curse's source, although it's often valuable to investigate. If you don't find the root of the curse, there's not much you can do but*

*bless the bearer of the curse and pray they find
some peace.*

I folded the lesson and replaced it in its envelope.
Grandma was a witch, sure, but she was a churchgoer,
too, which explained the talk of blessings and prayers.
She supplied the local church with altar flowers she'd
charmed to improve the sermon.

"What do you think, Rodney?"

His purring ramped up a few decibels, and he headbutted my chin.

"Sweet kitten." I combed my fingers down his body.

He flopped over on the kitchen table and showed me
his belly, where his birthmark, like mine, like Grandma's,
formed a brown star with an elongated top point.

"The mill burning down, now Fiona's disappearance—
they could have to do with a curse, if what Mrs. Garlington says is right. As for the curse doubling back, I can't
see how that would apply to land."

I pushed myself away from the table and walked into
the hall, where I could look down into the atrium and
onto the thousands of volumes shelved in the rooms on
the floors below.

What could they tell me about the mill site? My first
thought was of the tribes who'd inhabited the area for
centuries before Thurston Wilfred began harvesting the
area's timber. What if the mill had been built on a Native
American grave site? It was a gorgeous stretch of land,
just above the Kirby River. It could be a natural sacred
area.

The library had a good local history section. What
could it tell me?

I rested my hands on the banister encircling the third floor. "Books," I said down into the atrium, now lit only by the moon through stained glass. "Tell me about the land the old mill site is on."

Here, a shelf on the second floor whispered. *Come here.*

Padding down the service staircase, Rodney at my feet, I remembered the first time I'd heard books talking to me and how disorienting it had been—yet how natural. I'd always loved books. I'd always marveled at how a handful of paper could contain so much emotion and information. Grandma said my love of books was what unlocked their energy for me. When that meant simply recommending books for patrons, it was fine. I was still learning to harness the raw power that leapt out of control when I wasn't careful.

Over here, a shelf in the local history section said. *Tribal rolls*.

Psst, another book said. *Over here.*

The books were getting antsy. "I'm coming."

A volume popped forward from its shelf. I plucked it and settled into an armchair in the corner and clicked on the table lamp.

Rolls of Certain Indian Tribes, it said. The McChesney Rolls, an accounting of the Native American tribe that had lived in the region.

Us, too, a few other books whispered. Their spines glimmered with pale green light. I pulled them out and stacked them on the table next to me. Maybe here, maybe somewhere, I'd get to the bottom of the mill site's curse.

Hours later, I yawned and rubbed my burning eyes. I'd learned all sorts of interesting things about the local tribes—I even set aside a few books I thought Lewis Cruikshank would find useful—but nothing about the old mill site or a curse. When I asked the books specifically about the curse, they were silent. Unusually silent, in fact. No humor book tried to pass along a joke, no philosophy tome ruminated on curses in general. No, it was as if they refused to talk.

CHAPTER TEN

Last night's research had been a distraction from Sam's missing wife. This morning, amid the conversations and clatter of forks on platters at Darla's Café, there was no escaping the topic.

"They haul off Sam yet?" Duke asked the moment I settled at the counter.

"Duke!" I said. "Really?"

"I figured you'd see everything that goes down over there. You'd definitely know if they took him out in handcuffs." Duke's Brylcreemed hair was meticulously swirled today. He must have been counting on an audience for his retelling of finding the tire iron.

"Sorry I can't help you." I flipped over my coffee cup to the "yes, please" position. "Oatmeal, please, Darla. Could you fix it special?" Although these days even oatmeal was full of flavor to me, I couldn't resist amping it up. Darla was always happy to help.

"Hazelnuts and dried cherries. Hang tight," she said.

"Anyway, it's got to be the guy from the gallery," Roz said. "Otherwise, why would he go running off?"

"Unless he's dead, too," Duke said.

"Dead people don't drive," Roz said, gesturing with a fork with half a sausage speared on its tines. "His car is gone." Today Roz wore a polka-dotted blouse that emphasized her rounded features.

"Those rental cars have a tracking device in them, don't they?" Darla said as she slid a platter of biscuits and gravy in front of Duke.

"I'm sure Sheriff Beattie is following up on that," I said. Could Brett have been the man Mrs. Garlington saw? He might have switched rental cars from an SUV to a compact.

"The question is, why?" Roz said. "Why would someone from her gallery kill Fiona?"

"Jealousy, greed, revenge," Duke supplied. "Those are the usual motives. The artistic type isn't predictable. Mind you, my money's still on Sam."

Patty, the owner of the This-N-That and now the Sing-Along Salon karaoke lounge in the store's basement, took the seat next to me. Today she wore a powder-blue tracksuit with GET 'ER DONE emblazoned up the legs and across her chest, despite the fact that no one had actually seen her indulge in any form of exercise, ever. Side by side, Patty's resemblance to her big sister, Darla, showed in the no-nonsense set of their jaws and serious brows.

"How was the ESL class last night?" I asked her.

"Not bad. I gave them each a free pass to my karaoke club. Do them good to sing in English." She raised a finger to Darla. "I'll take the fitness special, please."

We all knew Patty had already eaten breakfast, and the "fitness special" was a malted milk shake. Darla tucked a stainless-steel cup under the shake mixer.

"So," Duke continued between mouthfuls of biscuit, "Sam still up at Big House?"

"With the baby," Roz said. "What a cute little guy Nicky is. All that curly black hair."

Darla gave Roz a significant look. "Sam never had curly hair. None of the Wilfreds did."

"And Sam's is quite a bit lighter. Maybe his wife has black hair somewhere on her side of the family."

"Maybe," Roz said in a way that read as "*and pigs fly.*"

"I'll pack the poor man a to-go box," Darla said. "Good morning, Lalena. Rough night telling fortunes?"

Lalena Dolby read palms and tarot cards from her trailer at the Magnolia Rolling Estates. Most mornings, including today, she didn't bother changing out of her bathrobe when she dropped by the diner. I wouldn't be surprised if she had more robes than dresses.

"Interest has exploded with Fiona Wilfred's disappearance," she said. "But, no, I was up late reading. Josie got me started on some vintage Mabel Seeley crime novels. Who knew the woods could be so creepy?"

"What do the cards have to say about Fiona?" Roz asked. She set her ever-present fan next to her plate and swiveled to listen.

"The cards say ten dollars for a three-card reading and

twenty-five for the full Celtic cross," she said. "Pancakes, please, Darla."

"It's the curse," Mrs. Garlington said. I hadn't seen her at the edge of the counter. She'd been unusually quiet. Maybe mentally composing a poem. "I told you the land was cursed."

I took my coffee mug and moved down a few stools to the buffer stool generally kept open next to her.

"Tell me more about this curse," I said.

She took off her glasses and trained her cornflower-blue eyes at me. "Well, the mill burned down. Then we found out the Buckwalter fellow had been killed there," she said, referring to a long-ago murder that had been uncovered last fall. "Now this. Poor Fiona Wilfred." She sighed a long one. "And remember the criminal element I encountered on my walk."

"You're sure it wasn't Tommy Daniels, the contractor?"

She looked at me as if I were barely smart enough to tie my own shoelaces. "I said he was tall, skinny, and dark, didn't I?"

"True," I said. "Did you happen to see the man from Fiona's gallery? He fits the description."

"No. Was he packing heat?"

"Not that I know of." Now it was my turn to sigh. "The mill has seen its share of trouble, but why? Who cursed it?"

"Beats me," Mrs. Garlington said.

That was it? "I thought you knew something in particular."

"Nope."

"How about a tribal curse? Maybe it was a gravesite or a holy area," Darla said.

"I thought of that and spent half the night reading up on local tribes," I said. "I couldn't find anything in the library's local history section that qualified as curse material."

"Doubt it was a gravesite," Duke said, wiping the last smudge of gravy from his platter with a piece of biscuit. "That land floods—or at least it did until the levee went up for the millpond, and sometimes that don't even stop it. You wouldn't want to bury anything there."

"Heads-up," Darla said in a low voice. "It's Sheriff Straightface herself."

The door opened, and we all turned to see Sheriff Beattie. "Good morning," she said, as if facing our stares was as normal as putting on her pants in the morning.

"Find out who used the tire iron?" Duke asked. "And on whom?"

"Active investigation. Can't talk about it." She slid into a booth and lifted the menu stuck into a holder with the salt and pepper shakers. "I hear your shrimp and grits are excellent."

"I'll bring you a bowl, and you can tell me yourself," Darla said.

"Got to be Sam," Duke said. "Motive and opportunity."

In the past months, I'd come a long way in appreciating Duke, but his manners still needed work.

"Not with her gallery friend running off like that," Roz said.

"Brett Thornsby?" As casually as if discussing an afternoon sun break or Dylan's cat having kittens, Sheriff Beattie said, "We found him."

CHAPTER ELEVEN

"You said what?" Duke said.

"I'm looking forward to that shrimp and grits," the sheriff replied.

"It'll be up in a minute," Darla said, tossing her dish towel on the counter. "But reel that back a second. You just told us Brett Thornsby had been found. Did you arrest him?"

Sheriff Beattie, her expression as placid as an elderly nun's, ruminated on this question. Finally, she said, "No."

"No, what?" Roz said. She picked up her fan and flapped it at her reddening face. We were all getting a bit tense.

"Why should I arrest him?" the sheriff said. "We found him, and he's on his way back to Wilfred for questioning."

"His 'way back'?" Roz asked. "Where was he?"

My thought exactly.

"We found his vehicle out of town and traced him through the rental car company. He'll be here soon. That's all I have to say." Darla slid her breakfast onto the sheriff's table. The sheriff dipped a fork into her bowl and tasted. "That, and this is delicious. What is that herb? Thyme?"

Patrons swarmed the library, though only a few actually wanted to check out books.

"Give me patience," I begged Marilyn's portrait as I passed through the atrium.

Here on the bluff above the Kirby River were the library, Big House, and Lyndon's cottage. Nothing else. Since the sheriff was holed up at Big House with Sam and Brett Thornsby, the library was the closest thing to a front-row seat. Thus, the surfeit of phony book browsers.

So far, there hadn't been much to see. The sheriff's SUV and Brett's compact were parked out front. Everyone was inside Big House and out of view. Once, the sound of a baby crying had drifted through a window, but moments later the window had been shut, and that was that.

I settled at the circulation desk to greet people as they entered and answer their made-up questions. Circulation was in the house's old parlor, just to the right of the entrance through the foyer. The room, like most in the mansion, had a fireplace. This one was marble carved in a Victorian Italianate style. However, in this room, French doors flanked the fireplace. At night, heavy brocade curtains covered them. Right now, silk chiffon, snagged here and there over the years, filtered the light but left a good view across the lawn to Big House. Yes, I kept watch, too.

Rodney was dozing in my inbox, barely suffering kids who said, "He's so cute!" and threatened to touch him. My interest in Rodney at this moment was more practical. If I wanted—and could get someone to watch the circulation desk—I could meld into Rodney's body and nudge him outside. Big House had a cat flap in its kitchen door. We might pop in and listen for a while.

Rodney lifted his head and fixed his whiskey-hued eyes on me. *No dice*, he seemed to say. *Lift my collar, and then we'll talk.* He tucked his head under a leg for an extended nap.

Just then, Big House's front door opened, and Sheriff Beattie strolled across the front porch and down the steps. Instead of getting into her SUV, she crossed the lawn, headed for the library. Patrons everywhere scattered like cockroaches under a light.

I straightened my papers and relaxed into what I hoped was a "busy, yet receptive" expression. The front door opened. Closed. Then there she was.

"Sheriff Beattie," I said. "What a surprise."

"Uh-huh," she said, without expression.

"How can I help you?" Even Rodney lifted his head and shifted his body to face hers.

"Upstairs, this side of the library. What books are up there?"

"The front room is Natural History, and the room toward the rear is the business collection."

"I wouldn't mind browsing some natural history, then."

Before I could reply, she'd ducked into the atrium, and the heavy tread of her boots retreated to the main staircase at the back of the house. In a minute, she'd be directly above me. And, like me, she'd be watching Big House. Sam and Brett Thornsby were still inside.

We didn't need to wait long. Brett exploded onto the porch. His voice sliced the afternoon drizzle.

"*You.* I'm not stupid. I don't care what you told the sheriff. You did it. You killed her."

I looked behind me. A few patrons lingered, including a young mother to whom I'd recommended a children's book on toilet training when she'd asked about gardening and a man to whom I'd handed a Persian cookbook when he'd expressed an interest in baseball history. They edged closer to listen. If the sheriff cracked the window upstairs, this conversation would be all hers, too.

I stepped to the French doors and pushed back the curtain. Sam's reply was too quiet to make out. I didn't see the baby, either, just Brett's broad-shouldered figure facing the wide doorway.

He shook his fist, like someone in a movie. "She told me you were cheating her out of a lot of money. She knew. She had an attorney lined up to look at the sale." He stepped closer, and his voice cracked with anger. "Where'd you leave her? Where's the body, huh?"

I couldn't hear Sam, but on the heels of his words were Brett's, at full throat. "You won't get away with it."

The thud of his footsteps on Big House's wooden steps

carried across the lawn. His brakes squealed as he pulled quickly into reverse, and he shot onto the highway in a passion-fueled burst.

I raised my eyes to the ceiling. Upstairs, beyond the plaster-carved molding, the sheriff had heard it all.

CHAPTER TWELVE

Poor Sam. His goose was cooked. A useful cliché. There must be a dozen more like it, I thought as I powered down my laptop that evening. No classes tonight. I could shut off the lights, check that the windows and doors were locked, and head upstairs for the evening.

The jig is up, a gangster novel said in a Brooklyn accent. *How's that for a cliché?*

"Not bad," I said. "But not true. Sam would never have killed Fiona."

Caught by the short hairs, another novel suggested. Other books jumped in, and soon the atrium hummed with voices. *Done to a turn. Got him over a barrel. Hung out to dry. Not a ghost of a chance. Open-and-shut case.*

"Stop it!" I yelled.

One more book chimed in. *The writing is on the wall.*

I sighed. Things did not look good for Sam. With Brett questioned and released, Sam had to have had a steel-clad alibi, if he were to stay out of jail. I winced, remembering Brett's accusations.

Someone knocked on the kitchen door. I flicked on the lights again. Sam's face and shoulders filled the door's window.

"Sam," I said simply, once the door was open.

The rain had stopped, and the last thrusts of the afternoon sun shed opalescent light among the clouds. I remembered the Japanese fable of the bride of the fox that Grandma used to read to my sisters and me. Only at magical times like these—between day and night, the rain and the sun—did foxes marry.

I opened the door. "Sam," I said simply.

"Mine?" Then, because I couldn't think of anything smart to follow it, I said, "Where's the baby?"

"Nicky's with Lyndon and Roz." He shook his head. "I still can't get used to the idea that they're a couple."

"It's an unusual relationship. Do you want to come in?"

"Actually, I want to talk to you. Would you like to come over for dinner? I'm making a vegetable soup. Spring vegetables—fava beans and greens, mostly."

My heart skipped a beat. "No Fiona, then? Maybe a call?"

He shook his head.

"Let me feed Rodney, and I'll be over in a minute."

Rodney's food was untouched. His hunger strike continued. Should I be worried? From my connection to him, I sensed he was okay, but what if I was wrong? I didn't want him to starve because of his collar. I ran upstairs for a can of tuna and flaked some on his kibble. That should do the trick.

Now for my own dinner. With Sam. As I crossed the lawn to Big House, I remembered Roz's words. "He's fond of you, Josie, but that's all."

Of course. He had a freshly dead wife and a very new baby. He also had a potential life sentence.

I knocked at the kitchen door at the house's rear, facing town and the river. For reasons Wilfredians never understood, Thurston number two had oriented Big House's face away from town, and the best view was from the tiny porch outside the kitchen door.

Sam gestured for me to enter. The kitchen smelled of garlic and basil. Two bowls and cloth napkins were set at the kitchen table, and *Tristan und Isolde*—or so the liner notes told me in a German accent—played quietly in the background.

"I heard Brett as he left yesterday," I said. Why not get it out into the open?

"You're not the only one." He set a wooden spoon onto a saucer and looked me in the eyes. "What do you think?"

"You mean, do I think you killed your wife?"

He nodded.

I smoothed my sleeves. "You know I don't."

He frowned—relief, maybe—and returned to the stove. "Thank you. But it doesn't look good. The sheriff was listening, wasn't she?"

I took a seat. "I think so. So what? He might have been playacting to put blame on you. Why did she let him go?"

"He must have an unimpeachable alibi. Sheriff Beattie would never have released him otherwise."

"I wondered about that. Do you know what the alibi is?" I asked.

"No. No specifics, anyway." He switched off the burner and sat across from me. "The sheriff has definitely set her sights on me."

"Probably," I agreed.

Rodney popped through the flap in the kitchen door. I didn't know who had installed it—maybe a long-ago kitchen maid—but Rodney was a fan. He strutted over and rubbed against Sam's legs. Sam absently reached down to pet him and sneezed.

"Our marriage was over, I admit. That doesn't mean I killed her. There's no way. The money didn't matter to me, as long as Nicky would be provided for. I—"

"I believe you," I said.

"No one else does."

"I'm not so sure about that, but I agree on one point. It doesn't look good for you."

Rodney leapt into my lap. I stroked his fur, soft as a nest of spiderwebs, and felt his purrs vibrate through his belly. He was far from skin and bones, despite his show of ignoring dinner.

"The sheriff will conduct her investigation. Until they have a body in hand, I doubt they'll take me into custody." His lips lifted into a vague smile, letting me know he was definitely unhappy. "I plan on asking questions of my own in the meantime."

"Why? You don't think Sheriff Beattie's investigation will be thorough enough?"

"She's settled on her chief suspect. Her work now is to line up evidence against me, not look for someone else. Meanwhile, the real murderer could be covering his tracks."

He drummed his fingers on the table a moment, then rose to dish up soup. He set a bowl of grated Parmesan cheese on the table next to one of the loaves of bread the PO Grocery had delivered daily from a Portland bakery.

I wasn't ready to eat just yet. "What does all this have to do with me?"

Rodney, still on my lap, his head above the table, looked with interest at the soup. I nudged him to the floor. If he was hungry, he could go home and try some of the tuna I'd left.

"People will hesitate to talk to me. I know that."

"Nicky is an entry," I pointed out. "He's already a big draw."

"Nicky is a good reason for them to want to put me away and make sure the baby has a safe home." He ripped a piece of bread off the loaf. "They trust you. They'll talk to you."

Sheriff Beattie, for all her cold-fish demeanor, seemed plenty competent to me. Then there were my inconvenient feelings. Somehow I had to wean myself off of Sam. "I don't know."

"Remember last fall?"

Of course I remembered. I remembered every second about that terrifying, exciting few weeks. I'd had a hard time forgetting certain details. Like how I'd found Sam, that first night, sleeping in the library with a Hardy Boys mystery in his lap, and how he'd snapped awake at my presence. Or how we'd made up his parents' bed together so I could stay there, safe. Or how he'd mentioned off-hand that his wife had called. That he even had a wife.

Not that any of this had crossed his mind since, I was sure.

"Sure, I remember it," I said.

"We worked so well together."

"I don't know," I said, but it wasn't convincing.

He set down his spoon. "You want to help, anyway. I know you do."

"What do you mean?"

"It's your sense of justice. If something's not fair, you can't let it stand." He caught my gaze. A tiny muscle in his jaw twitched, and it tugged some corresponding muscle in my heart. He was right. A strong sense of justice was in my DNA.

"There's one other thing," Sam said.

"What's that?"

"I didn't want to bring this up, but remember how you gave Fiona directions to the mill site?"

"Sure," I said warily.

"And how you and I went there that night?"

"You hadn't wanted to take me," I said. "Remember? I was the one who parked Nicky with Lyndon and insisted on coming along."

"I know. We can both tell the sheriff exactly that, but it won't make a difference."

"She'd hinted at all of this with me. And then she found us talking in my office with the door shut." I looked away.

"Exactly." He picked up his spoon again and dug in.

My heart sank, but at the same time, something kindled inside. I was in this, too. I had every motivation to see Sam—and me—cleared. It was what I wanted, both as a witch who was a truth teller and as someone with a huge crush.

Rodney milled at my feet, still purring in high gear.

"Okay," I said. "What do you want me to do?"

My goose was cooked.

CHAPTER THIRTEEN

As we were finishing dinner, Lyndon brought Nicky to Big House.

"He took his entire bottle," he said, chucking Nicky under the chin. "Little man with a big appetite, he is."

I'd never heard this tone from him before. When Lyndon did talk—which wasn't often—it was usually in a few gruff syllables. I liked this Lyndon.

"I gave him a tour of the conservatory. The baby seems to enjoy the larger tropical specimens." He handed Nicky to Sam. "He's a natural. He'll develop finer taste with time and start to appreciate less showy blooms."

We took the baby and two wool blankets to the kitchen's back stoop. I settled into a chair and drew up my legs. The lights of Wilfred shone below, on the other side of the river. Lalena was in her trailer at the Magnolia Rolling Estates, and Mrs. Garlington was parked in her drive, probably getting her weekly tarot card reading. Darla's Café was busy, although at this time of day, customers were probably more on the tavern side of the establishment. Lights went off at the PO Grocery. Way off to the left, out of sight, beyond the trailer park and the stretch of meadow to the river, lay the old mill site.

What had I just agreed to with Sam? "What can we do to find out what happened to Fiona that Sheriff Beattie can't?"

Sam held Nicky against his chest and tucked the blanket around him. The baby slept, three fingers hanging from his lip.

"We have a few advantages she doesn't. You know the town and the people."

"Assuming that someone here, um, you know—" It just didn't feel right to talk about murder with the baby here.

"I want to be frank with you about the divorce."

"Yes?" I said warily.

"We were having a hard time coming to terms. I'd think we had everything ironed out, then she would want more."

"I get it." I pulled up the blanket higher. "If money was a motive for, uh—"

"Killing Fiona," Sam supplied. "I appreciate your delicacy, but he's a baby, Josie, not a PhD in linguistics. He can't understand us."

I refrained from sticking out my tongue at him. "Then you'd have a strong motive. When you and Fiona divorced, you'd have to pay alimony, child support, and you'd share Nicky."

"Yes," he said in a matter-of-fact tone. "That's about it. I had no idea Fiona thought I was trying to cheat her by lowballing the mill site sale. Brett said she was having a forensic accountant go over the sale and was planning to sue. I didn't know about that, either."

"I bet that's why she wanted to see the mill site," I said. "She wasn't looking for landscapes to paint. She wanted to take photos to show her lawyer."

"Honestly, the money wasn't a big deal to me, as long as Nicky was provided for. I'd have thought she'd known that by now."

"Was Fiona like that? Suspicious?"

He let out a long breath. "No. Not really. She was fun to be with, impulsive. No matter where she was, something good would happen. People flocked to her. I'd always been such a loner, raised here in the country with no brothers or sisters. I saw something in her I wanted more of in myself. I met her in college, and we married right away."

He was introspective. Quiet. I could understand how Fiona's vivacity would grab him.

"The thing is, just like they say, what attracted me to her was what ended up driving me crazy. I'm sure it was worse for her. She wanted to go out when I wanted to stay in. She hated my music. Then she started disappearing. First for a few hours. Later, for days." He lifted Nicky's head to his lips. "But not since the baby. She'd promised me it was different now."

"Which is why you were so worried when she didn't come home."

We both faced the valley. Stars thinly iced the sky. Wilfred's quiet was something I was still getting used to.

"I'm not entirely stupid," Sam continued. "I knew it wasn't in Fiona's nature to be the devoted wife and mother, but she'd promised, and she had every incentive to follow through, at least until the divorce was final. Otherwise, I could make a case for full custody of Nicky."

"Brett?" I asked gingerly, leaving the rest of the question unspoken.

He looped his free hand around his tea mug. "I asked Fiona, and she said no. I believed her when she told me she wasn't having an affair with Brett."

Besides custody, an affair could threaten her child support and alimony. In novels, romance was tidy, and, except for landmark tragedies like *Romeo and Juliet*, all ended well. None of this squabbling over real estate and too-handsome gallery staff.

"Did you know him?" I asked. "Brett, that is?"

"I never met him. Fiona spent time with him last summer, but he hasn't been around since. I had the impression he'd done something to put her off. I was surprised when he showed up here, frankly."

"You never ghosted Fiona?" In the FBI, Sam had been a "ghost," tracking suspects without being tracked himself.

His tea mug steamed untouched beside him. "No. I couldn't do that."

"Well," I said. "The first step should be to check Brett's alibi. He's still the most likely suspect."

"Sheriff Beattie said they tracked his rental car. He was in Portland. He says he left Fiona sketching at the mill site, walked back here, and drove into Portland to meet an old friend. They were together all evening."

"He could have killed her before he left," I said.

"The contractor, architect, and the Waterses were at the site. They may have seen Brett leave or heard something."

"Brett would have had to find the tire iron, use it"—I

couldn't think of a more delicate euphemism—"then hide it in the bushes. That takes time."

"The woods may have muffled the noise of a struggle. Unless she was surprised."

I imagined Fiona sketching, and Brett's hand reaching around to cover her mouth. "Where would he find a tire iron? He didn't have one with him at the library, and they're not lying around at the mill site."

"That's something to look into," Sam said. "Could you talk with the architect and see if he heard or saw anything? You already have a start with him, and I think you'll have better luck with the contractor, too. If you get their stories—where they were, what they saw, and when—I'll double-check them."

"I can do that."

"Meanwhile, I'll look into Brett's alibi," Sam said.

"You know, Mrs. Garlington ran into someone suspicious at the mill site the morning before."

"No kidding. Who?"

"A stranger with a handgun. She was scared enough to hide until he left. To be thorough, I'll talk with her, too."

"We don't have much time," Sam added. "Just until Fiona's body is found or they've matched her DNA against the tire iron. Depending on how backed up the lab is, the sheriff will probably have results by the end of the week."

"Then you think you'll be arrested?"

"At least detained for a while." He tilted his head down again to look at Nicky, curled up in sleep. "For this guy's sake, I've got to figure it out."

"I have the next two days off. Why don't we meet tomorrow night to report back?"

"Thank you, Josie." He looked at me with warmth that made my blanket unnecessary.

"I'm really sorry," I said, feeling my face heat up. "For both you and Nicky. You know I'll do what I can to help." And try not to get sucked more deeply into my stupid infatuation. I shifted my gaze from the worried set of Sam's lips to the baby. "All that black curly hair," I said. "The Wilfreds must be part black Irish."

"Oh, no." Sam pressed his finger lovingly into Nicky's plump cheek. The baby opened his pink mouth into a yawn, seeming not even to wake. "Nicky's not mine."

CHAPTER FOURTEEN

"You mean, you're not his father?" I said once the shock had subsided.

Sam's hand enveloped the back of Nicky's head, and he stared beyond the river, into the valley. "I'm definitely his father, just not biologically." His voice was low.

"Oh."

"As I said, Fiona and I are divorcing. We haven't been—"

"I get it," I said quickly.

"—for a while. I was away on work assignments these past years, and I guess . . ."

This time I didn't supply a response. The faraway rumble of a diesel engine floated up toward us, muffled by the rustle of the wind in the trees.

"Sorry," Sam said. "I haven't told this to anyone. Anyway, Fiona got pregnant. It was just the one affair. She promised me it hadn't happened before and wouldn't happen again."

"Do you—do you know who his biological father is?"

"No," he said simply.

I nodded but couldn't help thinking of Brett. One look at Sam's expression showed a razor-sharp intellect, and his role at the FBI had depended on his knowledge of human behavior. Could he be that blind?

"I see," I said.

"You think I'm an idiot."

"I have to wonder," I admitted.

"Because of the guy from the gallery."

"He's attractive, you have to give him that. Plus, why would an art gallery send a staff person to help Fiona sketch? What was he going to do? Hold her pencil? He had to have wanted to come."

Shadows enveloped Sam's face. "I've known her for years now. Like I said, I believe she told me the truth. Anyway, as far as anyone's concerned, Nicky's mine." He stared down to Wilfred's quickly darkening footprint. "I only tell you this because I feel like you should know. Things might come out. I didn't want you to be surprised."

This hadn't been easy for him to say. He confided in me because he trusted me. That trust felt good.

I clicked on the light in the service staircase at the library's side entrance. Mulling over Sam's confession stirred up a strange combination of emotional fullness and loss. I felt like my chest held a tinderbox ready to collapse upon itself.

I mounted the stairs. The library was quiet, smelling of old paper and the lemon oil Lyndon used on the banisters.

I didn't know if I'd learn anything Sheriff Beattie couldn't, but there was one area in which I had the advantage: magic. Maybe if I could get to the bottom of the curse, I could untangle the situation, or at least prevent future tragedies. The lesson on curses had come up now for a reason. However, nothing I'd gathered from the library's collections about the tribes hinted at a curse on the mill site, and my attempts to get the books to give me any further hints had failed.

Sam was right that I had a strong sense of justice: I was a truth teller. Witches in my family had different qualities through which they funneled their magic. My mother had visions, and my sisters and grandmother were healers. My grandmother had a special way with plants. Like books talked to me, plants talked to Grandma. She'd made poultices and tinctures that could cure everything from night sweats to a cheating husband. She was even powerful enough to curb my magic when my mother had forced it.

Besides the fact that I was a truth teller, my star-shaped birthmark marked me as having especially intense powers. The combination made me the sort of witch who, in centuries past, ended up burned at the stake or bound and tossed in a river because she couldn't let the townspeople be victimized or a wife be abused. Or a curse go unresolved.

Not only did I have the need to see justice done, I had the responsibility. Sam didn't know about my full range of investigative skills. I intended to use them right now, starting with bibliomancy.

I shed my coat upstairs and then took the service staircase to the library's ground floor and stood in the atrium. Next to me was a Victorian table with a vase of pussy willow branches Lyndon had arranged. I glanced up at Marilyn Wilfred's portrait above the double doors leading to the foyer. I'd wondered once or twice if she'd been a witch, but I'd never had clear evidence one way or another. In any case, her presence was always a comfort.

Unsurprisingly, Rodney appeared at my feet. He wound around my calves, letting his tail touch me, even as he settled at my ankles. If I wasn't mistaken, he jingled his collar more than necessary and scratched at it, looking me straight in the eyes.

Not a light was on. Only moonlight through the stained-glass cupola three floors above gave the slightest illumination.

"Books," I said. "Tell me. Which one?"

To my right, a faint glow, barely perceptible, came from fiction. I followed the light and found a volume buzzing with energy on a shelf close to the fireplace. I pulled the book from the shelf. It was warm in my hands.

A slender volume, a horror novella, I noted, and had the sudden desire to cram it back into the shelf and leave. No. I'd asked for help, and this was what the books had provided. It was my duty to follow up.

As my grandmother had taught me, I closed my eyes and prepared to let my fingers shuffle through the book's pages. The book wouldn't open. My finger stopped at its title.

I took the book, my finger still lying on its cover, to a table lamp and clicked it on.

"*The Man in the Picture*," it read.

I opened to the title page. Although the novella had been written recently, it was set in the nineteenth century, the Wilfred family's world when they first came to the region.

The man in the picture. This was my clue. So, I was looking for a man?

Rodney slipped behind the fireplace screen and was batting a pen someone had left there, as well as purring, as he always did when I worked magic.

The man in the picture. At some point, it would be revealed.

CHAPTER FIFTEEN

I cracked open the window beyond my kitchen table, and moist air blew in from the river. It was one of those crystalline mornings that seemed to tumble out unexpectedly, like a pristine hardback novel from a sack of dog-eared paperbacks. Already the cottonwood branches were swelling, and soon tender green leaves would flutter from them.

I shut the window and turned away. Enough of this bluebirds and tulips nonsense. I had a murderer to find.

At the top of my list of interviewees were Ruff and Sita Waters. Presumably, Fiona had wanted to gauge the mill site's value to see if Sam was shorting her. She might have tracked down the Waterses to feel them out. They were at the mill site the afternoon Fiona was killed.

The problem would be finding them. They weren't in Wilfred, I knew that. They probably had a place in Portland, a good hour away. I imagined a house with a dedicated yoga room featuring a Burmese Buddha and a garage with an electric hatchback parked inside. Lewis Cruikshank might have their address.

I made my way down to the library's kitchen to start the coffee and set up for the day. Even though Roz was in charge on my days off, I loved the morning routine of opening the library. I felt like a travel agent to a world of stories and information, and I was preparing to hand patrons their itineraries.

I took the main staircase just outside the kitchen to the second floor, where I drew open the curtains and switched on lights. Next, I went to the ground floor, saluting Marilyn Wilfred's portrait as I emerged into the atrium. The conservatory needed a quick temperature check. The sun through the green glass ceiling warmed it—no need to put a log in its tiled woodstove this morning. Open went the curtains in Popular Fiction and, next door, in Children's Fiction in old man Thurston's original office. From there, I turned on the lights in the old drawing room and parlor—now Circulation and New Releases—and checked the clock. Five till.

How would I find Ruff and Sita Waters? When I did find them, what sort of excuse could I use for questioning them about Fiona?

A drive into Portland and back would take up most of the afternoon. As I pondered, I propped open the double doors into the foyer and unbolted the front door.

"Morning, Josie," Roz called from the kitchen.

"Morning," I replied. "I'm going out. Have a good day, and don't forget that the knitting club will be in after lunch."

A walk was what I needed to clear my mind. I turned

again to the front door and saw shadows moving behind
the doors' frosted-glass windows. Wilfredians loved their
library, but they rarely waited at the front door. Instead,
early morning patrons were more likely to come in
through the kitchen and help themselves to a cup of coffee. Sometimes they didn't actually want a book at all;
they wanted to shoot the breeze with Roz or opine about
town developments, like Patty's new karaoke lounge.

I turned the door's brass knob—set low, nineteenth-
century style—and froze. It was the Waterses.

"Are you open yet?" Sita said. The morning was bright,
but still a little chilly, and she rubbed her arms over her
Indian silk caftan.

"Come in." I motioned toward the atrium.

"It's shocking about Fiona Wilfred," Ruff said.

"You've heard?" I said, still startled by their presence.

"The sheriff stopped by last night to question us."

"It doesn't look good," I admitted.

"We knocked at Big House to see Sam, but we must
have missed him." Sita glanced at Ruff, as if looking for
confirmation. "Could we talk with you?"

A mother with twin toddlers came in with the back of
her stroller full of books. Roz stepped up to take care of
her.

I waved Ruff and Sita toward the rear of the library.
"Come to my office. We can talk in private there. Would
you like coffee?" They probably drank green tea chai
lattes, but I thought I'd ask. "Darla gets it from a local
roaster."

"No, thank you," Sita said. They filed into my office,
and I shut the door behind them. It was a squeeze, but we
all fit, including Rodney, who'd nosed his way out from
under my desk.

"We wanted to find out what was happening," Sita said. I'd noticed that although she and Ruff seemed to think as one, she often took charge. "The sheriff asked a lot of questions about the mill site and about Sam." She glanced at Ruff. "She made it sound as if Sam had something to do with Fiona's disappearance. I wonder—were we wrong to buy the land?"

"Wrong?" I said. "In what way?"

"Fiona implied . . ." She didn't seem to want to finish the thought.

"We got a good price on the land," Ruff finished. "Fair, but Sam could have asked for more."

"He knew you were doing something good for Wilfred," I said. The story was too complicated to go into right then, but Sam had been motivated to turn the old mill site—a constant reminder of how his family had run off in the middle of the night—into a driver for the town's reinvention. "He wanted you to have that land."

"That's what he told us when we closed on it. You don't think he was trying to cheat his wife out of anything, do you?"

"Absolutely not," I said.

Rodney was sniffing the hem of Sita's caftan and batted at its beaded trim.

"Should I tell her?" Ruff asked Sita.

"I don't see why not. We already told the sheriff."

Ruff tugged at his beard. "Fiona called us and said Sam had no right to sell the land without her agreement."

"That was his family's land," I said. "Besides, as far as I can tell, this was her first time in Wilfred. I don't think she even knew the mill site existed."

Sita continued. "She said she wanted a payout of the difference between what we bought the land for and what

she thought it was worth. If we didn't pay, she'd challenge the sale in court."

"She said fifty thousand dollars would be enough to
make it right—"

"Whoa," I said.

"—and we could pay her directly."

Rodney jumped to Ruff's lap, and he absently petted
the cat while Rodney seemed to focus on shedding all
over his white wool jacket.

"You're kidding," I said. I wondered if Sam had any
idea this had been going on.

"We were supposed to give her our answer within
forty-eight hours," Ruff said.

"What had you decided?" I asked.

"That we'd talk about it with Sam," Ruff said. "Paying
Fiona under the table didn't seem right, and we didn't
want to get in the middle of a marital dispute."

"And now she's dead," Sita said. "It's not the money.
We have the money. I just don't know about the land anymore. Maybe the retreat was a bad idea. I don't want to
build somewhere with that kind of energy."

"You didn't, by chance, see Fiona that day, did you?" I
asked.

"Sure, but we didn't want to hang around for a long
chat," Ruff said.

"Not after her threats," Sita said. "She was walking toward the stacking house with a man in a light blue
jacket."

"Brett. He's from her art gallery," I said.

"We waved, then we saw Lewis and headed toward the
millpond," Ruff said.

"The contractor was supposed to meet with you, too,
right?" I asked.

"He hung out in the construction trailer, and we met with him later, once we had the chance to get the vibe of the land," Sita said.

I hoped they'd come to some peaceful resolution of their disagreement over the architect's initial sketches. "I understand why it would give you pause, but I hope you won't give up on the retreat center yet."

"It really is a beautiful site, but can you imagine a meditation workshop where a woman had been murdered?" Ruff said. Rodney jumped from his lap and stretched his front legs. All of this talk about death meant nothing to him.

"Bad, bad energy." Sita shook her head again. "Like the land was cursed."

Curses on my mind, I found Roz in Circulation.

"What do you think Sheriff Beattie reads?" she asked.

"Why do you ask?"

"I don't know. I guess I was wondering about her, how she'd be as a heroine in a romance novel." She folded her arms over her chest. "A sphinx? That's an idea. A romance set in ancient Egypt. Beattie could be a queen known as the Sphinx. Until this pharaoh comes along, that is."

I let Roz brainstorm the next of Eliza Chatterly Windsor's romances while I decided which investigative task to attack next. In her lesson, Grandma said that curses weren't often about land, but about people. Could people have something to do with the mill site's curse? Maybe something from Wilfred's past?

"Roz?" I said, interrupting speculation about pyramids and a boudoir with asp-shaped bedposts. "Who knows the most about the mill site's history?"

"We have lots of stuff on local history here," she said.

"I don't mean dates and settlements, I mean the social stuff."

"Gossip. Scandal, you mean," Roz said. "You don't think people would be too stuck on the Elizabeth Taylor–Richard Burton vision if I did an Egyptian romance?"

"Say they did. What's wrong with that? And, yes, I mean dirt on the mill site."

Roz absently batted near her neck with her fan. "I guess you'd need to talk with Sarah Freeburger. She can't remember a thing past the Carter administration, but she can tell you about every family feud and broken marriage back to the Great Depression. What does that have to do with anything?"

"I want to know more about the mill site, get some context."

"You don't think Fiona's murder has anything to do with some old scandal, do you?" She shook her head. "No, it's about cash. Plain and simple."

Roz didn't know I was a witch, and she didn't share Mrs. Garlington's enthusiasm for curses. "It's the librarian in me," I said, hoping that would be explanation enough.

"Mrs. Freeburger's at the nursing home in Forest Grove. I'll look up the address for you. Call ahead and bring cookies. She has a real sweet tooth."

CHAPTER SIXTEEN

The Maple Grove assisted living center was a low, broad brick building intended to look like a house, but that couldn't hide its institutional function. One lonely maple—the ornamental kind, bent and pruned in a Japanese style—occupied a planter beside the front door. If there had ever been more to the grove, there was no sign of it now.

The home's glass doors slid open with a swish of warm air when I stepped close. A few minutes later, I was knocking on Sarah Freeburger's door. An attendant not much younger than I answered. She was tattooed up to her jawbones with twining flowers, and she chewed a slug of gum.

"You must be Josie Way," she said. "Come in."

Sarah Freeburger sat dwarfed in the corner of a white

sofa draped with granny-square afghans. I had no idea how old she was, but it had to be a number high enough that when she died they'd mention it on the evening news. Her eyes were milky and didn't seem to focus, and her skin was tender and white as a baby's, but creased with lines like crumpled parchment.

"Mrs. Freeburger?" I said. "You must be an artist."

The furniture looked generic—classic shapes, cream cotton upholstery—but the walls were crazy with oil paintings. About half were of beach scenes featuring a variety of stormy oceans, and the others were studies of the gaudiest of spring flowers.

"Used to be. Come over here." She patted the couch next to her. "I don't see so well, but I hear perfectly fine."

The small apartment was filled with light shining through a sliding glass door. The door let out onto a large, shared patio with pruned evergreens and hot-pink rhododendrons just breaking into bloom.

"Do you mind if I take care of a few things in the kitchen?" The caretaker tapped at her phone as she asked.

"No. No problem at all." Sarah was dressed in a pale-blue velour tracksuit with ivory scuff slippers. Her woolly white hair was clipped close to her skull. "Josie, you say?"

"Yes. I'm the librarian in Wilfred."

"Ah. Yes." She leaned back and closed her eyes. "Call me Sarah. Marcy—that was her at the door—said you wanted to talk about Wilfred."

"Yes. Specifically, about the mill. You lived in Wilfred, right?"

"Wilfred," she said, a vague smile playing on her lips. But that was all she said.

"Did you grow up there?" I prompted.

"Marcy?" Sarah yelled to the caretaker. "Where's my dinner?"

"It's not dinnertime yet."

"I want my dinner," she said and crossed her frail arms over her blanket. "Dinner. Dinner."

"Oh, all right," the caretaker said. She set aside her phone and pulled a plate from the refrigerator and set it in the microwave.

As the microwave whirred, I said, "I'd like to know more about the old mill. I hear there's been a lot of drama there."

"It burned down," Sarah said.

"Did you spend much time at the mill?" Maybe this was all a waste of time. Sarah Freeburger didn't seem to be the fount of gossip I'd hoped for. Not a fount of any conversation, in fact. Everyone knew that the mill had burned down. I wanted to know about the curse.

The caretaker arrived with a plate of anonymous chopped brown meat in gravy and mushy green beans. With her free hand, she shook open a TV tray. "All right, Sarah. Here's your dinner."

Mrs. Freeburger looked at it, stone-faced, and made no motion to pick up a fork.

"Sometimes she needs encouragement," the caretaker told me. "Here you go, honey." She held a fork of meat shreds to Sarah's lips, and the old woman sealed them firmly and closed her eyes.

Heeding Roz's advice, I'd stopped at the PO Grocery and picked up a box of donuts. I pulled one from the pink carton. "How about a cruller?"

Mrs. Freeburger's eyes flew open, and she grabbed the donut with both hands. When that was gone, I gave her a raspberry Bismark.

"Did you know much about the mill? Or maybe the Wilfred family, Mrs. Freeburger?" I asked her.

A smear of raspberry jam on her cheek, she said, "What do you want to know?"

Now her voice was sharp and clear. The caretaker took the armchair across from us and opened an anatomy text-book. The book launched into a discussion of the nervous system in a vaguely British accent. I tuned it out.

"Helen Garlington thinks the old mill site is cursed. I wonder if you have any idea if that could be true."

"Give me a cinnamon twist, and I'll think about it."

I handed it to her with a fresh napkin. "You have a bit of jam right there." I pointed to her cheek.

She dabbed at the jam and tore into the cinnamon twist. "Helen Garlington. Such a sensitive girl. Popular with the gentlemen, too."

Girl, I thought. She'd been collecting Social Security for a good decade already.

"Artistic type. Always did love a good story." Mrs. Free-burger leaned back. I prepared a chocolate-covered donut just in case. "The old mill site. Let's see."

The caretaker flipped the page of her textbook, and the book launched into a detailed description of a spinal cord.

"Daddy was in charge of peeling and planking down at the mill. He was one of Thurston's confidants. That's Thurston the second."

The one who'd built Big House. "I've heard about him." His heyday would have been between the World Wars. Sarah Freeburger was of a venerable age.

"A curse. A lot of things felt cursed."

"Like what?"

She stared at me, her milky eyes unseeing.

"Oh." I placed the chocolate donut in her hands.

She took a big bite and continued. "There were a few arms lost, fingers for sure, a life or two in the forest. Any mill, any logging operation has that to show. But a curse?"

"A curse doesn't have to be a lost life," I said, remembering my grandmother's lesson. "Maybe it's simply a life ruined in some other way. Or a feeling of . . . something not quite right." Somewhere in the apartment was a novel featuring a love story. It wanted me to know it was there. It was important now. But why? "Or love gone bad," I added, realizing that "love gone bad" might apply to every other house down the block.

"Marilyn Wilfred," Sarah said, this time blotting her face and hands thoroughly. "Now, there's one."

I sat up straighter. "Marilyn?" What would she have to do with a curse? "What do you mean?"

Mrs. Freeburger leaned forward, grasping the arm of the couch. Her voice dropped. "Whenever she's around, bad things happen. Real bad things."

"Like what?" She'd slipped into the present tense, I noticed.

"Milk sours, and cows lose their calves. People die."

Cold prickled the backs of my arms. "Wilfredians love her. She gave the town a library."

"Thought she could make things better with her money. I won't set foot in that place. Never. They warned me."

"She killed people?"

Mrs. Freeburger rested back, and the intensity drained from her gaze. "Marcy? It's time for my bath."

"What about Marilyn Wilfred?" I said.

"Bath," she insisted.

Marcy shut her textbook. "Bath means bath. If you want to talk more, you'll have to come back."

"All right."

Mrs. Freeburger looked away from me in dismissal, toward the patio, where a scrub jay splashed in a bird-bath. I glanced into the kitchen to make sure Marcy was safely out of view, then slipped a blank book from my bag to the shelf under the coffee table. *Do your work*, I willed it and covered it with a copy of *Painting Seaboard Sunsets*.

I reached for the box of donuts.

"Leave those," Mrs. Freeburger said.

The caretaker arrived and lifted Sarah from underneath her armpits. She grasped a three-legged cane.

"Nice of you to drop by," she said in a girlish voice.

"I'll be back soon," I said. "And I'll bring a layer cake."

"How about tomorrow?"

CHAPTER SEVENTEEN

Marilyn Wilfred. I didn't see how such a benevolent figure could be associated with a curse. Sarah Freeburger was still a vein to be mined, but it wasn't going to happen today.

I shifted the old Corolla into fifth gear on the highway connecting Forest Grove to Gaston, then to the tiny feeder road that led to Wilfred. I shifted down as I reached Gaston. Small towns around here were famous for their speed traps. The gears ground as I slowed. The Corolla was Darla's second vehicle, lent to me until I could come up with something of my own. Duke had given it a once-over and his approval, but the car and I were still on uneasy terms.

I parked at the library and walked down the hill. Instead of veering to the left of the old highway to stop in at Darla's, I crossed to the right and into the small neighborhood of wooden houses dotted with fruit trees. It was time to move the investigation along.

Mrs. Garlington lived in a tidy farmhouse whose orchard had long ago been platted for mill worker homes. An apple tree blossomed in its front yard. I'd only been here once before, to drop off some library books when Mrs. Garlington wasn't feeling well. That day, she'd instructed me to leave them on the porch. I wasn't sure how she'd feel about an unannounced drop-in.

I mounted the wooden steps and knocked on the screen door. Mrs. Garlington answered, her eyes watery with tears. From beyond her, I heard the voices of books whispering, sighing, and yearning. I also smelled violets. Whether it was an air freshener or the scent given off by purple prose, I wasn't sure.

"Mrs. Garlington! You're crying. Are you all right?"

She tapped a book. "It's Keats. Always touches the heart." She lifted a perfectly ironed handkerchief from her bosom and dabbed at her eyes before adjusting the waves of hair at her temples. I could never decide if her carefully molded curls and blue rinse were old-fashioned or strikingly hip. "Can I help you?"

"I hope you don't mind me stopping by like this. I had a question about the man you saw at the mill site."

She pushed open the screen door to let me in. "So you finally believe me. It's the sheriff who should be asking, not you. Come in. I'll make us some tea."

I followed her through a living room crowded with a baby grand piano and a few busts of composers, through a dining room wall to wall with buffets and display cases, to a homey kitchen with a blue-checked dish towel draped over the oven handle.

As she filled a kettle, she asked, "What do you want to know about the stranger?"

"Have you seen Tommy Daniels?"

"Yes, and as I told you, the man I saw was decidedly not him." She plunked the kettle on the stove and busied herself by heaping Darjeeling into a teapot commemorating the Queen's jubilee.

"And he wasn't—"

"Not the architect, either," Mrs. Garlington said. "Is that why you've come by? To ask me again? My mind is perfectly sharp."

"Sorry," I said. "I guess it's just wishful thinking that you'll have a different answer now."

"Come into the dining room while we wait for the water to boil."

I saw why Mrs. Garlington chose the dining room. The living room sofa was almost completely penned in by the piano, and besides an armchair by the fireplace stacked with sheet music, there was nowhere for visitors to sit. Mrs. Garlington must have spent most of her leisure time in the dining room. Half of the long table was covered with books and magazines, and a basket of knitting sat in one chair. On the buffet behind it was a studio photo of a man with 1970s lapels, gold aviator-style glasses, and pink scalp showing beneath thinning hair. A votive candle burned next to it, and a red silk rose lay in front.

Mrs. Garlington caught me examining it. "That's Martin. My husband, Derwin's father."

"I'm sorry. Did he die long ago?"

"Can't say." She lifted her chin. "He vanished in 1974."

"Oh, I really am sorry."

"I'm not," she said on her way to the kitchen in answer to the kettle's whistle. A moment later, she returned with the teapot and took two cups and saucers from the sideboard. "He was a loving man, and he gave me Derwin. I couldn't have asked for a better husband."

Now I understood Mrs. Garlington's tight grip on her son. "You say your husband vanished. You mean he ran away?" To anyone else, the question might have been insensitive. I had the feeling Mrs. Garlington would relish the opportunity to talk about it.

"Yes, honey. He sent a letter and a check every Christmas, and after a while, those stopped. I wouldn't say he ran away, exactly, but he went away. He's with the angels now."

"And you're not bitter about it."

Mrs. Garlington poured out our tea. "He filled me up with love. I knew I'd be content even if I never found love again. Besides, Lalena helps me communicate with him from time to time."

Whether it was Mrs. Garlington's story or the flickering candle beneath Mr. Garlington's photo or the crooning of the volumes of poetry, I couldn't help but feel a tug at my heart. One advantage of the years I hadn't had access to my magic was that my emotions had been dulled along with my senses. Now I wanted more—specifically, someone I couldn't have.

Mrs. Garlington slid a thin volume across the table. I didn't need to look at it to know it was Elizabeth Barrett Browning's *Sonnets to the Portuguese*.

"Take this, honey. Unrequited love is a bitch."

I nearly spit out my tea. "What are you talking about?"

"Do I have to spell it out for you? Sam Wilfred is a very attractive man in his way."

Once I managed to swallow, I said quickly, "So, this man at the mill site. Do you have any idea who he might be?" I knew by the heat in my face I was as red as the rose under the beloved Martin's photo.

Mrs. Garlington coolly sipped her tea. "I don't know. But he was looking for someone. And he was definitely looking for trouble."

"You don't happen to have any other information, do you?" I wasn't hopeful.

She set down her teacup and reached for her purse, a deep vinyl well that seemed to hold everything from an extra pair of socks to a gross of cough lozenges. "Since you ask, I do have his license plate number."

It was early evening, about happy hour, and I hoped I'd find Tommy Daniels tucking into dinner at the tavern. It was worth a try.

The café was empty except for the Tolsons, who were playing Scrabble over platters of fried chicken. Darla must have gone home by now. A prep cook did dishes in the back.

I stood at the entrance to the tavern, connected to the diner by a narrow open doorway. I didn't often venture into the tavern half of Darla's empire. To me, it was a beery hangout of men and televised sports. Where the café was full of light, the tavern was dark and smelled like a basement.

"Whatcha doing there, Josie?" It was Duke, calling from a booth on the far side of the room.

I wandered in, taking note of the dimly lit jukebox playing a Hank Williams tune and tattered indoor-outdoor carpeting. The café side was floored in freshly mopped linoleum.

"How are you?" I asked Duke and took the cracked Naugahyde bench across from him.

"How am I?" A Brylcreemed curl detached from his hair and swung forward. "Pretty great. You're talking to the new senior contractor for the retreat center."

"Congratulations," I said. "That's wonderful. Can I buy you a beer?"

This day had been a long time coming, I knew. Duke had irritating qualities—qualities I'd experienced regularly over the past months—but at his core he was a decent man.

"No, thank you. I'm set. What brings you here? We don't often have the pleasure of your company on this side of the establishment."

"I was looking for Tommy Daniels," I said. "I wondered if I'd be able to give him a hand at some point. I figured he'd take his dinner here."

"Instead of at the construction trailer. Only so much a microwave can do," Duke said. "I wouldn't be surprised if he'll be along shortly. He keeps a keen eye on sports."

Duke held my gaze just a few seconds too long. He was trying to tell me something.

"He like sports, does he?"

Duke winked. "That he does. Speak of the devil."

At the doorway stood Tommy Daniels. He hesitated only long enough to adjust his vision to the tavern's dark before striding, legs and arms wide, to the counter.

"Tommy," Duke said. "Over here."

Tommy turned, and a wide smile broke over his freckled face. His eyebrows were so blond they bleached into his skin.

"How are you, Duke?" He thrust a hand toward me. "Hi, Red. Don't mind if I call you that, do you?"

"You wouldn't be the first," I said. "How are you settling in? I'm in luck, finding you."

He took the seat next to Duke, where he could keep an eye on the television set. "I'm the lucky one."

"I wanted to make sure you know about the resources we have up at the library," I said. "Lewis Cruikshank has been by to read up on local history. I just thought if there's anything I can do for you—"

Tommy shook his head. "Cruikshank. He may be an artist, but he could use a good schooling on the practical matters of construction. No, the kind of info I use doesn't come in a book."

"I'm sure," I said, although I was certain anything could be found in a book, if you knew where to look. "He told me he was looking forward to talking with you, discussing how the retreat center would come together."

"Score!" Tommy said, looking at the screen. The game broke for commercials, and he returned his gaze to me. "Sorry. I have a few dollars riding on that game. What were we talking about?"

"Lewis Cruikshank. The architect."

"Oh yeah. I think we came to an understanding."

"About what?"

"He had all kinds of crazy ideas. Have you seen his sketches?" I nodded, and he said, "Then you know." He shook his head. "He needs to work that out with Ruff and Sita and leave the site prep to me. Get out of my hair. I know what I'm doing."

"Get out of your hair?"

"Foul!" His eyes were on the television again.

"What do you mean?" I asked.

His gaze was riveted to the screen. Even Duke shrugged at me.

Finally, Tommy said, "Cruikshank's all right. We might not see eye to eye on some matters, but that's the nature of the beast. He's a visionary, and I'm the more practical type, you know what I mean?"

I nodded. "You met up the day before yesterday. Did you happen to see Fiona Wilfred? I think she was out there at about the same time."

"Fiona? The broad who was murdered? I saw a cute brunette walking with another fellow, but I didn't know who it was at the time. The sheriff asked me the same thing, showed me a photo. The officers have been tramping through the woods all around the site."

"Maybe you heard something, then?" I asked.

He shook his head. "Nope. Lewis and I did a walk around the site with the property owners, then talked in the office. You don't think it will slow down construction, do you?"

"I hope not," Duke said. "I'm looking forward to that paycheck."

"The blue-haired lady," Tommy said.

"Mrs. Garlington?"

"She ever straighten out who she saw that morning? The tough guy with the gun?" He laughed.

"She insists she saw someone," I said.

"Probably saw Tommy, here," Duke said. "You know Helen Garlington. Imagination for miles."

Maybe a few days earlier, I would have thought the same thing and laughed with them. Not now. Not with a license plate number in my pocket. "We shouldn't underestimate her."

"Red, can I get you a drink?" Tommy Daniels asked, his attention again on the TV screen.

Tommy would be popular here. He was cheerful and open and practical. As far as Fiona's disappearance was concerned, he didn't know much and had zero motive, unless he had a connection to her from somewhere in the past, which didn't seem likely.

I rose. "No, thank you. I've got to be getting home. If you need anything—if I can help at all while you're in town—don't hesitate to get in touch." I reached for my purse, then turned back to Tommy, whose gaze was fastened on the television. "Say, have you seen Lewis lately? I was hoping to talk to him."

"He was poking around the site this morning," Tommy said absently.

"Probably picked up something at the PO to eat in the guest trailer. He strikes me as a bookworm," Duke said.

True. I'd given him a nice stack of research. "Well, have a good evening."

"Will do," Tommy said without seeming to listen. The TV flashed the game's final score. He was on his phone as I waved good-bye.

CHAPTER EIGHTEEN

That night, I couldn't put Mrs. Freeburger's words out of my mind. *"Whenever she's around, bad things happen. Real bad things."*

Had Marilyn Wilfred been a witch? And if she were, would she have cursed the mill site? I stepped into the hall outside my living room, where I could examine her full-sized portrait over the entrance. Moonlight through the cupola splashed blue and green diamonds over her straight-cut flapper gown. Marilyn had a strong connection to the library. I could feel it in the books and their reverence for her—even the volumes that had come in since Marilyn's death more than twenty years ago.

But a witch? The only witches I knew were in my family. Among us, I was the most powerful. I had the birthmark on my shoulder—as did my grandmother—that marked me. Marilyn's dress covered her shoulders, not that she'd necessarily share my birthmark. Frankly, I wasn't sure how witchcraft worked in other families.

I didn't know much about Marilyn Wilfred, except that longtime locals had called her Auntie Lyn, and she'd been beloved. She'd helped Darla learn to read despite severe dyslexia. She'd sheltered Wilfredians during the 1958 flood. And, most of all, she'd donated her family's mansion and her inheritance to making sure Wilfred had a library and community center.

I glanced back at my living room, with the standing lamp casting a warm circle of light on my worn mohair club chair with its seat wide enough for a cat to snooze beside me. Rodney wasn't there, though. He was standing at the top of the stairs to the library. "*Come on*," he seemed to say and leapt through his cat door.

What librarian ignores the call to research?

I followed Rodney down the bare wooden steps—the main staircase was three times as wide and carpeted—until we reached the atrium, where Rodney took a hard right into the kitchen. He stood near his full food bowl and meowed mournfully, jingling his collar.

"Rodney. Still on a hunger strike?" It had been a few days now that he hadn't eaten his kibble, and the tuna I'd laid out hadn't been touched, either. It was the same brand he'd always loved. Yet he didn't seem weak, and his hunger had a theatrical bent. I lifted him from his plump belly. "You have to eat, honeybun."

He yowled mournfully in response.

"Listen, I'm sorry about the collar—I truly am. But if you keep this up, you're going to the vet. That's a promise."

Rodney wriggled in my arms, and I set him on the floor. He trotted to the atrium, and I followed.

"Hello, Marilyn," I said, my voice strangely hollow in the empty atrium. "I'm going to learn something about you."

The books murmured appreciation. "Marilyn," they whispered with different cadences, making each syllable shush. A faint pink glow, sometimes golden, flashed from the library's various rooms of books. A happy sign.

"Thurston Wilfred's office," I said aloud, sure the books understood my intentions.

By the time I'd settled into the town founder's old office, his massive oak desk already had a few volumes for me to peruse with others floating in from the library's far reaches. I pushed open the curtains, not because the moonlight, dimmer on this side of the mansion, was bright enough to read by, but to have the moon's company. We'd become good friends on my regular nighttime trips to the old stacking house.

I snapped on the desk lamp. Rodney jumped up next to me and decided to clean his belly. I caught sight of his star-shaped birthmark, just like mine, as he bent into a goofy pose to groom the inside of a leg.

"What have you brought me?" I asked the books.

On the top of the stack was a bound copy of Wilfred's newspaper, the *Wilfred Searchlight*, which had gone out of business during the Great Depression. I gingerly opened it, and the pages unfurled to a birth announcement.

April 19, 1900. "It is with great sadness that Mr. Thurston Wilfred announces the birth of a daughter."

"Sadness?" I said aloud.

"Seraphina Miller Wilfred, Thurston Wilfred's wife, died in childbirth, leaving her husband and two sons be-

hind. Services for Mrs. Thurston Wilfred's passing will
be held at the Presbyterian church Sunday next."

The lamp seemed to dim as I read, and the books
sighed. So, Marilyn's mother had died in childbirth.

The next book in the stack was a yearbook for Gaston
High School. Again, the pages riffled open to a black-
and-white portrait of Marilyn, a bit younger than the portrait in the atrium, but with the same straight eyebrows
and full mouth. Sam's mouth, I noted. Her hair was shin-
gled in waves. She didn't smile.

"Marilyn Wilfred," the caption noted. "Debate, French
Club, and Shooting." This copy had no personal comments. It must have been archived straight from the high
school. I was ready to close it, when I heard a whisper.
Arlene, it said. *Arlene Alber*. A thousand other books
shushed.

I sat still a moment, unsure of what to do next. The
books had never been so firm about passing information
to me. Yet, they weren't urgent. Just insistent.

Finally, I said, "I'm in charge here," and flipped back
the few pages—there weren't many students—to the *A*s.
No Alber. Marilyn didn't go to school with her.

"Why do you want me to know this?" I asked.

The books were silent. Marilyn's hold over them was
strong.

The rest of the pile was made up of newspaper clip-
pings about the founding of the library and its donation to
Wilfred on Marilyn's death. A few, including some from
Portland's *The Oregonian*, were from the society pages.
In one, Marilyn was waving from a cruise ship in San
Francisco, bound for Hawaii. Another was an obituary
for her father, who'd died in the ax-throwing contest at

Wilfred's Timber Days celebration in 1950 at a hearty eighty-five years old. The accompanying photo showed Thurston Wilfred with a walrus mustache Lewis Cruikshank would have admired and a plaid wool shirt rolled up to the elbows. His arms were furred with wiry gray hair. He held an ax and looked straight ahead.

Knowing she must be in the crowd behind Thurston Wilfred or the books wouldn't have chosen this article, I scanned the photo. My eyes went straight to her. Marilyn stared at her father with an intensity that terrified me, even from a newsprint photo, even several decades later. Whatever had been going through her mind, it was dark. I set down the clipping and couldn't help checking to make sure I was alone. Except for the ticking of the mantel clock, all was silent.

I felt the books' tension. They wanted to tell me something, but they couldn't. Even Rodney sat still, alert.

"What is it?" I asked aloud.

Nothing. Not a word. Even the moon seemed to dim.

CHAPTER NINETEEN

Later that night, I was reshelving the books and articles on Marilyn when a knock on the kitchen door drew my attention. As I anticipated, it was Sam, ready for the day's report.

By the time I made it across the atrium, the kitchen's pendant light was on, and Sam sat at the long wooden table holding a bottle to Nicky's mouth. The baby lay back in a portable carrier, his dark curls damp on his scalp.

"Hello," I said. "That child has the most beautiful mouth." Now I knew where the term "rosebud lips" came from.

"Fiona's mouth," he said. "It is pretty, isn't it?" He smoothed Nicky's curls.

"And that tiny cleft chin. He looks like a cross between a cherub and Clark Gable."

"He's not so much an angel before nap time, are you?" Sam pulled a bottle from Nicky's bag.

"Well, I'm ready to fill you in. I've been busy."

He frowned slightly with amusement. "I'm listening."

"Biggest news first. Did you know that Fiona had called Sita and Ruff Waters the night before she died?"

"No." He set the bottle on the table. Nicky's arms flailed like a drunken man's. "What did she want?"

"She told them they'd underpaid for the mill site, and she was planning to sue for the difference."

Sam smiled. He was not happy. "Just like Brett Thornsby said. They never mentioned it to me."

"She asked them for fifty thousand dollars to be paid directly to her and gave them a deadline of two days to think it over. They'd decided to talk to you first. Then Fiona was killed."

He ran a hand through his hair and shook his head. "I don't know why she wouldn't trust me."

I didn't want to remind him that people who cheat usually suspect the same from others. Instead, I rocked Nicky's carrier gently.

"They weren't happy about it," I said. "Ruff and Sita, that is. They've been focused on building a retreat for months. All through the winter they'd stop by to take photos or show the site to friends. It's hard for me to imagine them killing Fiona for the land, but I suppose it's possible."

"Anything else?"

"Tommy Daniels said he saw Fiona and Brett in passing that afternoon, but that's all. He was busy with the architect and Ruff and Sita. I talked with him at Darla's, in the tavern. He likes his sports." I remembered his fevered attachment to the TV screen. "I wouldn't be surprised if he bets on games."

"Interesting," Sam said. "Not a motive to kill Fiona, but interesting."

"Last thing," I said. "This is good. I checked in with Mrs. Garlington about the stranger she saw, and she gave me a license plate number."

"No kidding? I'll have someone run it. If nothing else, we can ease her mind once we discover it was a lost vacationer."

"I'll text it to you." I pulled out my phone. "What about you?"

"I went into Portland and traced Brett's whereabouts. His story to the sheriff checks out. He drove into Portland to visit a college friend and arrived late afternoon. They went to a bar, and he spent the night at the friend's house before heading back to Wilfred. The friend backed him up."

"The friend could have lied."

"The car's GPS supports his claim, or Sheriff Beattie wouldn't have let him go. He still might have killed Fiona, then left town. We won't have a firm grasp of timing until her body's found, and maybe not even then." As he talked, he focused on Nicky, as if facing me would reveal too much emotion. His voice, though, was even and firm.

"You don't know Brett well?" I asked.

"As I told you, I don't know him at all. Fiona had mentioned him to me, but I never met him in person before he showed up here to accuse me of killing her."

"They were close enough friends to have talked about the terms of the divorce."

"I guess so." Nicky had gone to sleep, and a bit of formula pooled at the corner of his lips. Sam dabbed at it.

"Brett is not in the clear," I said, although Sam was going to need more to remove himself from Sheriff Beattie's list. "Can you tell me about Marilyn?"

"Auntie Lyn? That's a change of subject. Why?"

"She's such a presence in the house. I just wondered what she was like."

"I adored her," he said. "We moved when I was just a kid, but she used to send me letters and recommend books. I probably spent more time here, in the library, than at home at Big House. Sometimes she let me roll out a sleeping bag in Children's Fiction. She'd give me a sandwich and put the table lamp on the floor so I could read all night if I wanted."

I smiled at the story. The books would have been so happy. "As a person, though. How would you describe her?"

Sam leaned back in his chair and seemed to think it over. A calm perceptiveness settled over his face. He took my question seriously. The consideration, the insight, the patience showed that had made him so good at ghosting for the FBI.

"Loving, but she could be a little removed. Even with my father—her nephew. She was always friendly, but when she focused on something, she was completely fastened to it. You could see it in her eyes."

I had seen it, in the newspaper photo. "Go on."

"She liked tomato sandwiches and *I Love Lucy*, and

she adored cats—especially black ones. I've wondered if Rodney might be related to one of hers, in fact."

"He might be," I said. "They say he was a stray."

"Auntie Lyn tried to stay the weekend at the beach a few times each winter, too. She loved the ocean when it was stormy. Her perfume smelled like lilacs. Oh, and lemon candies. She always had lemon candies in a crystal dish. I wonder if that dish is still around?"

"I'll look for it," I said, entranced by his details.

"One thing, though. I couldn't help but wonder why my grandfather moved out of the Wilfred mansion and built Big House. In those days, a maiden aunt would have lived with the family, so I would have expected the next generation to stay here. The old house had plenty of room for everyone."

"She was a loner," I said.

"Yes—and no. If she was truly a loner, she wouldn't have turned the family home into a library."

"Do you think Marilyn and your family had a falling-out?"

"If they did, it was civil."

"*If* they did, you say."

He let out a long breath. "There was one thing."

"What?"

"She was always friendly, and people in town saw her as a benefactress, even when they'd given up on the rest of the Wilfreds."

"When the mill closed, you mean."

"Yes." Sam tucked a finger into Nicky's fist, and he clenched it, still sleeping. "But they kept a certain distance from her, almost as if they were afraid of her. Older folks, mostly. It was curious."

"You never felt afraid of her?"

"Not at all. Why would I be?"

"Seeing how others treated her."

He laughed once. "Josie, the Wilfreds were never beloved. Besides, that generation died off, and everyone else loved Auntie Lyn." His finger slipped from Nicky's fist and twirled into one of his curls. "Once, though . . . once I overheard a few people talking about her. I was on the sofa upstairs—"

"In Art and Music." I knew just the sofa he was talking about. It was a worn green brocade and backed up to the window. The perfect reading spot for a boy.

"Exactly. Two women were browsing the shelves on the other side, and they couldn't see me. They made a joke about watching out for Auntie Lyn. Said they wouldn't be alone with her or she'd give them the evil eye, like she did her father."

The image from the newspaper came back again. That level-eyed stare.

"His death was an accident, right? A mis-thrown ax? She couldn't have had anything to do with that."

"I know. Odd."

Sam's phone rang, and he glanced at its screen. "Mind if I get this? It's Fiona's gallery. I wonder why they're calling so late."

"Of course not."

"Thanks for returning my call." Sam turned away from me as he spoke into the phone. "Are you sure? You're certain?"

When he hung up, his expression had settled into neither a frown nor a smile. He drew his eyebrows together.

"What's wrong?" I asked.

"The gallery was closed yesterday and had a show opening tonight, so they couldn't return my call until now." He absently touched one of Nicky's curls. "It's about Brett."

"Yes?"

"They've never heard of Brett Thornsby."

CHAPTER TWENTY

So, he's a fraud," I said. "Who even knows if Brett Thornsby is his real name?"

"It's his real name, all right," Sam said. "I had him run through the FBI database. His record came up clean, and his ID matches."

"It didn't list where he worked?"

"He did gig jobs, mostly. Freelance design for small businesses and a few bit acting roles. It wouldn't have been that strange for him to take on a seasonal job at an art gallery."

Acting. The pictures. *The man in the picture*. I picked up my phone. "Let's call Sheriff Beattie."

"She already knows. They told me she'd called, too."

So, that explained it. Despite what Sam thought, Fiona and Brett were carrying on, and Fiona passed off her boyfriend as a gallery employee so her husband wouldn't find out. "It will keep you out of jail, anyway."

"Or get me there faster." Sam stood and shook his head. "Lots of husbands have killed unfaithful wives. That's not the case here. I'm sure she and Brett were legit."

Poor, poor Sam. Fiona had vowed she'd be faithful as long as they were still married, and the promise of a fat alimony check would have been strong incentive to stay the course. I dropped my gaze to the sleeping baby. But here was proof she was capable of all sorts of transgressions. Misleading Sam with words was the least of it. Fiona and Brett might have had a lovers' quarrel, with Fiona as its victim.

"A lot of unanswered questions," I said.

If Sam was hurt, it didn't show. He pulled Nicky closer. "I'd better get him home and in bed."

In the kitchen door, I stood facing Sam, already standing half in shadow. "One more thing." I shook my head. "You had better hope Brett Thornsby doesn't turn up dead."

I awoke drowsy, with Rodney splayed over a shoulder, his head resting on my neck. For a cat who refused to eat, he was getting plump. My family had never had cats— my mother was against it, no matter how much I and my two sisters lobbied—but my grandmother had always had them. Most cats smelled purely of love, I'd noticed over the years. Clean and soft, that was all. Black cats were special. They carried a hint of leather and vanilla. I breathed deeply from Rodney's fur.

I eased from under the cat's curiously boneless body and traded my nightgown for a denim skirt and cotton sweater, slipped my feet into my trusty clogs—perfect for standing most of the day—and went to the mirror over my dresser to wrestle my hair into an acceptable updo.

I took the bridge across the river and down the hill to Darla's. I had two goals for the morning: ask Lewis Cruikshank if he'd seen or heard anything the afternoon Fiona died; and talk with Brett Thornsby. No, make that three goals. I also needed breakfast.

As I'd expected, the diner was hopping in the way it could only when there was excitement in town. The yammer of conversation and clatter of cutlery on dinnerware filled the room. Mrs. Garlington's son might have heard something on his postal route that he could pass to Ruth Littlewood, who would somehow compare it to the life and culture of a species of bird. From there, Duke would figure out the mechanical angles, and Roz might opine on the human motivation. If Lalena, the town psychic, was around and not conducting palm readings in her trailer, she'd toss in a few words from the spirit world.

"What'll you have, Josie?" Darla asked as I took a seat at the counter.

"Clam fritters, please." With Darla's Southern cuisine expertise and the nearby Pacific Ocean's bounty, the clam fritters were a sure bet, even if they were an unorthodox choice for breakfast.

"Coming up."

I spun my stool toward the dining room. No Cruikshank here. Movement from the tavern drew my attention. Usually the tavern was dark this time of day. Instead, Tommy Daniels appeared to be peeling bills from a wad of cash, and he wasn't paying the bartender. A soccer match played on the television above his head.

Although Brett had the opportunity to kill Fiona, I couldn't figure out why he'd do it. Couldn't have been for money. With Fiona dead, he wouldn't be able to share in the fruits of the divorce settlement. He might have killed Fiona out of passion, but he couldn't be particularly jealous. Not if he was willing to visit his lover at her husband's house.

If I could find Brett, maybe I could feel him out about the situation. I scanned the room again. Nope. No Brett, either.

At least I was sure of a good meal. Darla slid a platter of fritters sprinkled with parsley. An old china teacup half full of homemade tartar sauce sat on the plate next to a pile of tart coleslaw. I'd have asked Darla's cookbooks for the recipe, but I knew she didn't use cookbooks. Not only was she a natural cook, due to her dyslexia, reading was a chore.

Duke emerged from the tavern, undoubtedly checking for updates to the grapevine before he left.

"Josie," he said, "See Sam lately?"

"Yesterday. Why?"

He leveled his gaze at me, his hair so stiffly Brylcreemed that I envisioned tiny surfers cresting its waves. "How was he?"

I used a ploy that had served women for centuries. "That baby is so cute. Honestly. Have you ever seen such a darling thing?"

Duke, not wanting to get caught in this net, turned to leave.

"Oh, Duke," I said. "Lewis Cruikshank hasn't been here this morning, has he?"

"Haven't seen him. You might try the guest trailer."

"How about Brett Thornsby, from Fiona Wilfred's gallery?"

"If that's his real name," Duke said.

"What do you mean?"

Duke leaned low, placing an elbow on the counter. "So, you haven't heard, have you? Turns out he wasn't with her gallery at all. Get my drift?" He winked, just in case I was too dense for innuendo.

"You're kidding." The word was already out.

"Yet another reason for Sam to do in his wife," Duke said. "Sure, the Wilfred baby is cute. Too bad his daddy is going to jail."

"You don't know that. Fiona hasn't even been found yet."

"'Yet' being the key word. Sheriff Beattie's dredging the millpond today."

"What?"

Duke chuckled with satisfaction at my shock. "At eleven this morning. The sheriff is sending over a search-and-rescue boat." He shrugged on his jacket. "You should stop by. Who knows what they'll find?"

After breakfast, I buttoned my jacket against the spring breeze and turned toward the Magnolia Rolling Estates, not far behind the diner, in the curve of the Kirby River.

On the bluff above the river stood the library's fussy angles, including its squared tower. Lyndon's cottage was hidden in the trees. Sun reflected off Big House's kitchen window. Sam was there, maybe feeding Nicky and listening to Verdi.

The trailer park's central drive was paved in gravel, and half a dozen trailers were parked off each side. Duke's was easy to identify from its lawn cut with military precision. Across from Duke's double-wide, roses still a month away from flower trellised Lalena's pink trailer. A blowsy lilac bush grew behind her hand-shaped sign painted PALM READINGS, APPLY WITHIN.

At last I came to Darla's guest cottage at the end of the right-side row. The porch light was on. I took the steps to the door and knocked. Somewhere in the distance, maybe across the road, a dog barked.

No one answered, so I knocked again. The trailer wasn't completely dark. Faint light shone from what I imagined to be the kitchen. Maybe the lamp over the stove.

I caught sight of the edge of a note tucked into the door frame, inside the screen door. The door squeaked as I pulled its aluminum frame open.

"*Dinner with friends in Portland,*" the note said in block letters.

Whom did he leave the note for? Maybe Ruff and Sita were supposed to meet him here? He surely wouldn't blow off his clients. Maybe he was due to meet with Tommy Daniels. I could definitely see Lewis preferring dinner in a Portland gastropub to what the Wilfred tavern had to offer—at least, if he hadn't tried the food first. He must have decided to stay the night.

Wherever he'd gone, he'd left his library books behind. I heard them inside telling stories of tribal camps, the photos swishing with wind in the pines.

I replaced the note and let the door close.

Standing in front of the trailer, the meadow stretched before me. In the distance was the hulk of the World War

II vehicle Duke had been bragging about. I could smell the cool moisture of the millpond, although it was too far away to hear the bullfrogs. Across the river was the old mill site.

Somewhere out there was Fiona Wilfred's body.

CHAPTER TWENTY-ONE

The day had steadily darkened, and by the time I made it to the millpond for the search for Fiona, it had started to rain.

Duke sniffed the air. "No downpour. Just drizzle."

Since moving to Oregon, I'd learned that rain came in many forms. A day might hold "showers" followed by "rain," as if they were different. Then there were downpours and drizzle, as Duke had mentioned, plus mist, sprinkles, and gully washers. I'd classify the current weather as a light rain—wet, but not enough to call for an umbrella.

At the edge of the millpond, two men positioned a raft. The search of the forest surrounding the mill site over the past day had yielded nothing—no Fiona, not a sign of her. The sheriff had sent a team through the woods, trampling brush and searching trees for stray hairs and dirt for foot-prints, and reports were that they'd come up dry.

Tommy Daniels joined us. He squinted into the rain and folded his arms over his chest for warmth, but still wore shorts and a T-shirt. "Red. Duke. So this is it, then?"

"When do they start dredging?" I asked.

"They're not going to. See that black doohickey?" He pointed to one of the machines on the raft. "It's a sonar device. They're going to run it over the millpond's bot-tom to see if they find anything interesting."

"There's got to be a lot of mud down there," I said. The millpond hadn't been used for logs for a good twenty years, and silt must have built up deeply. Any body that got caught in it would be difficult to pull up.

"Lots of mud," Tommy confirmed.

"It's only been a few days. My guess is she's floated over to the levee. I'm going to check it out."

With that, Duke took off. I watched his figure recede toward the bridge of boulders that spanned where the Kirby River fed into the millpond. He walked like Tweedledee crossed with Fred Astaire. Light and graceful and top-heavy. Tommy ambled to the group at the boat getting ready to push off.

"Anything happen yet?" Sam appeared beside me. Wind tumbled his hair, but his Pacific Northwestern up-bringing did him right, and the drizzle didn't faze him. The situation did, though. It showed in the shadows under his eyes.

"They're getting ready to launch the search raft."

Just as I said the words, the raft released into the millpond. A diver loitered at the pond's edge scrolling through his phone. I hugged my arms and hoped they'd find nothing more than old tires and lost fishing poles and have no reason to press him into action.

"I can't believe it," Sam said quietly, as if he were talking to himself.

I glanced at him, then turned toward the millpond. The pond was probably three football fields in size—large enough to be fun to canoe, but too small to call a lake. On the meadow side, a levee kept the river-fed millpond at bay against the meadow's slightly lower elevation. The millpond then siphoned into the river again and flowed north, eventually to meet the Columbia River and, ultimately, the ocean.

The earth below me murmured in low, ominous tones that vibrated in my bones. I shivered involuntarily. Some great energy was at work here, and it was uneasy. At this point, I couldn't connect it with Marilyn, but I wasn't through exploring.

"How are you?" I turned suddenly to Sam.

He smiled, then frowned. I could watch that mouth all day. I could watch him, guess at his thoughts, feel comfortable simply being near him. Unrequited love, Roz had called it. It had better fade away soon, or I'd melt into a puddle of longing.

"I don't know," he said. "I really don't know."

"Nicky?"

"At the library in Roz's care. He's Wilfred's hottest pastime."

I couldn't help but laugh, despite the gruesome setting. Wilfredians would be fighting over the baby as long as he was in town.

"I checked the license plate number you gave me from Mrs. Garlington," he said.

"What did you find?"

"Not much." The wind ruffled his hair. "It belongs to one Linda Mulvaney, owner of a 1998 Prius. No black SUV."

"Too bad. Maybe Mrs. Garlington misread the number," I said.

"Maybe."

The raft began a slow clockwise circle of the millpond. The rain sharpened, and I drew my jacket closer.

"I can't stick around. I have an appointment in Forest Grove," I said, thinking of Mrs. Freeburger.

Sam turned to me. He was close enough that if I'd wanted to, I could have pushed back the rain-soaked hair that threatened to fall into his eyes.

"Thank you for coming down."

"Of course," I said.

"Sam," came a voice from the distance. Sheriff Beattie. She walked toward us as untouched as Botticelli's Venus in a regulation khaki uniform. "Do you have a minute?"

"I'll go," I said.

"It's not private," the sheriff said. Nearer, she seemed curiously untouched by the rain. "The DNA report came back on the tire iron."

"And?" Sam said.

I waited for her to say, "It's a match."

Instead, she shifted feet and said, "It's not Fiona."

"Then who is it?" Sam said at the same time as I said, "What?"

"I don't know. A man. That's all we can say for sure."

CHAPTER TWENTY-TWO

I was half-regretful, half-relieved that I had a visit planned to the Maple Grove to visit Sarah Freeburger. After an uncomfortable pause with Sam and Sheriff Beattie not talking, but huddling against the drizzle and staring out at the millpond, pelted with rain, I made my break.

"I'm due in Forest Grove," I said. "You'll let me know if you find anything?"

"I'll definitely let you know if I need you," Sheriff Beattie said, but she seemed more concerned with Sam and the dinghy's grueling trawl over the millpond.

With each step from the millpond, emotional pressure seeped away. Whatever evil it was I sensed, it centered on the mill site's grounds.

My energy might have calmed as I put distance between us, but my mind continued to grind away. If the tire iron wasn't Fiona's murder weapon, then whom had it killed? And where was Fiona? If the sheriff didn't find her body today, they'd almost certainly launch another search for her—as a murderer. But, of whom?

At last, I emerged from the fir trees, and the library loomed straight ahead. All the gloom and dread of the mill site and the pond fell from my shoulders. Here, I was comfortable. Here, the books talked to me, and I helped connect them to readers. As I approached the library, the whole building beckoned, warm and welcoming. I breathed deeply and felt my lungs relax.

My next stop was to grab the layer cake Darla had set aside for me in the library's refrigerator. Half an hour later, I was at the retirement home knocking on Sarah Freeburger's front door.

This time it wasn't the tattooed medical student who answered, but a smiling Filipina in jeans and a crisply ironed blouse. "Come in!" she said cheerfully.

"Josie Way. I thought Sarah might like this." I handed over the layer cake in its box.

The caretaker popped off the lid and nodded in approval. "Perfect lunch," she said. "She'll love it. Mrs. Freeburger is on the patio."

I crossed the cramped living room and set my bag on the coffee table. The blank book I'd left the day before was still there. Good. I quickly slipped it into my tote before stepping out the open sliding glass door to the shared courtyard. The sky threatened more rain, but warmth radiated off the bricks, and Sarah leaned back in her lounge chair, eyes closed.

"Sarah?" I said.

"Donut lady?" she replied.

"That would be me. Today it's a seven-layer chocolate cake."

"Praise the Lord," she said, not even opening her eyes.

"I've been thinking about Marilyn Wilfred and the curse," I said. Maybe Fiona Wilfred had absorbed most of my mental space, but Marilyn was always there, too, filtering into the crevices.

"Ah, Marilyn," she said. Sarah sounded sharper than before. Morning must be a good time to find her.

"What was she like?" I said. "As a person."

"What else would she be like? A fish?"

I forced a laugh. "So true. But tell me. What did people in Wilfred think of her?"

The caretaker arrived with two fat slices of cake. Sarah grasped the fork, her fingers crabbed with arthritis, and stabbed at the cake.

"Thank you," I said to the caretaker and waited for Sarah to swallow her first few mouthfuls.

"Marilyn," Sarah said. "You really should talk to Arlene."

"Arlene?" There was that name again. "Arlene Alber." The books had told me.

"Dead. That's right. Arlene's dead." Sarah forked a slab of cake so large I watched with rapt anticipation of its tumble from her fork. She managed it perfectly, though.

"She's dead," I repeated. I needed to read up on Arlene Alber.

"Uh-huh." Sarah lifted her milky gaze to mine.

"Arlene knew Marilyn?"

"Said she was a witch," Sarah finished quickly.

There it was. Witch. "You mean, as in 'not very nice'?"

"No. As in evil. My mother used to talk about her," Sarah said. "Marilyn, that is. Not at first, not when my mother was young. But Mother fell to dementia, poor thing. Then the truth came out."

"What was so evil about Marilyn Wilfred?"

"It started at the beginning. Her mother died in childbirth. Then there was her father. And her brother. It was no secret she wasn't close to either of them. Both died in freak accidents. You tell me that isn't witchcraft."

I set my cake untouched on the side table between us. "You think Marilyn cursed them?"

"I'm just telling you what I heard, honey."

Across the courtyard, a glass door slid open, and a wheelchair motored out.

"Damn it, there's Lottie," Sarah said. "Hide the cake."

I pushed my slice back on the table, but there wasn't much more I could do. The woman Sarah called Lottie steered her wheelchair toward us.

"Good morning, Sarah." Her eyes were on my plate of cake. "Having a nice breakfast, are you?"

Sarah looked into the air, lips sealed.

Lottie reached toward the cake, and Sarah slapped her hands away. "Flora," she shouted into her apartment, "take this cake away."

The caretaker appeared, a pillowcase she'd been folding in hand, and removed my plate.

Lottie flipped a switch on her wheelchair, and it backed up, then swiveled to return to her apartment.

"You were saying?" Sarah said as she watched Lottie's retreat with satisfaction.

"I'm fascinated by Marilyn Wilfred," I said in an attempt to draw the conversation back. "Why would Arlene call her a witch? Can you tell me anything else about Arlene Alber?"

Sarah turned to me, her milky blue eyes innocent. Whatever sharpness she'd shown moments earlier had retreated. "How many dead is that?"

Returning to the library, I bypassed the kitchen door and entered through the front. After my surreal talk with Mrs. Freeburger, I felt the need to take the grand entrance, to see the library as strangers did and to be grounded in my own world again. I walked up the wooden steps to the broad porch and pushed open the double doors into the tiled foyer and inhaled its fragrance of books and old fir floor joists.

I passed through the second set of double doors to the atrium, all the time aware of Marilyn Wilfred's portrait above me.

"Hey, Josie," Dylan said from the old parlor to my right, now Circulation.

"Hey," I replied. "Have they found anything at the millpond yet?"

"Not that I've heard, but you have a visitor." Dylan smiled. I adored how he wore a vintage suit and bow tie to work.

"Really? Who?"

From the adjoining drawing room, a woman stepped in, her form a silhouette against the sun through the French doors. I blinked at the light, and my jaw dropped.

"Hi, Josie," said Fiona Wilfred.

Dylan, with his eye for style, stared at Fiona in awe. It wasn't often Wilfred hosted a woman who wore clothes from avant-garde designers.

"Where's Sam?" Fiona asked.

"With the team searching the millpond for your body," I said and struggled to regain my breath.

For a moment, Fiona froze, her expression static. Wherever she'd been, it hadn't been stranded in the woods. Her skin glowed with health and hot showers, and her angled gray dress was crisp. Then she burst into laughter. Damn it, even her laugh was beautiful.

"You're kidding. He thinks I'm dead?"

"You disappeared. You didn't answer your phone." My temper mounted. A title slid into my mind: *When You're in Love with a Narcissist.*

"Hmm." The dreamy expression returned to her face. "I lost my phone. Anyway, I was only in Portland."

"Really?"

If she heard the ice in my tone, she chose to ignore it. "Thought I'd see a friend."

"Maybe you'd like to use our phone to call your husband?" I struggled to keep the irritation from my voice and pointed to the old rotary phone on the desk.

"Sure. Thank you." She flashed one of those sweet smiles, full of warmth.

Still staring, Dylan got up from his chair and offered it to her.

"Don't be concerned about Nicky," I added. "He's fine."

Her smile dimmed, and she fastened me with her gaze. "I know. I just saw him. The caretaker—I think his name is Lyndon?—is giving him a lesson on root grafts." She pulled over the phone and dialed. The receiver looked chunky in her delicate hand.

How she could stand there with that half-smile flummoxed me. She had no idea that the town had rallied to find her, that Sam was suspected as her murderer. Either that, or she simply didn't care.

"He's not answering," Fiona said. "Probably doesn't recognize the number."

At that moment, my phone dinged. A text from Sam. "Body found in the millpond."

"It's not Fiona," I typed back as quickly as I could. I wanted to say more, but she needed to be the one to announce her arrival, not me.

"It's a man," he replied.

A man. My stomach dropped. Not Brett Thornsby, I hoped. He hadn't been seen lately. Sam would again be a suspect as the murderer of his wife's lover. Of course, now Fiona would need an alibi, too.

Both Dylan and Fiona stared at me. My shock must have shown on my face.

"They found a body," I told them breathlessly. "A man."

"Who?" Dylan said, wide-eyed.

With calm interest, Fiona perched on the edge of the circulation desk.

Another text dinged on my phone.

"Tommy Daniels IDed him. Lewis Cruikshank."

CHAPTER TWENTY-THREE

"**Y**ou should have seen it," I told Lalena later that night. "Total freak-out. When Fiona discovered the body was the architect's, she laughed so hard she started crying. Dylan sat her down and gave her his handkerchief."

"I can't believe it," Lalena said.

"Then Sam stormed in, smiling to turn water into icicle daggers. Fiona laughed the whole time. To her, it was a joke."

Sam had looked like he'd run the entire way from the mill site. He'd clasped Fiona to his chest, but he was angry—no doubt about it.

"Nicky," Fiona had said between laughing sobs. "Bring me my baby."

I'd jumped at the excuse to escape the emotional storm. Nicky was in his carrier next to Lyndon, who was pruning the banana tree. I brought the baby to Fiona, who lifted him out of the carrier and cradled him near. His expression stern, Sam picked up the carrier and ushered Fiona across the lawn to Big House.

I still didn't feel back to normal.

"You don't happen to know her astrological sign, do you?" Lalena asked.

"Narcissist with moon in nutjob, maybe?" I said. "They don't have a sign for her, unless it's in the *DSM*."

"Ha-ha," Lalena said.

"I'm being too mean. At the same time she was making light of it, Fiona was really upset. Sam, too. It was . . . strange."

We were upstairs in the hall outside my kitchen. Lalena bent over the railing, hands far apart on the oak banister. She wore a daffodil-yellow chenille bathrobe, and her hair was twisted into a towel. Lalena and I had taken to regular midweek dinners after her bath in the library's second-story bathtub. She liked a bath, and the trailer she'd inherited from her aunt—now the seat of her business as a psychic—had only a tiny plastic tub.

"I love it here when the library has closed," she said. "It's so peaceful. Especially after today's craziness."

Lalena was the closest thing I had to a best friend in Wilfred. Roz was a confidant, sure, but she was my employee—at least, as much as Roz was anyone's employee. Plus, she was my mother's age. I was on good terms with just about everyone in town, but no one really felt like a peer, except Lalena.

Her terrier mutt, Sailor, was chasing Rodney through the living room—they loved to play. Rodney knew that all he had to do was stop and face Sailor, and the dog would freeze in terror.

"I like it, too," I said.

"You don't get tired of living where you work?" she asked.

"Not a bit. This feels like home to me. Do you?"

"Not yet. Can you imagine me working in a cubicle?" Lalena went to the kitchen and helped herself to a glass of chardonnay from the box she kept in my refrigerator. "Want some?" she offered. "You might need it after today. One dead architect and one live Fiona."

"No thanks," I said, like I did every time she offered. "On second thought, yes." I rinsed out a glass and handed it to her.

"Was it a huge shock, seeing Fiona?"

"Are you kidding?" I said. "I'd just been down at the millpond, standing next to Sam while the sheriff's crew radared the pond's bottom. I was sure that any minute they'd start waving to shore to send in the diver. It was terrifying."

"I can imagine."

I tasted the wine. Round and sweet like bananas and apples. Every sensory experience was a pleasure these days, even boxed wine. "Then I walked in on Fiona, standing in Circulation like she'd simply been out for an afternoon of shopping. Meanwhile, Sam had almost been hauled off to jail for her murder. And she just laughed."

I still couldn't believe it. Sure, the situation was absurd, but too much drama had taken place to make it funny. I wondered how she'd explained her absence to Sam.

"A few people asked me if I knew who'd killed her," Lalena said. "I played it vague."

"Smart. Given that she's still in the flesh and all." I

reached into a cupboard for plates. "What's for dinner tonight?" Lalena usually brought something a client had dropped off for her. Last week it was some kind of casserole of canned beans and tomatoes layered in flour tortillas. Not gourmet fare, but satisfying.

"The manicurist from Forest Grove stopped by for a palm reading," she said. "Kale-quinoa salad. How do you feel about that?"

"Sounds nutritious." As always, I set Lalena's place so she had the view over the Kirby River to town. Besides the view, it was closest to the box of wine in the refrigerator.

Rodney sped into the kitchen and under the table, Sailor wagging from near the stove.

"Go on, boys," I told them. Rodney bounded out, collar jingling, Sailor on his tail.

"Where was Fiona all that time?" Lalena asked.

"In Portland. That's all she says." I'd pieced the story together from the little I'd heard directly from Fiona, plus secondhand bits from library patrons who'd fed at the café's gossip trough. I hadn't seen Sam since he'd left with Fiona, though I'd peeked through the windows to Big House from time to time. "She did a few sketches at the stacking house, then she walked into town and caught a ride to Portland."

"With strangers?" Lalena looked at me with sweet brown eyes and broad, almost Slavic, cheekbones that had invited the trust of scores of clients. "Someone would have seen her catching a ride in Wilfred, I'm sure of it."

"I know. She was vague. She also claims she lost her phone, and that's why she didn't get in touch with Sam."

"Even though her baby was here."

"That's what she says." I had a hard time believing it, too. Who left their infant for three whole days without checking in?

"Then the divers found the architect in the millpond."

"Yes. Not long after I left."

It had been a relatively speedy recovery. The millpond wasn't very deep, and the body hadn't been far from shore. Tommy Daniels had identified him, and the medical examiner had hauled off the corpse. Roz told me the word was that the back of Lewis Cruikshank's head was crushed, almost certainly by the tire iron we'd found. "They say he was tattooed like a sailor," she'd said.

"The curse of the mill site continues," Lalena said.

"What is that about, anyway?" I asked. "Mrs. Garlington talks about it all the time. Why would someone curse the land? I could see why a disgruntled mill worker might curse the mill or the Wilfreds, but the mill is long gone."

Lalena ripped a piece of bread in two. "Good point. People curse people. Land is rarely cursed, and when the person who curses it dies, the curse lifts."

"Right," I said, thinking of my grandmother's lesson.

Like everyone else, Lalena didn't know I was a witch. Her view of magic was pragmatic and had to do with people's hopes and dreams and expectations, and how she might earn a dollar from them. However, she was thoroughly book-schooled on witchiness.

"No," she said. "If anything, it's a land spirit."

"Land spirit? What's that?"

She turned to the refrigerator to refill her tumbler. She only needed to swivel, not leave her chair.

"Yes. Land spirit. The spirit that occupies a parcel of land. It was disturbed, and now it's bent on proving something."

"I still don't get it. Why would a piece of land need or want to prove anything?" I thought of the mill site and its cracked concrete foundation and the hooting of owls in the distance. And the deep rumbling I'd felt below my feet.

"It might have something to heal. Anger. Greed. It's hard to tell. A land spirit is a—a 'being'—that has its own character. They can be small enough to inhabit a city plot, or they can stretch out over a giant landscape."

Land spirits were not something my grandmother's lessons had covered. Not yet, anyway. "Tell me more."

"Okay, take the land spirit of New Orleans. It's known as 'the beast.' It pushes people to excess, which is great when it comes to creativity. Think of all the fabulous jazz that's come out of that city. It's not so great when it comes to partying." She looked in her tumbler of wine and pushed it aside.

"If there's a land spirit at the mill, what would it be like?"

"Hard to say. A land spirit sometimes simply wants to keep people away," she said, picking at her salad. "Other times it gives you the chance to prove yourself. You fail and die. Or you succeed, and the land spirit rests."

"You believe this?"

Lalena looked me in the eye. "What do you think?"

I smiled. To Lalena, magic was something her customers saw in the world because they needed it, and it was her job to point it out—for a price. Magic was not a gift doled out at birth, as it had been for me.

"You want to figure this out, don't you?" she asked. "You want to know who murdered Lewis Cruikshank."

"The sheriff is working on that," I said.

"That's not an answer." Sailor jumped into Lalena's

lap, and she dug fingers into the wiry fur between his ears. She fixed me with the gaze she must use for clients when she intuited their futures. "You think you have access to information she doesn't. That, and you can't help yourself. You simply have to know. It's about curiosity, and it's about justice. I'm right, aren't I?"

I swirled the wine in my glass as if I could read the future in its lemonade-hued surface, and I set it down. "You're better at this mind-reading business than you think."

After Lalena left, I prepared for bed. I made a small fire in my bedroom's fireplace, more for its cheer than to warm the room, which was already comfortable thanks to Lyndon's wizardry with the boiler.

Although books had a habit of appearing on my nightstand, I already knew what I planned to read. The books knew, too, and there next to the lamp was the blank notebook I'd left in Sarah Freeburger's apartment. I pulled the quilt over my chest, and Rodney hopped up next to me, and, gently purring, curled against my side.

I cracked open the book. As I'd hoped, it was filled with Mrs. Freeburger's writing, tidy and girlish. "I did it, Rodney."

This was magic I'd adapted from one of my grandmother's lessons, but I hadn't known if or how well it might work. The energy I drew from books came not only from the focus the author invested, but also from readers. In an old library like this one, the books teemed with power. However, a novel on the New Releases shelf chatted only quietly about its characters. Until it had passed through the hands of dozens of readers, its energy was barely strong enough to siphon to light a candle.

My idea was that a blank book—essentially, a book without any author energy—might be able to fill with the stories of someone nearby if I put a spell on it. The spell carried a few risks. First, I wasn't very good at writing spells. I was getting better at focusing and directing energy, and I'd become positively expert at talking to books, but something about spells felt too hocus-pocus to me. Rhyming spells were the worst. My best spells came from passages from books I loved. For instance, a passage from *Sleeping Beauty* read to me when I was a little girl had cast a spell strong enough to lock my magical powers until only last fall.

For the blank book, I had dipped again into *Grimm's Complete Fairy Tales*, this time to "Rumpelstiltskin." Instead of asking the miller's daughter to spin straw into gold as in the fairy tale, I wanted the blank page filled with memories. I had relaxed into the story, remembering the words I'd read so many times as a girl. I was the king in the story, and the blank book was the straw. "Now set to work," I quoted the story, "and if by the early morning you have not spun this straw to gold you shall die." I'd flinched at that last word.

Using magic to control people or delve into their brains was ethically questionable, and, as my grandmother's letters had warned many times, should only be undertaken for a greater cause. In this case, I figured that lifting the old mill site's curse was vital. Lives had been lost. Also, Mrs. Freeburger's mind was fraying. This might be the only way to collect her story.

I'd seen that the blank book had picked up writing, but

would it be useful at all? My intent was to record bits of Mrs. Freeburger's life related to the curse, but other stories might have elbowed their way onto the page.

There was only one way to find out.

I adjusted the quilt and patted Rodney before getting down to business. Rather than read each word, I scanned the pages, then held the book to my chest and let the stories wash through me in Mrs. Freeburger's voice. I could go back and reread any part that needed extra attention.

Mrs. Freeburger's writing plunged into the middle of a scene from when she was a schoolgirl. In Chicago. From Roz's brief description, I'd thought Mrs. Freeburger was a lifelong Wilfredian. Another girl was teasing her about not having a father. Cold winters, a one-bedroom apartment above a print shop, her mother—dark-haired with a serious gaze—tired as night fell.

Who was her mother? Something about her was familiar. She must have resembled someone I knew from Wilfred today. I couldn't pause too long to wonder—the stories rushed on.

Now Mrs. Freeburger, older, was back in Wilfred, wearing a belted, full-skirted dress of the 1950s. I searched for her mother, but she was gone. Wilfred was busier. The mill still churned out tens of thousands of board feet of timber, and bloated pickup trucks and cars with fins traveled the main drag. The summer sky was as blue as Florentine end papers.

My breath caught in my throat. There was Marilyn Wilfred looking on as Mrs. Freeburger held a young man's hands. Marilyn was handsome more than pretty and must have been in her fifties. She searched Mrs. Freeburger's face for something—a resemblance?—and

Mrs. Freeburger and the young man pointedly turned away.

A few other gauzy memories swept by, including a wedding, an easel set up at the beach, a baby's face, but they vanished in seconds to be replaced with images of pastries. Donuts, cupcakes with thickly piped icing, sleeves of grocery store cookies, and a stack of buttered pancakes dripping with maple syrup. That was it.

I slipped the book to my nightstand. Fascinating, but not super useful. At least, not yet.

CHAPTER TWENTY-FOUR

There was only one place to be that next morning: Darla's Café. What, with a dead architect in the mill-pond and a presumed-dead woman reappearing, Wilfredians had a lot to talk about.

Thor and Buffy were taking advantage of the audience. Thor's cape now sported a jagged edge, and "The Fluoridator" was written on its shoulders in magic marker. "I did it on purpose," Buffy said. "It looks more fierce, don't you think?"

"Choose a card. Any card," Thor said once I'd fished a dollar from my handbag.

I randomly selected the Queen of Clubs and handed it to him, facedown.

"Thank you." Thor's tongue protruded from the side of his mouth as he concentrated. He returned the card to the deck and put the deck behind his back while he closed his eyes. Buffy peered around him.

"What are you doing back there?" I said, as if it wasn't clear he was putting the card I'd just chosen under the top card in the deck and pretending to shuffle.

"It's, um—"

"It's part of the suspense," Buffy supplied.

The front door opened to Ruff and Sita Waters. They made their way past me and the child magicians straight to the cash register at the end of the counter.

"We came as soon as we heard," Sita told Darla. "I can't believe it. Something was feeling off base over there. The energy has not been good."

"It's a shame," Darla said. "I admit to misgivings about Cruikshank. But he was a decent guy. He even had a suggestion for a new patio." She pointed to his patio sketch, which she had now taped behind her below the black cat clock with its swinging tail.

"Have you seen Tommy Daniels?" Ruff asked. "We'd hoped to catch up with him."

"Here I am," Tommy said from a booth.

The Waters couple slid into the bench across from him. I drew my attention back to Thor.

"Is this your card?" He pulled the Nine of Hearts from the top of the deck.

"Close enough," I said, keeping an eye on the table with Tommy and the Waterses.

Mrs. Garlington sat in the booth just behind them. Her son must have just left for his postal route—a licked-clean platter with a wadded-up napkin sat across from her.

"May I sit with you?" I asked. Normally I would have

left her in peace to compose a sonnet to the dead architect or something. Today I had some eavesdropping to do.

"Certainly. In fact, I'm glad you're here. I wanted to talk to you about the music room."

"Sure," I said as Darla poured me a cup of coffee.

"What'll it be today?" Darla asked.

"Oatmeal, please."

"My sheet music keeps disappearing," Mrs. Garlington said. "Students have been delighted by 'One Little Fishy,' and now it's vanished. Plus, I found 'Red River Valley' behind the organ last week, and I have no idea how it got there."

This could go on for a while. Mrs. Garlington didn't expect an engaged conversation. I nodded vaguely and focused on the talk at the table behind me.

"—I'd seen him just that morning. It blows me away," Tommy Daniels said.

"A life lost. On that land, and because of our project," Sita said. I imagined her shaking her head, her beaded earrings swaying.

"Fiona Wilfred threatened to challenge our ownership, too," Ruff said.

Something in their conversation triggered a memory. What was it? Something wasn't quite right, but I couldn't put my finger on it.

Mrs. Garlington tapped her plate with a fork to get my attention. "Are you listening to anything I just said? If 'Pop Goes the Weasel' goes missing again, I'm going to file a complaint with the library trustees."

Rodney's work, no doubt. His new collar seemed to bring out the worst in him. I noticed how he became scarce during organ lessons. I wouldn't put it past him to drag the sheet music off and hide it somewhere in an attempt for peace and quiet.

"I'll see what I can do, Mrs. Garlington."

"Don't let it stop you," Tommy Daniels said from behind me. "Cruikshank's death was some kind of accident."

"With a tire iron?" Sita said. "Head bashed in?"

"Well, the Wilfred woman disappeared right after, remember," the contractor said. "Odds are good they'll figure out she did it, and she'll be locked up. Problem solved all around."

Tommy was hell-bent on making sure the retreat center went forward. He undoubtedly counted on the income, especially if he was going to be handing out packets of cash as I'd seen him do the other night. But he had an intriguing theory, one Wilfredians would be sure to embrace. She hadn't been clear about where she actually was.

"You're eavesdropping on them, aren't you?" Mrs. Garlington said.

My attention snapped to her. "I couldn't help but overhear a few words."

She looked smug. "Writers are observant people. You can't get anything past me. I suppose that's why you wanted to sit here."

"Oh no," I lied. "It's busy today, and I thought you'd be nice company."

"Anyway, it's clearly another strike of the old mill's curse."

My oatmeal arrived, this time with a sprinkling of pecans and honey. I gave Darla a thumbs-up.

"Speaking of curses, was there ever talk about Marilyn Wilfred and curses?"

"Oh, vague chatter. She was a warm woman. She dedicated her life to bettering Wilfred. That was the Marilyn I knew. I'd heard talk—early on, when I was a young woman and the Wilfreds still lived at Big House—that she was the black sheep of the family."

"In what way?"

"Tragedy seemed to follow her like a malicious hound. Hmm." She withdrew a pad from her purse and jotted "malicious hound" inside with a purple pen. "And, of course, she wasn't married." Mrs. Garlington fixed me with a significant look.

"Lots of women aren't married," I said.

"They say she fell in love once, but it didn't work out, and she never got over it."

"Don't make a hasty decision," Tommy said to Ruff and Sita behind me, raising his voice. "Don't let emotion take over. You don't want to do something you'll regret later."

"We're thinking things over carefully, and we'll let you know how they stand. Soon," Ruff said.

"We need to spend some time here, seek inner guidance, feel the energy," Sita added.

Thor whisked to the Waters couple, his cape flapping behind him. "Care for a trick?"

I needed to think. I took the long way back to the library—down to the trailer park, through the meadow, and over the levee to the old mill site. From there, I'd walk the trail through the woods along the bluff.

The trail through the meadow was really no more than a rut in weeds and grass. It siphoned runoff and was potholed enough that I kept a keen eye on the ground to avoid twisting an ankle. If Ruff and Sita went ahead with the retreat center, they'd have to gravel it properly.

It sounded like their decision had a lot to do with Fiona. Fiona, popular contender for Lewis Cruikshank's murder. I remembered her frantic reaction to the news of his death. If that wasn't guilt, I didn't know what was. Yet she seemed unwilling to defend herself by revealing where she'd been and with whom.

The dew on the morning grass wet my ankles as I trudged up the road. Why would she kill Lewis Cruikshank? It made no sense to me. Could she have known him from, say, art school?

To me, Brett was the likelier suspect as a murderer. He'd already lied about being employed at the gallery. Maybe Cruikshank had found him out, and Brett killed him to cover up his and Fiona's affair.

Tommy Daniels had been at the site, too, for at least part of the day. There, too, motive was a problem. Daniels had made it clear this morning that he wanted the retreat center to go ahead as planned. Offing the architect was a fast way to put a halt to the project.

I climbed the embankment to the levee, with the millpond wide and serene on my right. The levee wasn't much more than a pile of rocks meant to keep the millpond put and to siphon overflow to the Kirby River. I could imagine old man Thurston directing the placement of the granite boulders more than a century ago.

Almost immediately, I felt a tremor in the ground beneath me, as quick and steady as a hummingbird's wings, and building in intensity. It wasn't an earthquake; it was energy.

I pulled my arms close. Maybe Lalena was right, and the mill site wasn't cursed at all. A land spirit, sleeping since the mill burnt down, had somehow been awakened. I had no idea what power a land spirit might possess. All around me, rocks might fly, or tree branches take to the air. Heck, I might be swallowed up in a sinkhole.

"Land spirit?" I said, not exactly sure how one talked to an amorphous entity.

The humming beneath my feet continued, rattling my leg bones. Gathering my courage, I crossed the levee, being careful to keep my footing over its rocky crown. I knew that just behind me, across the meadow, the view opened to Wilfred proper and the valley, rimmed with foothills. From here, I faced an abandoned industrial site and the forest's sharp rise behind it.

"Land spirit?" I tried again.

The trembling deepened, and I gasped. "What do you want?"

The sky was calm, and a hawk circled overhead. It would have been a peaceful spring morning, if not for the anger beneath my feet. Sun glanced off the surface of the millpond. The millpond from where, I reminded myself, Lewis Cruikshank's body had been pulled out the day before.

"What is it?" I asked again. "What do you want?"

The anger beneath me intensified. All at once, birds scattered from the trees, cawing, and flew over the meadow. My breath caught in my throat.

"Is it the construction? You don't want anything built here?"

The rumbling traveled up my legs, and I had to focus to remain standing. Other than the exodus of the birds, the landscape appeared the same: placid, with the barest wind rippling the millpond.

I tried once more. "Are you unhappy? Can I help you?"

Motion on the ground six feet or so to my right caught my eye. Green on green—a snake with diamonds running down its back. A rattler.

Blood iced in my veins. I stepped back, and the snake lifted its head and curled its body rapidly into a coil, its tail rising and rattling at a pace to match the earth's tremor. Images whipped through my brain of lightning storms, screaming wind, and suffocating fire.

Staring into the snake's eyes, I was frozen. Its tongue licked out, and its head drew back. I couldn't move. Couldn't even close my eyes against the strike I knew was coming.

"Greed." This single word rose from the rattlesnake's parted mouth.

Then the snake rippled over the weed-strewn ground toward the woods and was gone.

CHAPTER TWENTY-FIVE

All day, the memory of the snake and its warning chilled me to my core. Some large presence inhabited the mill site, and something had awakened it. Unless I could somehow help, I planned to stay far away until it returned to sleep.

The day's work was, as always, a welcome distraction. Dylan's father came in for a thriller, and I sent him home with a furnace repair manual. Two sisters who went to Gaston High asked where they could find something on Impressionist painters, and I bypassed Monet for the Pre-Raphaelites, which they loved. Another patron stood in front of the shelf of DVDs for half an hour until I plucked *Auntie Mame* off the rack for him. He didn't know he wanted it, but he did.

But every once in a while, the memory of the snake's

glassy eyes and freakishly deep voice shivered through my gut.

Then Sam came in, and warmth edged out fear—at least for the moment. I hadn't seen him since he'd stormed off with his wife the day before, and I realized I'd missed him. He was fond of me, that's all, I quickly reminded myself. "How's Fiona?"

"That's why I'm here," he said. No baby this time. Nicky must be with his mother. "I need your help. Again."

"What kind of help?"

"Lewis Cruikshank was murdered."

"Yes," I said uneasily.

"I'm worried."

"Why do you have to deal with it? Fiona's home," I said, suspecting what he'd tell me next. "You're off the hook."

"She won't tell me where she's been all this time." He paced, staring at the floor. "Three nights she was gone."

"I thought you said she went off from time to time." I kept my voice soft, but neither of us was stupid. It didn't look good for her.

He smiled slightly. Trouble. A patron browsing new releases lifted his head the better to listen in.

"I'll meet you in the kitchen in a minute," I told Sam, nodding toward the patron.

After the patron left with a memoir of a war hero under his arm, I found Sam, arms crossed, looking out the kitchen door's window toward Big House. I couldn't tell if he was watching someone or simply lost in thought.

"Sam?"

He swiveled toward me. "Fiona hasn't done this since

the baby was born. I thought—I'd hoped—she'd changed. She's still Nicky's mother."

"The important thing is that you're his father."

"Yes." He wouldn't meet my eyes.

"Did she come clean to Sheriff Beattie?"

"I don't think so." He pulled out a chair and sat. "Fiona is her own person. She believes she can do anything and not suffer the consequences. That's what made her so attractive—that wild spirit—and so infuriating. I'm sure she told the sheriff it's none of her business and expected that trouble would simply wash off her. It's always worked in the past."

"So, she won't say what she was doing or whom she was with, except that she was in Portland."

"That's about it."

"Nothing else? Nothing at all?"

"Well," Sam said, "she told me she'd decided to go into Portland to see an art exhibition and have dinner."

"Out of the blue? She never mentioned this to you earlier?"

He shook his head. "Brett left, and she caught a ride into town."

"With whom?" I said.

"That's where she gets vague. If I press her, she says it's her life, and she can do what she wants."

"She wouldn't even tell you where she stayed?"

"No. Assuming it was a hotel, that'll be easy enough for the sheriff to trace through her credit card."

I sighed. "If Fiona refuses to say where she was—"

"I know," Sam said. "She becomes the primary suspect in Lewis Cruikshank's death. I just keep thinking of the baby. Fiona isn't perfect, but she's no murderer."

I drummed my fingers on the counter, then leaned

back on it, arms folded across my chest. "What do you want from me?"

"We're friends."

Straight for the jugular. I did my best to look indifferent and nodded. "And?"

"I hoped you would talk to her. She likes you. She told me so."

"You're kidding." I didn't even register in her world. I knew it. "You think she'd tell me where she was, when she wouldn't tell you or the sheriff?"

Rodney strolled into the drawing room and wound himself around my legs before strutting to Sam to beg for pets.

"It's worth a try. Then I could let the sheriff know, and she would confirm it." He stroked Rodney down his back.

It wasn't right. Yes, I wanted to find the person who killed Lewis, and I wanted Sam to be happy. But I refused to get in the middle of Sam's marriage. Besides, I needed to back out emotionally. As it was, living next to Sam and seeing him so often was like tossing matches on a mountain of tinder with only a Dixie cup of water to put out the flames. Yet seeing his hopeful expression tore me up.

"No," I said reluctantly. "It's up to her to come clean, and I won't pretend to be her friend to weasel information out of her."

"She wants to go to Patty's karaoke lounge tonight. Why don't you come with us? Maybe ask a friendly question or two. That's all."

Sam wanted me there. It was so hard to say no. "All right. I'll come tonight, but no questioning."

"Thank you. It means a lot to me." Rodney headbutted Sam's leg. "Hi, guy. Want more chicken? I bet you do."

"You've been feeding him?" I said.

"Nearly every day now, right at dinner. I hope you don't mind."

Rodney. The little son of a gun. Faking a hunger strike.

"I'm happy to come and check out the lounge, but, remember, I'm not spying for you." I dropped my hands to my sides. "I'm sorry. I know you're in a tough spot, and you're worried about Nicky, but this is between you and Fiona."

Sam looked at me for a long time. Finally he said, "You're right. I understand."

CHAPTER TWENTY-SIX

I'd disappointed Sam. I knew it, but it couldn't be helped. There was one way I could help, however, and that was to investigate the mill site's curse or land spirit or whatever it was. If I could dissolve that, maybe the trouble swirling around the site would dissipate, too.

Right now, my most promising lead was a complete stranger: Arlene Alber. Once I finished the day's chores of cataloging and paying bills, I'd turn to the matter of researching her.

Later that afternoon, I climbed the main staircase to the second floor, letting my hands brush the banister's satiny finish. I passed the old house's bathroom—no visiting bathers this afternoon—and rounded the corner to the dressing room that served as our music room. No organ music, either, but I did hear voices. This was surprising, since, despite the comfortable couch, most patrons avoided the music room unless they were focused on sheet music or lessons with Mrs. Garlington.

I popped around the corner. "Hello?"

Ruff and Sita Waters lifted their heads. Sheaves of what might have been legal documents lay on the coffee table in front of them, and the standing lamp gave the room a cheery glow, despite the cloudy afternoon.

"You don't mind if we spread out a bit here, do you?" Sita asked. Today she wore yet another gypsy princess outfit—this one with fluttery sleeves and a bodice that skimmed her slender figure. Indian ribbon trimmed the hem and neckline.

"No, that's fine," I said. "That's what we're here for."

"We want to spend more time in Wilfred over the next few days, until—" Ruff began.

"—until we figure out what's going on," Sita finished. "There's really nowhere else to talk privately, except the library."

True. Everyone in the diner would strain to catch the Waterses' conversation if they had any idea a juicy tidbit might surface.

"It's no trouble to hang out here." A thought rose. "Darla's extra trailer will probably be cleared by the sheriff soon. Lewis Cruikshank was the last guest. I don't know if you'd be interested in staying in town. Or maybe it's too gruesome for you."

"He didn't die in the trailer," Sita said calmly. "We could cleanse it."

I imagined what Darla would say to find the trailer smoky with sage and glittering with crystals hung in its windows. "Just an idea. At least you'd be close by and could feel like more a part of goings-on."

Once I'd passed along Darla's phone number, I stopped

by Local History in the house's old dining room on the ground floor. When I'd looked into Marilyn's background, it had been evening, and all I had to do was go to old man Thurston's office, knowing the materials I'd need would have collected themselves. Books flying through the air wouldn't do for business hours. I'd have to do this the old-fashioned way.

First I checked the Wilfred family files. Over the years, Wilfredians here and there had assembled a loose history, collated in binders. Pages held taped-on newspaper articles, birth announcements, photos of houses, and even an amateur sketch or two.

Other history, like that pertaining to specific families and buildings, was sorted by file folders in a two-drawer wooden file cabinet that might have dated from the house's construction.

The Alber file was thin. According to a church newsletter, Carl Alber, a mill worker, assumed the post of church deacon in 1915. At the time, he had a wife, Zelda, and a daughter, Arlene, aged five. That would have made her ten years younger than Marilyn.

I reached for the Gaston High yearbook the year Arlene Alber would have graduated and flipped to the index. There she was, a tall, thin girl with short dark hair and freckles. Her eyes were unusually small and dark as coffee beans. She was in Future Farmers of America but didn't have any other specific mentions.

I couldn't make out any link to Marilyn, except that they both lived in Wilfred. Marilyn would have been town royalty, while Arlene was the daughter of a laborer in Marilyn's family business. In a larger town, they wouldn't have mixed socially. Maybe it was different in tiny Wilfred.

Next, I'd try periodicals to see if we had any references to newspaper articles about Arlene Alber. Maybe she and Marilyn had been in a civic or church group together.

As I passed into the hall ringing the atrium, the sound of Fiona's name stopped me.

It was Ruff Waters's rich baritone. "This is extortion. She can't do this to us."

Sita's voice was too soft to make out. I wavered between deciding to clomp past their door to make sure they understood they could be heard or to stay in place. I stayed.

"I know," Ruff replied to whatever Sita had said. "That doesn't make it right. We can't let her get away with it."

"Ms. Way?" Dylan yelled up from the atrium, where he could clearly see me frozen, head tilted toward the music room.

Ruff's voice stopped abruptly.

Damn it. I leaned over the railing. "I'll be right down."

Fiona had the Waterses by the neck somehow. Was she still pressuring them for money, even with her demands now out in the open?

Dylan led me to the circulation desk, where a young mother needed recommendations for her four-year-old daughter. I relaxed my mind, and images of rodents scampered through my head.

"Does your daughter enjoy mice?" I asked.

Once E.B. White's *Stuart Little* had been checked out and settled into the delighted girl's arms, I wandered to the card catalog, still turning over Ruff's words in my mind. I flipped through the index for the Forest Grove and Wilfred newspapers. The card index stopped in the 1990s, and the library's trustees had promised the funds to subscribe to the online database, once we had a few computer terminals set up. For Arlene Alber, it didn't matter.

I struck gold. A feature article, it looked like. The index card had yellowed, and its hand-typed entry had faded.

A chill gripped the backs of my arms. The card read, simply, "Arlene Alber's disappearance."

I glanced at the mantel clock. The article would have to wait until later. I was due for karaoke.

CHAPTER TWENTY-SEVEN

I reluctantly made my way down the hill to the Sing-Along Salon in the basement of Patty's This-N-That.

These days, the storefront window was stacked with spools of ribbon. Patty sold whatever caught her fancy. It was bells for a few months, then scissors, then old band uniforms. She kept equally capricious hours.

On the building's right side, steps led down to the Sing-Along. A red light bulb glowed over the entrance, and strains of "God Bless America" in a warbling soprano wafted toward me as I pushed open the door.

It took a second to get my bearings in the dim light. To my left was a stage barely larger than my kitchen, and Mrs. Garlington was on it, singing her praise of the country's oceans and prairies and mountains white with snow. At the table closest to me, Buffy and Thor performed magic tricks for Tommy Daniels. I'd have expected him to be ensconced in the tavern side of Darla's, but I guess everyone needed a break sometimes, and the new kara-oke lounge was Wilfred's only other entertainment. He was laughing with Thor and good-naturedly pulled a card from the deck Buffy proffered.

Just behind him at a bistro table were Ruff and Sita, and they didn't look happy. I doubted it was because of Mrs. Garlington's singing, either. No, the black cloud floating over their table had been seeded by Fiona, who was at the room's one large table against the rear wall. She was laughing and holding court with Duke and Roz. Sam sat at the table's other side. When he saw me, he waved me over.

Patty waved from behind a makeshift bar with a tiny refrigerator on the counter behind her stocked with bot-tled fruit juice. Two stools were at the counter. The fluffy gray sweater over one seat marked it as Mrs. Garling-ton's.

Sam rose to give me the chair closer to Fiona. I shot him a look meant to communicate that I would not be questioning her.

"You just missed Tommy Daniels singing 'My Way,'" he said. "Frank Sinatra's job is safe."

Fiona looked at Sam, then me, and said, "I can't be-lieve you people really thought I was dead."

Mrs. Garlington examined her microphone, as if she wanted to crank up the volume. Patty manned the con-trols from her counter and wasn't having any of it.

"We had a bloodied tire iron and a body," Duke said. His expression was worshipful. Fiona had that effect on people. Certainly men. "Naturally we searched the millpond. The levee needs work, though, I'll tell you that. Examining it from the boat . . ." He shook his head.

Fiona laughed and tucked a lock of hair behind an ear. No wedding ring, I noted. Maybe she and Sam had fought. "Dead. Me? That's crazy."

"What were we supposed to think?" Roz said, her stare icy. Good old Roz.

Fiona ignored her. "What a laugh! I took a few photos, made a few sketches, decided to go into town. No biggie."

The door opened to Brett. Even with shadows under his eyes and eerily backlit by the red light outside the basement door, his looks earned a double take. He adjusted to the dark before crossing the room to our table. Everyone stared. The last time we'd seen him, he'd accused Sam of murdering his wife. Now, Fiona waved and smiled as if her last interaction with Brett was a "see you later" at the grocery store.

Sam tensed and drew back. Without even looking at him, I knew he was smiling.

"Anyway," Fiona said, eyes on Brett, "I may as well have fun tonight before the sheriff hauls me off, right?"

"Hi, Fiona." His gaze swept the rest of us before returning to her.

"Hey, Brett," she said. "Nice to see you."

We all watched intently. No last-second touchdown or nail-biting movie reveal and certainly no karaoke number had earned this caliber of rapt attention.

"I tried to call, but it went straight to voice mail," Brett said.

"Oh, sorry I haven't been in touch. I lost my phone somewhere," she said in the most casual voice.

"Still in town?" I asked Brett.

"Sheriff Beattie asked me to stick around another night. Not that I'm legally obligated." He fastened his eyes on Sam's. "But I thought I would. Make sure Fiona is all right."

I looked around nervously. The last thing I wanted was for Brett to take a chair next to Fiona. It was clear from his unflinching gaze toward her that he wanted to, and she seemed to neither discourage nor welcome it. We didn't need more drama.

Meanwhile, Buffy had taken the microphone and was belting out an energetic take on Beyoncé's "Single Ladies." Oh, to be a clueless six-year-old.

"There's an open stool at the counter," I said. "Why don't you have a seat?"

Brett flicked a glance at me, then at the empty stool. "Okay. I'll stay. Just to keep an eye on things."

"Come on, Josie," Patty said, clearly in an attempt to draw attention from Brett. "After Buffy. I have the perfect song for you."

"Uh-uh, no thanks. I'm just here to watch."

"Yeah, Josie," Roz said, tearing her gaze from Brett. "Why not give it a try?"

I was an introvert, not a Broadway star. The acme of comfort for me was a vintage detective novel and a soft armchair—no audience. "I've never done karaoke. I wouldn't even know where to start."

"It's not hard," Roz said. "Don't you sing in the shower?"

Sam watched, a faint frown playing on his lips. "How about 'Witchy Woman'?"

Last fall Sam had told me my FBI code name was "Broomstick," for my hair. He knew I didn't like it.

"She doesn't want to do it, Sam," Fiona said. "Leave her alone. Not everyone is cut out to take the stage."

"Exactly," I said.

"Maybe 'Witchcraft'?" Duke suggested.

"She's a librarian, for God's sake," Fiona added. "Not a party girl."

"That old business of hair-in-a-bun and glasses-on-a-chain isn't true anymore," I said, feeling my pulse jack up a few notches. "Not that I want to sing, but one of my library school classmates just scaled Mount Everest. Another one keeps the music library for the Rolling Stones. Librarians aren't boring. Right, Roz?"

"I'm not getting up there," she said.

A frown of amusement hung on Sam's lips. I was happy to see he'd been distracted from Brett's arrival, at least for the moment. "Why don't you prove it to us? Knock that old stereotype on its head."

Everyone looked at me, waiting for me to react. "Okay. Fine." For the reputation of librarians everywhere, I snatched the microphone from Buffy as she stepped down. "Not 'Witchy Woman,'" I told Patty. "I don't know why everyone is so stuck on witches."

"Got it," she said. "Try this."

The sultry opening strains of Nina Simone's "I Put a Spell on You" wafted over the basement's sound system. "That's not funny, Patty," I said.

"Come on, it's a good song."

My father loved jazz, and I knew this song well. "Okay," I said. "I guess."

Spotlights nearly blinded me, but that was all right. I didn't want to see the audience. I sang. Not perfectly, but with feeling, and it was surprisingly easy. The lyrics—a woman telling her lover not to play around, that she'd bound him to her—felt right. Lights in my eyes, I could see only the audience's bottom half: Sita's gauzy hem, Duke's work boots, Fiona's ankle boots with the Japanese sole, Sam's beat-up oxfords, Thor's dragging cape. The song was over before panic set in.

Sam welcomed me back to my seat and patted me on the back. Roz gave me a thumbs-up.

"I know. I'll sing something," Fiona said. "What do you say? We should be celebrating that I'm alive."

"Sing, Fiona," Brett said from the bar.

"I love to hear that voice," Duke added.

Ruff audibly sighed from his and Sita's table behind us. I thought of Lewis Cruikshank's body at the morgue, maybe this very moment, with the medical examiner hunched over it.

"I'm going home," Sam said in a low voice.

I'd been getting used to his warmth next to me, his elbow jostling me from time to time. *Stop it*, I told myself.

Fiona ignored him and stepped next to Brett at the counter. "Patty?"

"Hmm?" Patty was pouring seltzer into a glass for Brett.

"I'd like to sing next."

"All right. What song?"

Fiona turned to us and flashed a million-watt smile. "How about 'Killing Me Softly'?"

"'Killing Me Softly,' coming up," Patty said.

I felt Sam stiffen. "Fiona. No."

She laughed. "It's a joke, Sam. Chill. Don't you think it's funny?"

Sam rose abruptly, his chair knocking mine. He faced the table as if he was going to say something, but when his gaze fell on Fiona, he simply turned and left. The door closed firmly behind him. Fiona watched him, and for a split second her eyes widened before softening again.

Any doubt Fiona might have felt had clearly vanished. She picked up the microphone from the bar and took the stage with a smile that enveloped the audience. She had committed. She was going through with it.

Brett swiveled his stool to face her. Tommy Daniels leaned back, hands clasped over his belly. Duke was rapt. I glanced at the Waterses. Ruff studied his fingernails, and Sita closed her eyes and appeared to mutter some sort of mantra. Emotionally, I was with Sam. This was a very bad idea.

The song flooded the room and led straight into vocals. Fiona missed the first few words, but when she picked up the lyrics, it was with gently swaying hips and a voice clear and casual. I couldn't watch.

The Sing-Along Salon might not have fancy furnishings, but Patty had not stinted on the sound system. The easy swing of the guitar and gentle harmony of the background singers played true. Despite the complete lack of sensitivity, the song was a good choice for Fiona, and she sang it well. Still, she shouldn't have been singing it at all.

As the music played, Patty shooed Buffy and Thor upstairs with a mouthed *brush your teeth and get to bed*.

Mrs. Garlington leaned over the counter and said something to Patty, then took charge of the kids. Thor's cape flapped behind him as he disappeared into the hall to the stairs. His and Buffy's feet tapped up the steps, Mrs. Garlington's heavier tread behind them.

Now the song reached the middle eight, where the lyrics consisted of "oh" and "la la la." Would it ever end?

Roz exchanged a meaningful glance with me. Sam had to be most of the way to Big House by now.

Fiona was in her own world, basking in the attention, relishing the joke. She swayed and winked at "killing." I couldn't stand it any longer.

I lifted myself from my chair, ready to say something to Patty, when the music abruptly cut. The room went black. Someone yelped—Sita, maybe?—and someone else gasped.

"What happened?" Roz said into the dark.

I felt for my chair and sat again.

"Hold on, folks," Patty said. "We must have tripped a circuit breaker. Don't move—I'll get it." A few chairs creaked as people shifted, but otherwise we obeyed.

"My phone," said a voice from my left. Tommy Daniels. "Let me find the flashlight function. That'll help."

I fished in my purse for my own phone, and soon more shafts of light joined ours in crisscrossing the basement lounge. Within seconds, they converged in one place: on Fiona Wilfred's body collapsed on the stage.

CHAPTER TWENTY-EIGHT

Roz screamed at the same time Patty said, "Got it," from the circuit breaker box. With the return of the lights, the instrumental track resumed for "Killing Me Softly."

When I could unclench my jaw, I said, "Turn that thing off." Patty, eyes wide, rushed back to the bar to cut the music.

Tommy led the gathering around Fiona's limp body while I called 911. Brett moved slowly to the stage, as if in a dream.

"I have a first aid kit." Patty held up a small white plastic box.

My suspicion that its contents of bandages and alcohol wipes weren't going to save Fiona was confirmed when Roz said, "She's gone."

Ruff and Sita backed against the wall. Roz, staring at Fiona's body, returned to her chair.

I'd hoped an ambulance might be needed, but that idea was quashed when Brett rolled Fiona on her side. Through her back, under her left scapula, was a wound rimmed in scarlet. Her arm flopped to the stage, sending us all leaping back. Worse were her eyes, open, unblinking. Brett gently cradled her head in his lap and brushed the hair from her cheek.

Despite the horror, somehow she remained beautiful, delicate. Her face was as unblemished as the inside of a porcelain teacup, and her honey-hued hair lay in waves. If it weren't for those eyes—and the blood—she might have been asleep.

"We need to stay," I said, ripping my gaze from Fiona.

"The volunteer fire department will be here in minutes," Duke said.

"We need to wait for the sheriff," I said. "She—Fiona—was murdered. It had to be one of us."

As I spoke, I searched the room. Could someone have reached through a window somehow? No. The two windows on the basement's street side were at least six feet from the stage and fastened shut. The room's dropped ceiling would never bear the weight of a man. No, it was just us.

And—I couldn't help but feel grateful at the thought—not Sam.

But then, who? And how?

I ruled out Patty and Roz right away. Patty had been behind the counter, and Roz sat on my other side. I would have heard if she'd rushed to the stage. Besides, neither of them had a motive.

Nor did Duke. He was light enough on his feet to have skipped to the stage and stabbed Fiona. Just because he could have done it didn't mean he had a reason to kill her. Tommy hadn't been far from the stage. I could see no reason why he'd kill Fiona, either. He didn't seem particularly interested in her one way or the other when she'd been missing.

Russ and Sita huddled together near the wall, not far from the circuit breaker box, which was still open. Considering that they wouldn't even eat a fried egg, because it came from an animal, it was hard to picture them murdering someone. But with Fiona's threats to sue for ownership of the land if they didn't pay up and the bit of conversation I'd overheard that afternoon, they had reason to want her dead.

Finally, there was Brett. If the room were an emotional map, its edges would be thick with fuzzy red shock, and the center, where Brett held Fiona, would pool the deep blue of grief. Had he returned to take her life?

As we waited, no one spoke. Even Roz held her tongue, as if this situation was even worse than the disasters she regularly prophesied.

Eventually, sirens wailed nearer, and pulsing shafts of red light pierced the basement windows. Brett rose as the basement door opened, then sat again. Two EMTs were at Fiona's body before anyone could greet them.

"It's too late," Duke said.

One of the EMTs was already on the phone, undoubtedly calling the sheriff. It was going to be a long night.

Behind me, Sita swallowed a sob.

* * *

Sheriff Beattie took charge. She looked fresh, and her uniform was cleanly pressed, as if she were an action doll, not a law enforcement officer in charge of a quickly deepening murder investigation.

"I'm going to talk with each of you separately. I'm also going to ask you to let a deputy pat you down. Okay?" she said.

"Not okay," Brett said. He'd returned to his stool and shoved his clenched fists into his pockets. "You're not searching me without an attorney present."

"Noted," the sheriff said. "Anyone else object?"

None of the rest of us did.

"Soda water for everyone. On the house," Patty said and pulled bottles from the minifridge behind her.

While we waited our turns to go upstairs for an interview, two deputies—another had arrived shortly after the sheriff—searched the karaoke lounge. We all stayed put, except Patty, and she left only for a moment to check on Buffy and Thor. A deputy accompanied her. We didn't talk much, but the room felt divided, with Brett on one side and the rest of us on the other.

"Josie Way?" Sheriff Beattie said from the hall leading upstairs to the This-N-That shop on the ground floor. At last, it was my turn.

Surrounded by bolts of grosgrain ribbon and every kind of trim from sequined to bobbled, I took a hard-backed wooden chair across the sales counter from the sheriff.

"Where exactly were you in the room?" she asked.

I pushed aside a length of sky-blue satin ribbon. On a sheet of notebook paper was a hand-drawn map. Due to its tidy lines and accurate scale, I judged it to be Duke's work.

"There," I said, pointing to the large table near the counter. "Roz sat behind me, nearly at the wall, and Duke was on the other side. Fiona's chair was next to his."

"And at this chair?" She tapped the *X* next to my seat on the map.

"Sam. Until he left."

"When did he leave?"

She surely already knew the answer. "When Fiona told Patty she'd sing 'Killing Me Softly.' He couldn't bear it." And rightly so, I thought. "He went home."

The sheriff walked me through everything that followed, from the lights being cut, to their return, to Fiona, crumpled on the floor.

"Fiona probably never even saw it coming," I said.

"How's that?"

"The stage lights are blinding. I sang before she did, and all I could make out were feet." I shifted in my chair and pulled a three-inch length of rickrack from under me. "How did the murderer do that with the lights? It all happened so fast."

"Can't say. That's what I'm here to find out."

Then she let me go.

CHAPTER TWENTY-NINE

I walked up the hill. The night was startling clear, and the stars pierced the sky with slivers of light. Wind shushed through the cottonwoods by the river and rose to the oaks and fir trees ringing the library and Big House.

A sheriff's SUV was parked in front of Big House. A deputy would have knocked on the house's wide door, asking if he could come in, and saying he had bad news. My heart went out to Sam.

I took the side entrance to the library and went straight up the service staircase to my apartment. Rodney waited for me at the top of the steps. It was long past dinnertime. I opened the refrigerator and shut it again. Food didn't appeal.

Maybe Fiona wasn't the most responsible mother, and maybe she'd cheated on Sam, but at one point he'd loved her. And she was still Nicky's mother. Remembering the few minutes Fiona and I had spent together when she'd reappeared, I knew she could be kind, too. And vulnerable.

I wondered what would happen next. Wilfred now had two active murder investigations. Could they be linked? If so, Brett was the most likely suspect. He was at the old mill site the day Lewis Cruikshank was murdered, and he was at the karaoke lounge tonight. He was hostile to Sam and refused to be searched for a knife.

But why would he have killed Fiona? Could Fiona have refused his advances? I could imagine her leading him on. She'd promised Sam she'd be faithful until the divorce was final. Then again, she hadn't been wearing her wedding ring.

The sound of a car door thunking closed drew me to the living room window. The county sheriff's SUV backed out of Big House's driveway.

Sam now knew he was a widower. The kitchen light at Big House flicked on. He might turn to a beloved opera or start cooking an elaborate recipe, despite the time. Or he might simply sit at the kitchen table and stare into space. I reached out a hand, as if I could stretch across the cool night and into the kitchen's warmth and rest it on his cheek.

One thing I knew for sure was that he'd want to find Fiona's murderer.

Sam had asked for my help, and I'd refused. Maybe if I'd talked to her as he'd asked, she wouldn't have wanted to take the stage. She might still be alive.

I had to help. Sheriff Beattie knew her job, but I had magic.

I went down to the library's ground floor without turning on the lights. Moonlight was ample for now. Diamonds of jewel-toned light splashed over Marilyn Wilfred's portrait and onto the atrium floor.

From the kitchen I took a candle and stuck it in a worn silver-plate candlestick, and I crossed the atrium to old man Thurston's office.

I set the candlestick in front of me and pointed my index finger toward the wick. "Fire," I whispered, and the candle burst into flame.

This was an amateur move, one I'd learned early on through my grandmother's letters. Although it was barely more than a parlor trick that focused the books' energy, it scared me. The autumn before, when I'd learned I could cause fire, the library had almost burned down, and it had terrified me enough that I'd sworn I'd never use magic again. To overcome that fear, I forced myself to light a candle with magic from time to time.

Rodney leapt to the desk, and I took the chair. He purred and rubbed his face against my hand. My birthmark tingled. Five days earlier, we'd had a weapon and no body. Now we had a body and no weapon. We'd all been searched, save Brett, and nothing had turned up except the paring knife Patty used to slice limes. It was clean.

"Books," I said aloud, "help me find the murder weapon."

Posing an open-ended question was a new approach for me. Normally I asked for specific information the books might contain, and they revealed it. Sometimes they revealed it when I didn't even know I needed it, like their hints at Roz's double life as Eliza Chatterly Windsor or even my own identity as a witch.

Tonight, the books murmured and hummed, but none spoke out.

I tried a different tactic. "Books."

Yes, yes, yes, they whispered from the library's corners.

"Where could a person hide a knife in the basement of Patty's This-N-That?"

An Agatha Christie novel and two other mysteries sailed into the library and landed delicately on the desk's corner. Rodney, still purring, tapped one with a paw as it settled into place.

Another book, this one a biography of a circus geek, flew in next to join the stack. I pulled its still-warm bulk toward me, and it opened to a page a third of the way in. Apparently, this circus geek swallowed knives.

"Nice try," I said. "I'll check the mysteries, too, but how about something more practical that doesn't require an English manor and a secret staircase?"

A book almost as big as a catalog moseyed in, only three feet or so above the floor. With effort, it rose to the desk's level and landed with a thud directly in front of me. *Practical Application of Furnace and Cooling Systems*, it read. I wondered if anyone but Lyndon had ever cracked its cover.

The book groaned softly and heaved open to a diagram of ducts feeding into and out of a furnace. Ducts hidden by a false ceiling, just like at the Sing-Along. Now we were on to something.

If what the books suggested was right, the knife could be hidden somewhere in the basement's ceiling—and the murderer might come back to claim it before someone else did. If he hadn't already. Which was a big "if." Books occasionally played practical jokes on me, and although with their collective knowledge they could answer questions I didn't even know to ask, they couldn't read minds. Except mine, that is.

I had an idea. If I could get into the ceiling, I could search it without tearing anything apart. A person was too large, but a cat was perfect. If I found anything, I'd tell the sheriff.

"Rodney," I told him. "We have a job to do."

He strutted to me, his collar tinkling, and held his neck up high.

"Okay, okay." I unbuckled his collar and dropped it on the desk. "Satisfied? Let's go."

CHAPTER THIRTY

By now, it was nearly two in the morning, and clouds thickened in the sky, dampening the moon that had lit my walk home from the Sing-Along.

Rodney scampered along at my feet. He stopped to sharpen his claws on a tree, then ran ahead to sniff at a rock. As we drew nearer to Patty's This-N-That, he stuck closer to me.

Wilfred slumbered like a town in a fairy tale. Although in Oregon, bars could stay open until two in the morning, the tavern side of Darla's rarely kept the lights on past midnight. The building was dark, and only one car was parked in the gravel lot out front—the Rutgers' sedan, which broke down everywhere. The narrow two-lane highway that served as Wilfred's main street was a highway only in name, and traffic not bound specifically for Wilfred rarely passed through. It was dead quiet now.

Could the murderer be watching, waiting to return? I didn't see anyone, but just in case, I hurried to the side of Patty's This-N-That and pressed against the wall leading to the basement door to the karaoke lounge. The red light was off now, and police tape bound off the entrance.

Rodney was practically standing on my feet. Above me, Patty and her grandkids slept.

I took my phone from my bag and ran its light down the building's side. I just needed a way in. The door was sealed tight, as I expected it would be. The two slender windows facing the street, barred, were latched from the inside, I remembered.

I crept to the building's rear, where a surprisingly lush backyard of container plants, including a few palm trees, surrounded a cedar deck. This must be where Patty lounged mornings watching televised aerobics in her ath-leisure wear before heading across the street to Darla's for her faux-smoothie. Just around the corner, right where the bathroom would be in the basement, was another barred window, but this one was ajar. I eyed the bars, then cast a measuring glance at Rodney.

"Can you do it, little guy?" I whispered.

Just then, a light snapped on in the room above me. I flattened myself to the siding. Water ran inside. Maybe it was the kitchen, and Buffy had called out for a glass of water. The light clicked off, and the backyard was again in darkness.

When my pulse steadied, I knelt at the basement win-dow and reached between the bars to push it farther open.

"Okay, Rodney," I said. "This is your moment of glory."

Then I sank to the ground and centered myself, one hand on Rodney's back. For a few seconds, my consciousness flickered, first here in the cool dark yard, concrete under my jeans, then down low, peering into the window.

Then I was in. As Rodney, colors in my vision flattened, but with the somber tones of night, it didn't matter. Besides, everything was sharper. A spider on the deck grabbed my attention, and I caught a whiff of raccoons and possums.

"Focus," I whispered to Rodney.

Rodney—I—shoved my body between the window bars to the bathroom's sharp aroma of pine cleaner. I leapt to the sink, then floor, with a grace that rippled through my muscles but didn't jar my bones. The floor was cool under my paws.

I pushed through the bathroom door onto the indoor-outdoor carpet in the karaoke lounge and paused at a set mousetrap.

"Carry on, Rodney," I urged and flashed to the cool midnight yard. *Focus.*

I was back in the basement again, padding into the lounge itself. A handful of street-level windows let in only the barest amount of light. The chairs were pulled out and scattered, and the stage was uncomfortably bare, calling attention to its last performance. The scent of raw blood and stale fear drew me closer, then I pulled away.

I looked up. The ceiling tiles lay smooth on their metal frame. From here, they were so far away. Yet the ceiling wasn't really so high—to a person.

How to get up there? I jumped to a bar stool, landing like a fly, then to the counter. The ceiling was still a good four feet over my head. A half-dead philodendron hung from a hook over the counter, but that wouldn't support my weight. I briefly considered putting Rodney on a diet, but Rodney firmly resisted and even refused to budge until I let the idea go.

"Don't quit," I urged him.

No, the plant wouldn't support me, but its macrame hanger would. I stood on my rear legs and hooked my front claws into the jute. The ceiling tile should be light. It would be a leap of faith. One, two, three! With a quick hop, I used the plant hanger as a split-second ladder and, with my head, bumped the ceiling tile aside. I was now standing inside the false ceiling.

It was as dark as the basement stacks at the Library of Congress here. Dusty, too. But that aroma of blood on steel called to me. I gingerly set one paw in front of the other as I made my way across the ceiling, feeling rather than seeing my path toward the scent. Step after step, careful and light.

Then there it was. An open penknife with a mother-of-pearl handle and a blade pungent with blood.

"Bring it to me, Rodney," I whispered from the backyard.

I just wanted the knife moved. Preserved. If someone came for it now, I wanted it gone so the sheriff could examine it later.

As Rodney, I grasped its slick body in my teeth and made a retreat toward the ceiling tile I'd bumped off track.

The sound of scraping, then an opening door stopped me. Someone was coming in. Whoever it was, he wasn't supposed to be there. The door was sealed off with police tape and locked. It couldn't be Patty. She would have come down by the interior staircase. No, someone had picked the lock and was coming in.

As Rodney, I should be safe hidden in the ceiling. Or was I? When the killer discovered the knife missing, would he look further? Plus, the ceiling tile over the bar had been moved. The thought of something happening to Rodney made me frantic with fear.

"Come back," I urged him. "Through the ceiling, back toward the bathroom."

Rodney stepped like a dancer over the ceiling tiles, the knife still in his mouth. To the right, a ceiling tile abruptly popped up, then another, and I—as Rodney—moved to the ceiling's opposite side.

Quietly, I continued in the direction I calculated as toward the bathroom. It was so dark, so confusing in the false ceiling that I wasn't entirely sure where I was.

Behind me, ceiling tiles continued to lift and fall back into the aluminum frame. The stranger—whoever he was—wanted the knife.

I continued away from the lifted tiles, stopping once to readjust the knife in my mouth. Then I came to a wall. The ceiling tiles ended. I extended my claws and lifted up the tile in front of me. Below was the bathroom door. Carefully, I pushed the tile aside and jumped to the ground. The knife fell from my mouth and skittled to the corner.

"Who's that?" a voice growled. I couldn't tell if it was a man or a woman.

I pushed into the bathroom, leapt to the counter, and squeezed through the window's bars.

Then, with a deep inhalation, I was me again.

CHAPTER THIRTY-ONE

I rolled out of sight of the basement window and breathed deeply to calm my racing pulse. Rodney paced in front of me.

I scooted to the corner of the building and listened. After a few minutes, a quiet creaking told me the basement door was opening. I gave the intruder time to get to the highway, where he couldn't look back and see me. When I thought I was safe, I poked my head around the corner. No one. Whoever it was had moved quickly.

I'd heard steps leaving the shop, but no car engine. The intruder had come on foot. I stood and stretched, shaking out my limbs before I peered around the building's street-side edge. The faint mercury light from across the street in Darla's parking lot revealed no one.

I crept up the side of the building past the basement door, once again carefully taped off. I couldn't see that anyone had been inside. Would Sheriff Beattie be able to tell? I looked up and down the highway. Wilfred was fast asleep.

Where did he go? He couldn't have vanished.

My plan now was to stroll confidently toward the library. If I ran into anyone, I'd say that due to Fiona's murder, I couldn't sleep. Tomorrow I'd let the sheriff know to search the Sing-Along's hall for the knife.

The temperature must have dropped ten degrees since I'd left home, and I shoved my hands in my pockets for warmth. I crossed the highway and was headed toward the bridge when I heard a voice behind me.

"Hey, Josie. Walk of shame, huh?"

I just about choked. I turned to find Lalena at the entrance to the trailer park, Sailor on a long ribbon. Rodney trotted over to him.

"What?"

"Ha-ha. Just kidding. As if." It looked like Lalena wore two bathrobes. Maybe one was her outdoor robe.

"As if, what?" I asked. She was only teasing, but I didn't like it. Librarians had a heavy burden of prissiness to bear, and this was the second time in the last eight hours I'd had to deal with it.

"You seem more like a woman of the page than the flesh. No one notices if I ramble at night. I'm the town psychic. They expect stuff like this. But you, what are you doing up? It's got to be three in the morning."

"I couldn't sleep. Did you hear about Fiona?"

She stopped, and Sailor tugged at his ribbon-leash. "No. Did she disappear again?"

"She was stabbed to death." I filled her in on the night's events, minus Rodney's trip through the Sing-Along's false ceiling. I had to hand it to her, she was an excellent audience, her eyes wide all the way through the story.

"I can't believe I missed all that," she said, still rapt. "No murder weapon, huh?"

We both turned to face Patty's building across the street. No one seeing it now would ever guess what had happened earlier in the evening.

"I wondered if the killer might return for it. Have you seen anyone else out tonight?"

She cocked her head. "No. Just you. Well, I did hear someone about half an hour ago, though. He—or she— walked right by the trailer." She shook her head. "Fiona, murdered. This is too much."

"You didn't see who it was?"

"No. I need to ask Duke to fix my porch light."

We both swiveled toward the Magnolia Rolling Estates. "What do you think?" I asked.

"I think we check it out," she said. "Come on, Sailor."

Silent, we walked past Darla's to the entrance to the trailer park, marked by twin cedar trees underplanted with roses. The park was laid out simply, with a gravel road as its spine and half a dozen trailers feeding off each side. Lalena's trailer was a few places up on the left, and Duke's was directly across the road.

Lalena nodded toward Duke's trailer. It was completely dark, and his truck was parked in the driveway. I imagined Duke inside, dreaming of eight-piston engines and the two-step. I knew from experience he had a motion-sensitive light mounted near the door, so I didn't go closer.

"Looks like he's in and asleep," Lalena said. "Should we check on Roz?"

"Might as well. To be complete," I whispered back. Rodney let me know he was still with me by wrapping his tail around my calf.

Roz's trailer was two spaces behind Lalena's. As we approached, I stopped and held up a hand to halt Lalena, too. "A light's on," I said in a low voice.

"In the kitchen," Lalena said. "Look."

Two shadows passed by the blinds. "That's Lyndon. How much you want to bet they're doing a jigsaw puzzle? She probably couldn't sleep after tonight."

"See what I mean about librarians?" Lalena whispered.

"I'm going to ignore that. Let's check the guest trailer," I said. "See if Sita and Ruff are in."

The guest trailer occupied the last space on the right. It, too, was dark.

"I bet they're sleeping," Lalena said as we drew near.

I stopped cold. "Their car is gone."

Could it have been one of them who broke into the Sing-Along tonight? When they didn't find the knife, maybe they left town. I hadn't heard their car, but Sita might have parked it north of town and waited for Ruff to retrieve the knife.

We stood on the far side of the guest trailer, with the meadow to our backs.

"I never would have pegged them as killers," Lalena said.

"Me, neither, but listen to this. Fiona was threatening to sue them unless they paid her fifty thousand dollars. When she disappeared, they might have felt enough glorious relief that they wanted her gone again—for good. It's a solid motive," I whispered. "I heard them complaining about it just this afternoon."

"I guess you'd better break in, then," Lalena said matter-of-factly.

"What?"

"Maybe there are clues in there."

"You mean, like an open calendar with the entry 'knock off Fiona' on today's date? This isn't a Trixie Belden mystery, Lalena."

"Fine." When I responded by putting my hands on my hips, she added, "How are we going to find out unless you look? Go ahead and let them get away with it."

The night was damp and cold. Lalena's second bathrobe seemed to be keeping her warm, but I was chilly. I rubbed my arms as I looked at her, then at the trailer.

"Maybe I'll just peek in the windows," I said.

"That's more like it. I'll stand guard. Be quiet—remember, Roz and Lyndon are still up." She moved to the trailer's front, facing the road, where she'd have a clear view of anyone coming.

I mounted the wooden steps—every trailer at the Magnolia Rolling Estates had them to get up the four-foot cinder-block foundation to guard against flooding—and gingerly opened the screen door. Through the door's window, I made out the living room and kitchen, with a hand-painted WELCOME, Y'ALL sign over the couch. One of Darla's Southern touches. A stack of library books sat on the table. Everything looked tidy and undisturbed.

The bedroom would be the real tell. I walked around the back of the trailer. Could I get up to the window? This end had the trailer hitch. I hoisted myself up on it. Not quite high enough.

I went around the front of the trailer again. Lalena was staring into the distance.

"Do you have a ladder?" I whispered.

"No. Besides, don't you think that would be suspicious, dragging a ladder down the trailer park?"

"I'd like to get a look in the bedroom."

"I just got a psychic hit. Try the front door," she said.

"You're joking."

"Seriously. Not everyone locks up here. I was kidding about the psychic thing, by the way."

"I'll try."

I turned the handle, and the door opened so quickly that I nearly fell in. Lalena mouthed, *I told you so*, and returned to her station out front.

Inside, I hurried to the back of the trailer. Ruff and Sita might roll up any minute, and even with my imagination, I couldn't think of an excuse to be nosing around in here.

The bed was rumpled, but the closet was empty. No brightly colored saris over a chair or chandelier earrings on the bedside table. No toothbrushes or shaving things next to the bathroom sink, either.

That was it. Thirty seconds of illegal entry was all I could stand. I was almost out the door when a page ripped from a magazine caught my eye. It was on the coffee table, askew, as if it had been perused and tossed aside.

"Museum to feature Los Angeles artist," the article said. Accompanying it was a photo of Fiona Wilfred. I leaned closer, pointing my phone at it for light. The article was dated a few months earlier.

In seconds, I was back in the night air, the guest trailer shut up behind me. Sailor and Rodney were chasing each other at the meadow's edge. Rodney trotted over and looked at me expectantly.

So did Lalena. "Well?"

"No sign of them. They totally skipped out." Deep in thought, I scratched Rodney between the ears. "Should we call the sheriff?"

"And get ourselves tossed in jail for breaking and entering?" Lalena said. "Bad idea. Besides, it's too late now. They're gone."

CHAPTER THIRTY-TWO

In the morning, the rain began, and did it ever. Instead of the moody drizzle enveloping the past few months, this rain was a flat-out downpour. The lamps—floor lamps, table lamps, chandeliers—in each of the library's rooms were warm against the dim day, but the conservatory's glass roof beat like a drum circle.

"Lyndon?" I said. I found him checking the glass panes for leaks.

"Hmm?" he replied, pressing a linen cloth to a seam and checking it for moisture.

"I'd like to make a bouquet for Sam. Something to express how sorry I am about Fiona."

Normally Lyndon averted his gaze when talking to me—or to anyone, except Roz, really. Now he looked me straight in the eye. "That's a fine idea."

"What do you recommend? Not a lot is in bloom right now. I saw some daffodils."

"Sign of everlasting love," he said.

"So, maybe not daffodils. What else do we have?"

He scratched his chin as he considered my question. "I could cut some camellias for you. A fine bush of red camellias is in bloom on the west side of the house."

"What do camellias mean?"

"That you offer the recipient your regards."

"Regards" were more acceptable than "everlasting love," but still didn't feel quite right.

Just as I was about to ask for another suggestion, Lyndon said, "How about purple hyacinths? We have some in the bed out front. They mean 'sorrow.' They won't last much longer in this rain, anyhow. Cut them all, if you'd like."

"Thank you, Lyndon. That's perfect."

I took a pair of scissors out the front entrance and returned, wet, but with six purple hyacinths rich with fragrance. I bound their stems with ivory yarn, left after a knitting club meeting, and hesitated over what I should write on the accompanying note. I decided on a simple "Dear Sam, I'm so sorry. Josie."

I left the bouquet leaning against Big House's kitchen door, where it would be protected from the rain. "If you give him five seconds of distraction, you'll have done your work, little flowers."

Then I ran back to the library to call the sheriff's office.

* * *

Most Wilfredians had chosen to stay home and dry. So, when I found Brett staring out the window in Natural History that afternoon, I almost dropped the treatise on spotted owls I was supposed to shelve. We were in the library's second floor, in the old bedroom directly above Circulation. He wore a light blue jacket that fit his runner's body well.

In a novel, Brett's eyes would glisten with tears over Fiona. Surely, they were having an affair, and he was the grieving lover. But if his eyes glistened at all, it was with anger.

"Can I help you?" I asked, putting on a cheerful voice.

"No," he said curtly.

"Rainy, isn't it?"

He didn't even favor that remark with a response.

"Maybe a cup of coffee?" I said. "There's a fresh pot in the kitchen."

"Do you have a problem with my standing here?"

I set the book on the oak desk next to me. Not everyone expressed grief through tears, I knew. "I'm so sorry about Fiona."

Rain-muted daylight from the window behind him threw him into relief. He looked at me a moment before speaking, as if he were trying to explain something complicated, but in the end he simply whispered, "Fiona."

I didn't need to do more than breathe in sympathy.

"She . . ." Now the pain was setting in. Those almond-shaped eyes dipped low.

The books were catching some of my energy and began to hum baritone notes, like a funeral dirge.

"You really cared for her," I said. I had the sense I was

holding a hummingbird and my slightest movement would set him flying. "You're Nicky's father, aren't you?"

He looked at me in surprise, as if he'd momentarily forgotten I was there. He laughed once and turned his head. "No, I'm not."

"But you loved her. You were having an affair with her."

He shook his head. "She wouldn't have me."

"Oh," I said. We might have formed a lonely hearts club. We stared at each other, and I felt like I was watching a movie playing in his eyes: desire, disappointment, grief. Then, again, anger. His eyes narrowed, and his arms tightened at his side.

"Someone murdered Fiona. When she'd disappeared, I thought for sure it was her husband. Sam. Now I know better."

He knew something. "Who, Brett? Who killed her?"

"Think about it. It's not so hard to figure out. Who benefited from her death?"

I could see the passion gathering like a tornado, and I involuntarily stepped back.

"Who was there?" he said.

"The Waterses," I whispered, remembering their absence from the guest trailer.

"That's right." His voice was quiet but razor sharp.

"It's just conjecture."

"That's not what Fiona thought," he said.

"She said something to you?"

"Only not to leave her alone whenever they were around."

The books' humming gathered in intensity, and my breath quickened. *Calm*, I willed them. *It's all right*. The books fed off of Brett's simmering anger and my fear of it. To control the energy, I clenched and released my fists and slowed my breathing.

"You couldn't save her," I said. "No one could."

"She was afraid something like this would happen. I was there, but . . ." Without warning, Brett slammed his fist on the desk's edge, just inches from me, and I jumped. Adrenaline fizzed in my bloodstream.

He rushed from the room. I forced myself to move slowly, with measure. I knew from sorry experience that if I wasn't careful, books would fly after him, crashing on the walls where he ran—if they didn't hit him first.

Downstairs, the front door shut with a bang. He was gone.

Hands shaking, I picked up the spotted owl treatise again and noticed that the desk listed a bit on the side he'd pounded. Great. That desk had endured more than a hundred years and thousands of students, and now it was busted by some ill-tempered Lothario.

Fiona had told Brett that she was afraid Ruff and Sita would kill her. I let that sink in. Should I take that information to the sheriff? All I had was hearsay and the fact that they'd left town. Leaving town at suspicious times seemed to be everyone's MO these days.

As I pondered, I wiggled the desk's back leg. Nothing looked broken, just detached. Lyndon could probably peg it back together. But something rattled under its surface. Had Brett derailed a drawer, too?

I slid the drawer forward and back. It seemed all right.

Then, on a hunch, I pulled it all the way out. I knelt in front of the cavity the drawer had left, but it was too dark to see all the way in, so I gingerly reached into its depths. And touched metal. A skeleton key.

I held the key between my palms. I'd never had much luck with objects telling me about themselves, but the key had been so near books, maybe it had absorbed some of their energy. I closed my eyes and cleared my mind.

Two words slipped into my consciousness: *Arlene Alber*. Her again.

Downstairs, I slipped the key into my desk drawer. I'd give it a thorough examination tonight, but not until I'd found that newspaper article on Arlene Alber's disappearance. Last night's events had gotten in the way of reading it.

"Josie?" Roz called from the conservatory doorway as I passed.

Today she was working in the library, spending the morning as Eliza Chatterly Windsor, romance novelist. She often passed her writing hours in the conservatory. Before last fall, it was so she could surreptitiously watch Lyndon rake leaves or wheel mulch across the yard. Now writing here was a comfortable habit, and she could easily segue into her position as assistant librarian after lunch.

"Come in," she urged me.

The little woodstove in the corner wafted gentle heat, occasionally ruffling a leaf of the banana tree in its giant ceramic pot nearby. Rain drummed on the green glass roof and windows. A small but fragrant bouquet of snow-drops, daffodils, and daphne sat on a side table. Lyndon's work.

"What did Brett want?" Roz asked, cutting to the chase. "I heard him slam the door on the way out, and I watched through the parlor window as he stormed off. He's not going to make trouble, is he?"

"I don't think so. He was upstairs, staring out the window. I don't know why he was here, actually."

"He can't go anywhere else," she pointed out. "He's not a favorite at Darla's. Tommy's started a pool in the tavern. Three-to-one that Brett's arrested before the week is up."

"You know, I think Brett really misses Fiona."

She tilted her head. "They were having an affair?"

I shrugged. "He said she'd rejected him."

"You believe that?"

I took the chair nearest Roz. "Sam told me Fiona had sworn she was through with all that."

"Would you believe a word that came out of her mouth? I know her kind." Roz set her lips in a firm line. "I've cast her type twice, as Catherine de la Brassière and Mimi Borne. Catherine was a heartless courtesan. Irresistible and self-centered. Mimi was the younger sister of Forster Borne, billionaire adventurer."

"Mimi," I said. "Aptly named."

"That kind of woman takes what she can get and doesn't care who's trampled because of it. Pathologically insecure. I saw it right away. Fiona was so pretty and lively. Entertaining. But a lousy listener and couldn't even be bothered to take care of her own kid."

Rodney padded in, wet from the rain. He plopped over next to the woodstove and splayed his belly toward the heat. If it had been a warm, dry day, he would have hopped into the kindling box. He stretched his neck luxuriantly. He was back to making short work of his kibble, now that he was free of his collar.

"None of that matters now," I said. "Brett did mention something interesting, though. He said Fiona was afraid of Ruff and Sita. He thinks they killed her."

We both sat a moment, silent, remembering the night before.

"I'd be surprised, but stranger things have happened," Roz said finally. "Sometimes it's the folks you least suspect who are the guiltiest. Some New Age-y guru probably preaches a take on 'the ends justify the means.' What's a dead blackmailer compared with the benefits of years of yoga retreats? Sita is supple enough to assume the Warrior Pose and stab Fiona at the same time."

"Have you seen Sam?" I asked, wondering how he was faring and if he'd received my flowers.

"No. He has a lot to think about right now." She looked straight at me, as if trying to read my mind. Maybe she was sizing me up as a character. A spurned lover, perhaps.

"I know," I said before she could give me another lecture on unrequited love. "His wife was murdered. But he's looking to settle in Wilfred again. At least, he was. I wonder if he'll stay?"

"If he gets the sheriff's job, he will."

If he found his wife's killer, it would boost his candidacy. I thought of him over in Big House, dealing with last night's aftermath. Again, I wondered if things would have been different had I agreed to talk with Fiona.

"Do you mind if I take an hour off this afternoon?" I asked Roz.

"No. Why?"

"I want to run an errand."

"Fine with me. The rain seems to be keeping patrons away, anyway."

Lyndon came in, leather work gloves in hand. Roz lit up, and Lyndon caught her gaze. An outsider might take in his placid expression and distance and conclude he and Roz were coworkers. Reading Lyndon was a sport for the observant. The micro-millimeter lift of a corner of his lips and his pause before reaching for the poker to stoke the fire told me he was happy to see her. That and the bouquet he'd placed close to her desk.

"Warm enough?" he said.

"Perfect," Roz said, keeping her eyes on him worshipfully. Hot flashes kept her temperature up anyway.

"Rain's getting heavier," he said. "Gutters are clear, and the library is pretty well buttoned up." His heavy eyebrows scrunched together. "I don't like the looks of the river, though."

"The weather forecast says it's supposed to let up later on," Roz said. The clouds rumbled in response.

"A good thing, too," Lyndon said.

"Thanks." I rose from the chair. "I'd better get to work."

"Oh," Lyndon said, slipping the poker back into its rack. Rodney hadn't moved during the whole procedure. "Word down at Darla's is that Sheriff Beattie found a knife at the Sing-Along, just outside the bathroom door. An anonymous call on the tip line led her to it."

"The murder weapon," Roz said. "I knew it had to be somewhere."

"Strangest thing. They found feline saliva on it."

Rodney licked a paw and drew it behind an ear. He was dry now, and I knew his fur would be as warm as fleece pulled from the dryer.

"Cat spit?" I said. "Weird."

CHAPTER THIRTY-THREE

Midafternoon, I set off on foot from the library toward the old mill site. Maybe Tommy could tell me something about the night before at the Sing-Along that would shed light on the murder. He'd spent more time with the Waterses lately than most of us had.

Rain fell steadily, and although I'd learned Pacific Northwesterners scorned umbrellas, I brought mine along anyhow, a plaid collapsible number with a nickel-sized hole in it that I'd found in the library's lost and found box. Today it served me well. Rain pelted even through the forest's canopy where the trees usually sheltered me from the weather.

I hesitated at the edge of the woods and looked over the mill site. A slither of green passed through the corner of my eye, but it might have been the wind in the brush. I steadied my breath.

"Is it all right?" I asked the earth. "May I come in?"

I felt no response, just a steady subterranean grumble.

Taking that as a yes—or, at least, not a no—I emerged from the woods to the mill site's clearing and hurried through the rain to the construction trailer. I rapped on the door.

"Hello?" A space heater hummed inside the tiny trailer.

"Red?" Tommy said.

I pulled down my umbrella and set it near the portable steps. "May I come in?"

Duke stood at a dining table that looked like it converted into a bed at night. He rolled up a large drawing, probably a site map. He didn't seem relaxed and happy, as if he'd been talking about pouring concrete or whatever filled a contractor's heart with glee. No, I'd almost have thought he and Tommy had been arguing.

"Josie. What brings you here?"

I'd prepared this bit. You didn't just walk into a strange man's trailer ready to ply him with questions unless you had cover. I smoothed the water from my denim skirt.

"Last night at the Sing-Along was awful, especially on top of finding Lewis Cruikshank. I'm so sorry you had to be here for that, Tommy. I wanted to see how you were holding up and bring you something to take your mind off the evening."

I held out a hardback copy of *A Solitude of Wolverines*, a thriller featuring a wildlife biologist. My witchy instincts had told me this was the one for him. I had the very barest vibe of other books in the trailer. Besides the thriller, I sensed some kind of machinery manual. That was it.

"Hey," Tommy said. "I was hoping to read this one. How did you know?"

Even Duke looked at me with respect. "She has a reputation."

"Your DVD of *Singin' in the Rain* is overdue, by the way," I said.

"I don't have a library card," Tommy said.

"Don't worry about it. I know where you live." I looked around the tiny trailer. Besides this dining-room-slash-bedroom, the rear of the trailer held a desk, chair, television set, and a bathroom. It was a cozy scene, personal, but the uneasy vibration of the earth beneath us kept me on edge. "If you ever have the yen for a proper bath, just come over to the library. We have a six-foot clawfoot tub."

"I prefer a shower myself, but thank you. Have a seat? Duke was just leaving."

"We weren't really finished—"

"We were finished," Tommy said. "I tell you, I've been building sites like this for twenty years. We're fine."

Duke rose slowly and tucked the plans under an arm. He shrugged on a light jacket. "All right. See you tonight at Darla's?"

Tommy gave him a salute. "For sure."

When the door closed behind Duke, I took his seat at the built-in bench. "I wouldn't mind drying off just a minute before I go back to the library."

"Of course." He picked up the novel I'd brought and read the back. "Thanks again."

"It's no trouble. I'm just sorry you got mixed up in Fiona's death."

Tommy was a solid man—not especially large, but dense—and even in the cold rain he stuck to shorts and sandals. He had the mobile expression and affability of a salesman, but his callused fingers were those of a worker.

"Stuff happens," he said. "I was just glad to be able to help out a bit."

"I don't know how the power cut out."

"Someone must have thrown a circuit breaker," he said. "That would be my guess."

"Wouldn't we have seen him?" I asked.

"Or her."

"Or her," I corrected. "Fiona had a lot of spirit." I tried to find the right words. "I don't suppose you knew her before?"

"Why should I?" He looked genuinely perplexed.

"She was fairly well known. In artist circles, that is," I said. "Los Angeles."

"Not my scene." Tommy shook his head. "Poor lady. Looks like her husband is up for some questioning, but between you and me, he's clean."

"I agree. Besides, he'd left by the time Fiona died." I leaned back. "I heard there's a betting pool at the tavern, and the short odds are on Brett. Why him?"

"First time I saw her was here at the site, when she'd come with that—her assistant. Brad."

"Brett," I said.

"Right. When it turned out the architect knew her, Brett looked like he was going to blow a gasket. I say it was a crime of passion."

"Lewis Cruikshank knew Fiona?"

Tommy shrugged. "Sure. When Brett left, she and Lewis wandered around the site a bit."

"No kidding. Where?"

"I don't know. I had work to do."

We both looked out the aluminum-framed window at

the rain splattering over the mill's cracked foundation and siphoning into the heavy green millpond.

"What are the odds on Ruff and Sita Waters?" I said.

He laid a freckled arm on the table's Formica top. "Three-to-one. Not a long shot, but not the favorite, either—that is, unless new information surfaced."

He looked me squarely in the eyes as he delivered the last part of his statement. I had the feeling his interest was less about the case and more about wondering if he should spread his bets.

"There's been some general talk that they didn't get along," I said.

"Hardly motive for murder." He drummed his fingers on the tabletop. "But then . . . No."

"No, what?" I said.

"Something isn't kosher between them, you have that right."

"What do you mean?"

He placed both palms out in a stop position. "I don't want to say anymore, especially if it would slow getting the project underway. The sheriff knows her business. She'll find the perpetrator, I'm sure."

"What about me?" I asked.

"What about you, what?"

"What are the odds on me?"

Tommy slapped a thigh and guffawed. "The dark horse, huh? No. You're a librarian. No one would put money on you as a murderer."

"The sheriff suspected me," I said. "Briefly, at least." I was starting to feel like I needed to rob a bank or run off with a race car driver or something to add some spice to the librarian reputation.

"Nope. Brett or the Waterses," he said.

Through the window, the millpond, normally the placid home of bullfrogs and kids skipping stones, convulsed with the Kirby's runoff. Only a few days earlier, Lewis Cruikshank's body had surfaced there.

"Speaking of Sita and Ruff, have they hired a new architect yet?" I asked.

"Not yet. I hope they do soon. I've worked a lot of projects over the years, and very few have been trouble-free. But this one?" He sighed and pushed the thriller to the side. "I'm doing everything I can to keep this project rolling, but it's like something bigger than all of us refuses to let it go on."

That night, I left my dinner dishes in the sink and went downstairs with the key I'd found in Natural History.

It was still raining with an intensity that would have qualified as a hurricane back home, had it been windy. I was glad reports forecast it petering out tonight. The relentless storming on the cupola window was a constant reminder of the weather. If this rain kept up, the library risked becoming a Victorian ark and washing down the valley.

Had this room been Marilyn's bedroom? It might have been. It was large and at the front of the house. I clicked on a table lamp. Overhead lights hadn't been added over the years, probably due to a combination of expense and lack of a need, since the library was rarely open after dark. That suited me fine. The pool of light from the glass-shaded lamp felt friendlier, anyway.

"Hello, books," I said and received a chatter of hellos in return.

Now, what would the key open? If it had been Marilyn's, she would have kept the object close, in her room. Now the room held the old desk and a bentwood chair to go with it, two armchairs and a side table near the fireplace, and shelves and shelves of books. At one time, it would have had a bed, dresser, and probably a wardrobe, since the house was too old for closets.

I turned the key in my palm and traced the filigree on its looped top. It could be a key to a wardrobe, in which case it was no good now. Only one of the house's wardrobes had survived, and it was full of office supplies. Every one of its corners had been explored over the years.

I knelt to examine the desk. Could it hold a secret compartment? I pulled out its drawers and examined the bare woodwork. There was no room for anything wider than a slip of paper, and nothing on the sides or backs of the drawers.

Maybe there was a secret compartment in the walls. In Nancy Drew mysteries, it seemed like they larded every other house, along with hidden passageways. The Wilfred mansion was certainly old enough.

I pressed the wainscoting and examined the fireplace for loose bricks and woodwork. I came up dry. Maybe I was completely wrong. After all, once her home had become a library, Marilyn had converted the servants' rooms into an apartment and moved upstairs. If she had something valuable enough to lock away, why would she have hidden it in her old bedroom?

Rodney slipped into the room and rubbed against my legs. Instead of staying near me, as he usually did, he sauntered to the wall at the front of the house and plopped against a bookshelf. He fastened his unblinking gaze on me.

"What? You're too good for me now?"

No grooming, no batting at the wadded-up gum wrapper near him—I'd have to do a better job with cleanup—just a stare.

Then it occurred to me. "Oh no. Not there."

He wanted me to examine either the wall or the floor where he sat. It meant unloading and moving a heavy oak bookcase and possibly peeling up the rug.

I crossed the room and sat down next to him. He purred in response, and his tail flicked the air. I was on the right track. Whatever Marilyn had locked with this key contained stories, I knew it. I held the key and listened.

Up filtered whispering. I heard a girl's voice and a woman's voice, sometimes elated, often sad. I couldn't make out the words, but the feelings came through loud and clear, like hearing radio shows through faraway speakers.

Whatever the key opened, it was right where we sat. I groaned. This wall, without a window and facing the fireplace, was the logical place for a bed. A girl would naturally hide something valuable near where she slept.

"Move, Rodney. We have work to do."

An hour later I had the bookshelf nearly unloaded, and stacks of books surrounded me. I'd also found a love note from the 1980s, from one Tristan to Carrie, hidden on a bottom shelf and apparently never retrieved, plus a few dead pens. I was reaching for *One Hundred Years on the Tundra*, when my phone rang.

I glanced at the screen. Roz. "Hello?"

The clatter and conversation at Darla's played in the background. "You'll never guess what happened."

"What?" It was so quiet and dim here, with nothing but the humming of the books as I worked among them and the rain's steady beat. It was easy to forget about the society just down the hill.

"Tommy Daniels came in. Someone totaled his construction trailer."

CHAPTER THIRTY-FOUR

"Okay," Roz said. "Maybe not completely destroyed."

"Then what?" I said. Judging from the background noise, jaws were flapping at Darla's.

"Vandalized. Someone broke the windows—every single one—and spray-painted 'I see you' on its side. In orange."

Instantly rose the memory of the snake lifting its head, its tongue flickering. "Greed," it had said. Did the curse—or land spirit, whatever it was—strike Tommy, too?

"That's awful. How's he taking it?"

"He's on the tavern side applying beer to his mental wounds. He's a contractor, so I guess he won't have trouble boarding up his windows, but still. Two murders and now this?"

After Roz hung up, I set my phone on the desk and returned to the shelf I'd mostly emptied, but I didn't finish the job right away. Instead, hands on hips, I stared at the stacks of books.

What was going on around here? Greed had certainly motivated Fiona. She'd wanted more money out of Sam. Had greed driven Lewis Cruikshank, too? Tommy had said he'd greeted Fiona as if they knew each other. Maybe he was in on her plan to squeeze money from the Waterses.

I went back to work removing the last few books. I tested the shelf's weight. Even empty, it was heavy. It was going to have to be moved, though, for me to check the wall and pull up the rug.

By rocking the bookshelf back and forth, I was able to hobble it away from the wall. A few pieces of scratch paper and a lot of dust stuck to the wallpaper. I jogged to the bathroom for an old washcloth and wiped it down. I pressed my palms over the cool plaster and felt nothing unusual. No bumps, no areas obviously repaired.

That left the floor. I peeled back the rug to an oak finish still in great condition, thanks to being covered all these years. I pulled over the desk lamp for more light and got on my hands and knees to really examine the floor. Rodney sat next to me.

"Where is it, baby?" I asked him.

He gave me a blank look.

"Thanks a lot."

Then I saw it. The baseboard molding was loose. I pried my fingernails behind the wood and jiggled, then lifted. A section about a foot long came away, exposing where the hardwood flooring met the wall. Cooler air met my fingers as I pried here, too. Maybe the floorboard would come up.

It did. About six inches of flooring lifted, allowing me to feel around between the joists. I tried not to think of spiders and mice. Deciding it was a game, Rodney stuck a paw in after my hand.

"Keep your paws to yourself."

Ah, here was something. I knew by the tingle in my fingers it was a book. I pulled out a diary. I blew dust from its cover and set it aside to feel around some more. By the time I'd plunged my entire arm into the opening, I'd harvested five diaries. None of them were locked, however. They were all notebooks. None of them needed a key.

Could there be anything else hidden beneath the floor? My hair was already full of dust and the strange lint-like matter that accumulates in closed-off spaces over time, but I pulled the desk lamp closer and lay down flat to squeeze an extra inch of arm into the opening. I flailed my fingers back and forth, hoping to get something other than splinters.

Bingo! I touched metal. But I couldn't get enough of it to grab.

I sat up straight and pondered. The poker. I grabbed it from the rack of tools on the hearth and fed it into the opening. I heard it hit metal. Carefully, I felt for an edge. It took three tries, but eventually I succeeded in nudging the object into view. I tipped it on its side and pulled it out.

It was an old metal box about the size of an encyclopedia, and it was locked. Whether it was excitement or exhaustion, I wasn't sure, but my fingers trembled as I fitted the key into the lock's mouth and turned. Even after all these years, the lock worked perfectly.

Inside were a dozen or so letters, all written in the space of two years in the 1920s. All were from Arlene Alber.

Night had long fallen, and I couldn't bear the thought of getting the room back into order. It could wait. I took the diaries and box of letters upstairs and prepared for bed.

Tonight, my nightstand was empty of novels, but two bound volumes of the *Wilfred Searchlight*, too large for the nightstand, leaned by the bed. Curious, I looked at their spines. I'd expected one from the year Arlene Alber had disappeared, but here was another, too, dated five years later. I set the diaries aside for the moment and pulled the first volume of newspapers to the bed. It opened to the article I'd been waiting to read, the one on Arlene Alber's disappearance.

The rain beat on my bedroom windows. Rodney circled and settled on the pillow next to mine.

"Arlene Alber Disappears," the article's title read. It was dated July 2, 1928. A grainy photo of a schoolgirl headed the article. Her chin-length hair was tied back with a fat ribbon, and her eyes were small and dark and expression solemn. The photo looked like it had been separated from a larger family portrait.

Wilfred girl Arlene Alber, 18, daughter of Carl and Zelda Alber, disappeared June 30. She was last seen crossing the bridge to the Thurston Wilfred home after school.

Sheriff Sweet told the Searchlight *that he has questioned business owners and family friends*

*widely without result. The Wilfred town council is
organizing a search of the woods.*

    *Anyone with information is urged to contact
Sheriff Sweet's office directly.*

The article kept to the facts, but the town would have
been whirling with speculation about Arlene. At church,
in the grocery store, at lunch at the mill. The article didn't
mention Marilyn Wilfred, except for the reference to her
house. She would have been twenty-eight years old
then—ten years older than Arlene. What could she have
to do with a teenage girl?

I opened the second volume of newspapers, and its
yellowed pages flipped to one covered in small items. I
let my finger draw the correct article to me. There it was,
a tiny announcement boxed in a thick black line: "Carl
and Zelda Alber request your presence at a memorial service for their daughter, Arlene, who disappeared in 1928.
Her body was never recovered, and it is now time to lay
her to rest."

Mrs. Freeburger remembered this story, even though
she was just a baby when it happened—or possibly not
yet born. Somehow Marilyn had been involved. How?

Turning this over in my mind, I opened the first of
Marilyn's diaries, a schoolgirl's notebook with loose scrawls
nearly too faded to read. The first entry was dated February 10, 1912. Marilyn would have been eleven going on
twelve then. The mill had been in full force, with horses
dragging timber from the forest and peeled logs filling
the millpond. February. Cold and rainy.

    *Dear Mama, I need a friend. My brothers are
too busy to talk to me, and Father is always away.*

*I'm too old to talk to dolls anymore. You died when
I was born, but I will talk to you here. You will be
my friend.*

The entries told of a lonely, perceptive girl who found
solace in books. I could relate to that. She did well in
school but didn't seem to be rewarded for it. The mill-
workers' kids wouldn't include her in their games. Apparently, where Darla's was now, there had been a
pharmacy with a fountain. Marilyn had often sat alone.

Of her family, she hadn't written much. Old man
Thurston was simply called "Father" and appeared in the
pages as a presence at church and too rarely at the dinner
table. Marilyn was friendly with the cook at Big House,
but even there she was shooed away when her eldest
brother thought she hung around too much.

No wonder she'd been seen as an outsider. She'd felt
like an outsider—at least, when she was young.

I'd read through four of the diaries and was as far as
the 1920s when I set them aside. It was three in the morning, and this was my second late night in a row. I yawned
and stacked the diaries and letters on the nightstand and
rested a hand on them to feel Marilyn's spirit, lonely and
loving.

CHAPTER THIRTY-FIVE

When morning came, it was still raining, and now thunder rattled the air. From my kitchen window, through the trees I glimpsed the Kirby River muddy and surging like I'd never seen it. As far as I could tell, the library was holding up well against the storm.

It was Monday, and the library was closed. I was alone. I planned to finish Marilyn's diaries over coffee, then walk down the hill for a leisurely breakfast at Darla's. Plus, I could get the latest on the damage to Tommy Daniels's construction trailer and see if anyone had heard from Ruff and Sita. I still wondered if I should have told the sheriff they'd left town.

For a moment, I considered taking the diaries to my living room and making a fire. Crackling warmth in the hearth would be perfect for a stormy day like this. If I did,

I knew I would be drawn to the window that looked down at Big House. I hadn't seen Sam since the night at the Sing-Along, two days earlier. I refused to be a lovesick woman watching for lit windows or movement behind curtains from a man who was fond of her but never thought of her except as a babysitter and sounding board. No, I'd take the diaries to the conservatory on the other side of the house and spread them out on the table there.

Downstairs, a light was on in the kitchen. Maybe Lyndon was double-checking that the house was sealed up tight. A baby's coo told me it was Sam, with Nicky. Foiled again.

"Good morning." I set the diaries and box of letters on the table. "How are you?"

Such a simple question, but today it was a ladle dipping into a stream of emotion. I watched potential responses come to his lips, then be rejected.

"I'm all right," he said finally. "Considering everything. You?"

"Better than you, I'd guess."

"Thank you for the flowers." Sam held Nicky over a shoulder.

"I'm glad you like them." I walked around to see the baby's face, eyes wide, taking in the room. Poor little guy. "Can I hold Nicky?" I found myself saying.

Sam handed me the warm bundle of baby, and I cradled him where I could see those petal-pink lips and adorable cleft chin. Nicky's fist, which he'd lodged into his mouth, shot up and reached for one of my curls.

"I came over for coffee," Sam said. "We were all out, and I'm not quite ready to face the crowd at Darla's. You don't mind, do you?"

"No, that's fine," I said in a baby voice as I stared at Nicky, which I abruptly cut off when I realized what I was doing. "I mean, that's perfectly fine. Anything new?"

Sam filled the coffeemaker as he talked, and I swayed to rock the baby. "Sheriff Beattie found the knife that killed her." No need to say Fiona's name.

"I heard. On the floor."

He nodded. "Apparently, the murderer shorted out the electricity by sticking a paper clip in an electrical outlet. It flipped the circuit breakers."

"Where was the outlet?" I asked.

"Against the back wall, opposite the bar."

Within easy reach of Ruff and Sita or Tommy. Far from Brett, though. "Would the short have happened right away, or could it have been a delayed reaction?"

"Right away, almost certainly."

"Or, could the paper clip have been a decoy? Maybe the power was shut off another way." Nicky was falling asleep, still gripping my hair in his wet little fist. "I can't figure out how Lewis Cruikshank's and Fiona's deaths could be related." I looked up to see if hearing his wife's name had ruffled Sam, but he appeared lost in thought.

"I know. I've gone over it a hundred times," he said. "All they share is the old mill site and the retreat center. Cruikshank was designing it, and Fiona had threatened to hold it up."

"The architect didn't want to hold it up, though. He was excited to see it built." I bit a lip as I thought it through. *The man in the picture.* The words I'd found during my try at bibliomancy came to mind. That, and Ruff and Sita's midnight exodus. "Maybe Fiona saw the Waterses threatening Lewis Cruikshank. Or worse. She might have used that information to increase her pressure on them, especially once he was killed."

"Why would the Waterses kill their architect?"

"I'm not sure. Not yet."

Wind and rain rattled the windows behind Sam. "I like your creative thinking, but Fiona was always focused on her own world. She wouldn't have noticed anything but light on the millpond or the shape in the opening of the trees."

"She went to the mill site to document it, Sam, not to sketch it," I said quietly but firmly. *Greed*. The vision of the snake was lodged in my mind. "She wanted to make sure she wasn't getting ripped off in the divorce settlement."

Sam continued, "She left for Portland straight from the mill site. Why would she do that if she'd seen something? No, I think she was being Fiona, that's all." He poured himself a cup of coffee. It hadn't taken him long to make himself at home in the library's kitchen, just like everyone else in Wilfred. "I did find out where she stayed. She had a receipt for the Heathman Hotel in her wallet."

The Heathman. A boutique hotel for long dinners and lovers' assignations, yet she hadn't been there with Brett. I remembered Fiona sketching the skull as she talked to me, a skull with *memento mori* written under it.

"Interesting. Did you—did you happen to see Lewis Cruikshank's body?" I asked.

"Yes. I was there when they pulled him out, but I didn't recognize him."

"I heard he had a lot of tattoos. Did he have one of a skull, by chance?"

"He might have," Sam said. "Yes, I think he did. Why?"

Tommy had told me Lewis had greeted Fiona like they'd known each other. I glanced at Nicky. Could it be? I opened my mouth to share this idea with Sam, then closed it again. It might be interesting speculation to me, but for him it could be painful, and I didn't have proof.

"I thought I caught a hint of a tattoo on his arm, that's all."

Sam waited for me to say more. When I didn't, he gestured the mug toward the diaries and metal box. "What are those?"

"They belonged to your aunt Marilyn. The box is full of letters." I handed Nicky, still sleeping, back to him, and our arms touched. My heart beat double-time, but Sam didn't seem to notice.

"I've never seen them before. Were they in the apartment?"

"No, actually. Marilyn had the front bedroom on the house's west side when she was growing up, right?"

"I'm not sure."

"This key fell out of the desk in what I guessed was her room." I showed it to him. "I wondered what it might go to, and last night I found these things hidden under the floor where the bed probably was."

I thought of the mess upstairs. At least the library was closed, and I'd have time to reassemble it.

"How did you know where to find it?"

I tried for a puzzled look. "Just a shot in the dark." I cringed at the expression. Then, to move along, "Have you heard of anyone named Arlene Alber?"

"No. Never. You're full of questions this morning. Did Arlene live in Wilfred?"

"I'm not sure." I topped off my coffee from the pot

Sam had just made and went to the refrigerator to splash in some half-and-half. "The diaries and letters are yours now, if you want them."

"But you want to read them first."

"If you don't mind."

He frowned faintly. He thought my nosiness was funny. "That's fine. You'll tell me the juicy bits, right?"

I laughed. "It's a deal."

CHAPTER THIRTY-SIX

By the time I got to Darla's, I was soaked. The café's windows were damp with condensation, and rain shed from jackets left puddles in the entry.

Everyone was here. Something about natural disasters brought people together, and the past few days of rain, with a couple of murders tossed in, felt like one. Mrs. Garlington and her son were in the booth closest to the counter. Her son was in complete postal rain gear and was fastening his cape around both him and his mail bag. Patty and her grandchildren occupied another booth. Thor's cape was drenched. Patty's sweatshirt read BORN FOR SPEED. No Brett, and, naturally, no Ruff or Sita.

Duke sat at the counter and turned to the door when I entered. He bent over his coffee when he saw me. I took the stool next to him.

"Disappointed it's me?" I asked.

"What will you have today, Josie?" Darla filled my coffee mug.

"You choose," I said. I knew it would be good, whatever it was.

"You're all right," Duke said. "I'm waiting for Tommy. He said he'd meet me here." His plate was nearly empty. He'd been waiting awhile, apparently.

"I heard about the construction trailer. Who could have done that?"

"I have no idea. At least, not officially."

"What does that mean?" I asked.

Duke raised his eyebrows. "It could be that certain property owners have an incentive to do a certain thing to a certain person."

"You're joking," I said, lowering my voice. "The Waterses wouldn't vandalize their own contractor's trailer."

"Wouldn't they? It'd be a way for them to get out of the retreat center. They scare off the builder, they can cancel their contract with him and give up on the whole project. Plus, no one has seen hide nor hair of them since Fiona's murder."

"You really think so?" The image of Sita in her spangled silk caftan wielding a can of spray paint was too ridiculous to take seriously. Yet, Brett had basically accused them of murder, and they were making noises of backing out of the retreat center.

"However, at this very moment, we have a bigger issue." Duke tapped the rolled-up site plans next to his platter.

"What's that?"

"If this rain keeps up, the levee will never hold. The levee goes, and we'll have the Kirby River lapping at our doors."

"You think it would be that bad?"

"The trailer park, the houses south of town, even the café—I wouldn't be surprised if they were all swallowed up. It wouldn't be the first time, you know."

I'd seen photos in the library's archives of horses standing chest-deep in water, their carts of logs nearly submerged. "One of the Wilfreds rebuilt the levee, right?"

"Sure. A century ago. It needs work, and it was my understanding that was step one of the retreat center plans. The county insisted on it."

"They did," I said, remembering the Waterses talking about it. "It's not in the plans, is that what you're saying?" Surely the Waterses weren't that shortsighted.

"Oh, it's in there, all right, but it's not part of Tommy's plans. Something isn't right, and I'm afraid he's being railroaded."

"What do you mean?"

Duke shook his head. Say what you would about him, he took pride in his work. "He hasn't planned for the materials, labor, or time to make that levee right."

"And you think he's being held back. By Ruff and Sita."

"Think it? I know it. We need to have a serious pow-wow before it gets worse. Shoring up the levee is mandatory. We can't cheap out on building materials, either. Tommy agrees. Or at least he will once I've pointed it out to him."

Oh boy.

"Pecan waffles and bacon." Darla slid the platter to me with one hand and moved to the register to cash out Mrs. Garlington's son.

"I'll leave you this seat for Tommy, then. I have to make a call."

I took my plate to the opposite end of the counter. At last I did what I should have done sooner: I dialed Sheriff Beattie's number.

Message left, I looked for a place to settle in for breakfast. I'd asked Sheriff Beattie to meet me at the café as soon as she could.

"Mind if I join you?" I asked Mrs. Garlington. "It's busy in here today."

"Indeed," Mrs. Garlington said. "In fact, I've been wanting to talk with you."

I hoped it wasn't about the sheet music Rodney had been hiding. "How can I help you?"

"Fiona Wilfred may not have been my idea of sterling womanhood," she said, "but she was married to a descendant of the town's founder, and we must do right by her."

"I agree."

"She'll have a service."

"Perhaps you'll write something for it?" I asked, taking her opening.

"Funny you mention it." She snapped open her purse and withdrew a folded piece of lined paper. "I've sketched out a few ideas."

"I'd love to hear them." I kept a receptive expression. Her talk would fill the interminable minutes until the sheriff arrived.

She cleared her throat. "Oh, fairy queen of the sylvan glade with golden falls of song, how we raptured in your—"

I bit off a piece of bacon. The Waterses could be anywhere by now. The sheriff might have asked them to stick around, as she had me, but they weren't legally obligated to stay. They might have taken a flight the next day and were drinking margaritas on a Mexican beach this very moment.

I glanced toward the counter. No Tommy yet. I wouldn't mind checking Duke's assessment of the site plans with him. I closed my eyes in faux appreciation of Mrs. Garlington's literary efforts.

"Josie?"

My eyes flew open, and I sat up so fast I bumped my arm on the table's edge. Sheriff Beattie stood next to me. Mrs. Garlington cut off her epic poem mid-stanza.

"Your call sounded urgent," the sheriff said.

"Excuse me, Mrs. Garlington," I said. "Such a beautiful tribute to Sam's wife."

Mrs. Garlington cast canny eyes at the sheriff, then at me, and closed her notebook. "I'll leave you two to talk."

Sheriff Beattie slid into Mrs. Garlington's place across from me. "What is it?" she said.

"Would you like anything to eat?"

"I have to make this quick. We're investigating two murders, remember."

"Right," I said. "Well, I won't waste your time. I have reason to think Ruff and Sita Waters—one or both—are responsible for the murders."

Her expression was unchanged. "And why is that?"

I leaned forward on my forearms. "Take Lewis Cruikshank. They hated his ideas for the retreat center."

"So, they killed him because they thought his sketch was ugly."

"That's not all. He threatened to keep his retainer if they fired him."

"He did, did he?" She clasped her hands on the table and didn't look overly impressed. "Do you know how much that fee was?"

"No," I admitted.

"I do. It was five thousand dollars."

She stared at me, letting it sink in. From the heat on my neck, I knew I was reddening. "Okay, so that's nothing to kill someone over. But really it's Fiona's death that convinced me."

"You mean because she tried to extort fifty thousand dollars from them?"

"Yes," I said weakly. "How did you know?"

"Sam Wilfred told me, and I verified it with Sita and Ruff. They're more than solvent and could have afforded it, but they had no intention of paying Fiona off, anyway. They consulted an attorney who told them she didn't have a case." The sheriff's phone beeped, and she glanced at the screen. "Is that all?"

"Duke's concerned that the materials they've authorized don't include what's needed to rebuild the levee, even though it's a condition of building on the site. Maybe Lewis Cruikshank found out, so they had to kill him." I was beginning to sound desperate.

"Okay. I'll look into that. Anything else?"

Heartened, I nodded. I'd saved my biggest reveal for last. "Ruff and Sita have disappeared. They cleared out of Wilfred sometime the night of Fiona's murder." The most incriminating evidence of all. Skipping town when you were a murder suspect was as good as hanging a GUILTY sign around your neck.

"I didn't tell them they had to stay in Wilfred. I knew how to get in touch with them."

I leaned forward. "But why would they leave, unless they were guilty? You said they have plenty of money. They might have left the country. Do you have any idea where they are now?"

I lifted my gaze to Sheriff Beattie's, but she was look-ing past me. She waved. "Hello, Mr. and Ms. Waters. We were just talking about you."

My face prickled with heat. I sucked in a breath and turned to the door. Sita was shaking the rain off a Peru-vian wool maxicoat, and Ruff was smoothing water from his beard. They came to our table.

"I hope the drive from Portland wasn't too bad in the rain," the sheriff said. Was that a hint of a smile? "Would you like a seat? I'd better get going." She lifted herself to her full height of five-foot-two. "If any of you see Brett Thornsby, would you let me know? We need to talk to him. It's urgent. No one seems to know where he's gone."

"Glad to see you, Josie," Ruff said once he was seated.

"It's nice to see you, too," I replied, feeling like a solid-gold idiot. Of course the sheriff had checked every angle. Of course she'd know where they were. What had I been thinking? "You went back to Portland?"

"We moved out the night Fiona died and drove home," Sita said. "We just couldn't stay. It was too horrible."

"The look on Fiona's face." Ruff shook his head.

"The sheriff told us it was fine to go," Sita said.

"I see," I said. "But you're back."

Sita and Ruff looked at each other and seemed to come to an agreement.

"We're thinking of giving up the project," Sita said. "When we decided to build the retreat center here, we thought Wilfred was something special. Seeing how peo-ple rallied to save the library when we were considering that location—"

"—it told us this was the right place to make a home.

This was where we belonged. I just don't know anymore," Ruff said. "I just don't see how we can go on."

"Fiona's no longer a problem," I said with hesitation.

"It's not that," Sita said. "I mean, it was—"

"But it's bigger now," Ruff interrupted. "Every time we look, something with the project goes bad. The architect dies, then Fiona—"

"—and something is just plain not right about the land. I can't say what it is," Sita said, "but I feel it."

I looked from wife to husband. "So, you want to throw in the towel? Completely?"

"We've been 'round and 'round on this. We committed to the town, and we don't want to disappoint them," Sita said.

"So we donate the land to the town as a park or something," Ruff said.

"The energy. There's such bad energy there," Sita said. Her bangles tinkled as she pulled a strand of hair behind an ear. "I never felt it before. In fact, it had always felt good. The earth wanted us there."

"I know," Ruff said, the defeat clear in his voice.

If they dropped the project, it would not go over well. The retreat center was to be Wilfred's ticket out of the economic pit left when the mill had shut down. So many people were counting on it. Not just Duke, as the lead contractor's right-hand man, but everyone he'd hire. Plus the new business at Darla's. Plus the bike trail the county was talking of putting in on the old railway line along the river.

"We'd lose what we spent on the land, but it might be worth it," Ruff said.

"The bad energy," Sita repeated.

I couldn't admit that I'd felt it, too. The land spirit—if Lalena was right in her assessment—was not happy.

"It's a shame," Ruff said. "Lewis left a stack of library books in the guest trailer about local tribal culture. They're so inspiring."

I remembered them, with the magazine article about Fiona resting on top.

"We'll return them, of course," Sita said quickly. She shifted her legs, releasing the tinkle of tiny bells. They must be sewn on her hem. Rodney would hate that. "Maybe we could have had a local tribal member design the retreat center. It could have been so wonderful. We could have done so much to heal the world. Aura reading workshops, vegan cooking weekends, music camps."

"I'm worried we'd end up throwing good money after bad," Ruff said.

"We have to decide now," Sita said. "We can't string Tommy and everyone else along." She shook her head, her beaded earrings swinging.

What could I tell them? Even if the retreat center went up without a hitch, would they ever get the bad taste of the past week out of their mouths? Would they ever feel the same connection with Wilfred that they'd had earlier? A retreat center was their lives' dream. It should feel right to them.

I opened my mouth to reassure them if they wanted to pull out, Wilfredians would not be happy but would eventually adjust, when the front door flew open and Lyndon ran to the back counter.

Lyndon never ran anywhere. If he had a family crest, it would have said "slow and steady" under the image of a tortoise. His eyebrows were drawn together, and his

Angela M. Sanders

mouth was set in a firm line. He had a few words with Darla, and her face blanched. She tossed her dish towel to the side and stepped up on a chair.

"Listen here, everyone," she said.

Duke rose and banged a spoon on his water glass. "Hush up, Darla has something to say."

"The Kirby is about to jump its banks, and we don't know how long the levee will hold up."

"Told you," Duke said under his breath.

"Anyone who lives at the Magnolia Rolling Estates and the houses west of the highway, all the way down to the river, had better get out and get out now."

Cries of "no" and gasps went around the room. Chairs scuffed against the linoleum as people rose.

"Lyndon and I are library trustees, and Lyndon talked with Sam. That's three out of five trustees. We're opening up the library if you need a place to stay. The diner is closed as of right this minute." Darla stepped down from the chair. "What are you waiting for? Hurry!"

CHAPTER THIRTY-SEVEN

I ran back up the hill, the rain pounding on me and all around me. In the past hour, the Kirby River had doubled in size.

The library and Big House were safe up on the bluff. My apartment's living room could hold two overnighters on the floor, and ten people could easily bed down in the atrium. Here and there among the stacks, Wilfredians with sleeping bags might find a spot to pass the night. Lyndon had surely thought of this already.

He had. By the time I arrived, he was hauling wooden cots from the basement, cots I hadn't even known were in storage. Sam appeared to be organizing it. Sheriff Beattie lingered a few steps behind him. Embarrassed by my earlier accusation of Ruff and Sita, I stepped out of her line of sight.

"Darla will stay upstairs with you, if you don't mind,"

Sam told me. "She's driving up with supplies from the café—oh, there she is now. The PO Grocery is bringing more, plus first aid kits."

Dripping with rain, Darla hauled in a box of eggs, milk, and bread. "There's more in the car."

"Do you mind helping her?" Sam asked.

He was a different person now. In charge and caring for his family's town. With all the uncertainty that swirled around him, it must have felt good to take control.

I ran out to fetch boxes of supplies to turn the library's kitchen into a commissary.

On Darla's heels, Wilfredians began to arrive. Duke jumped in to help Sam, and I noticed the duffel bag in his hand. Lalena and her terrier mutt, Sailor, were close behind him. Lalena held up a silk bag with a tassel. "Tarot cards," she said. "I'll set up shop in old man Thurston's office, if you don't mind."

Mrs. Garlington came in pulling a suitcase on wheels and holding a pet carrier with a fluffy white cat inside. She lifted a box of electric curlers. "I need to set my hair. I hope the power doesn't blow."

"I thought you were on the other side of town, away from the flood zone," I said.

"Better safe than sorry," she replied. My guess was she didn't want to miss a party.

Still more Wilfredians continued to show up. All the residents of the trailer court were accounted for, including Ruff and Sita, who'd decided not to brave the drive home to Portland.

Within an hour, I counted twenty-five adults, eight children, four cats—not including Rodney—six dogs, and a canary. Plus, someone had set up a chicken coop out front.

I found Sam in Circulation, checking notes. "Hmm?" he said.

"Sam. Have you seen Brett?"

He checked off something on his list and wrote something else down. "No. Why?"

"There's still a murderer on the loose, remember. Sheriff Beattie had mentioned he was missing."

"You're right," he said quietly. The arm holding the checklist dropped to his side. "Sheriff Beattie is staying the night. I'm putting her up at Big House. We'll stay alert."

I wandered from room to room, greeting people and reminding them not to set their sandwiches on the books. In the old dressing room, now the music room, Mrs. Garlington was rolling her hair into curlers. Her suitcase included a fat stack of sheet music. Apparently, tonight would be musical.

"Sam's opening up Big House for overflow," Lyndon said, as he caught me in the atrium. Not that it would matter to him. By bedtime he'd be snug in his cottage with Roz, probably working on a puzzle of "License Plates of the World" or "A Thousand Shattered Teacups" as they tucked into a tofu stir fry.

People seemed to being doing well without me. I'd go upstairs and take a break for a moment, maybe make tea and clear space in the bathroom for Darla's toothbrush. Before I ducked into the service stairwell, I glanced at Marilyn's portrait. I could have sworn she was enjoying the scene.

"Josie?" Ruth Littlewood stood in the atrium, hands on hips. "Why isn't that cat wearing a collar?"

* * *

Escaping Ruth Littlewood, Rodney darted for the service staircase. I followed. My humiliation was still too keen to let me be comfortable hanging out downstairs where I'd bump into Sheriff Beattie.

Up here, the voices and activity in the library were muted. Rodney stretched out on the Victorian sofa. His tail flicked the velvet upholstery. Marilyn's diaries had moved from their box in my bedroom and were now stacked on the side table, waiting for me.

"Okay," I said and clicked on the floor lamp to a rumble of thunder and a surge in the rain's beating. "Got it."

Brett was still missing, but Sam and the sheriff had an eye out for him. The more I thought about it, the more I could imagine him killing Fiona. He loved her, and she didn't return his feelings. He had a quick temper, as I'd learned in Marilyn's old bedroom. He'd likely followed her to Portland when she'd disappeared, but he hadn't found her. Heck, he'd come all the way from Southern California to be near her, yet she hadn't seemed to care one way or another. His jealousy of her prior friendship with Lewis Cruikshank might have driven Brett to kill him, too.

Sheriff Beattie could take care of the hard evidence. I knew that. But maybe I could help with my magic. I still held out hope I could dissolve the curse and ease her work.

If the answer was anywhere, it was in the diaries. Rodney plopped against me and vibrated with a soothing purr that softened the rain's edges. The ruckus downstairs fell away, and even the thunder became merely background noise.

I reached for a diary and picked up where I'd left off.

It was 1926. Marilyn continued to feel out of step with Wilfred. By now she was a young woman, in her mid-twenties. She believed people avoided her, thought she was strange. Maybe they'd simply seen her as the boss's daughter, I thought.

Wilfred's mill continued to run, and old man Thurston had found wider markets for his timber. Marilyn fell in love with an artist, and I flipped through the pages, tracking her hope and joy. The artist had painted her—the portrait downstairs, I realized with a jolt as the past and present snapped together. He'd moved to New York. They wrote, but he never returned, and the letters stopped. My heart ached for her. In these pages of her loose handwriting, I came to know her better. Yes, Marilyn could be moody and cryptic—she mentioned long walks in the woods and quiet hours alone, reading. She couldn't understand her purpose in life. She seemed to feel she was different from other people.

Then she met Arlene Alber.

"Josie?" Darla said from the doorway.

I hadn't even heard her. Somehow the hours had slipped away, and now it was nearly dark. "How are things downstairs?"

"All right, I guess," Darla said. "Thor and Buffy are cleaning up with their card tricks. Pity more than mastery, of course. The bathroom will be getting heavy use. And the rain . . ."

With her suggestion, the sound of rain battering the windowpanes, punctuated with streaks of lightning, woke me from my dream connection to Marilyn's world.

"Any sign of Brett?"

"None. He must be in Forest Grove or Portland or who

knows. How about a bowl of gumbo?" Darla set it on the table in front of me. "I didn't want to disturb your work. What are you reading?"

"Marilyn Wilfred's diaries, if you can believe it," I said. Gosh, I was hungry. I'd missed lunch, and the morel mushrooms in the gumbo—Darla would give it a Pacific Northwest twist—were irresistible.

"No kidding." She straightened, hands on hips. "I'd love to hear about them sometime. I'm going down to feed the masses now."

"Leave the door open, please."

I forked gumbo into my mouth and listened to voices, laughter, and organ music—"You Are My Sunshine" was the current selection. A dog howled along.

Was that Ruff Waters I heard laughing? Yes, and Sita's voice had joined his. Good. At least they were getting a break from their stressful decision-making.

After my gumbo, I'd go down and join the crowd, especially if I could find a room without the sheriff. But for now, I wanted to take a quick look at the letters.

The first letter was dated in 1928 and was postmarked in Chicago. Before I slipped out the letter, I marveled at its two-cent stamp, the same red and white as the Spode eggcup in my kitchen. I glanced at the last page. Yes, it was signed Arlene Alber. The words started to whisper to me. I almost didn't need to look at its pages to know their message. Arlene needed Marilyn's help. She was in desperate straits. She was pregnant.

In a few seconds, I'd absorbed her emotion and her story. She'd met Marilyn while walking along the river trail through the woods. Despite their ten-year difference in age, they became friends. Marilyn had always wanted a sister, and Arlene was desperate for an ally. Her parents ignored her, a situation Marilyn understood all too well. They were strict and fiercely protective.

That spring, Arlene thought she'd found love with a boy who drove one of the logging trucks. She ended up with a pending baby and no husband. If her parents ever found out, she'd be turned out of her home, she knew it. Marilyn gave her money to stay with an old school friend in Chicago and had helped smuggle her to the train station in Portland. A final letter mentioned a baby girl. Arlene had named her Seraphina, after Marilyn's mother.

I didn't need to read on to know what had happened. Arlene and Marilyn had been known to be friends, and Arlene had disappeared. Wagging tongues had attributed it to Marilyn. After all, they'd have said, she'd killed her mother when she was born. She'd stared at her father as he was slaughtered in a freak accident. Now Arlene.

Marilyn could never tell anyone the truth. The secret was Arlene's. I stood and stretched my arms above my head.

I pulled down my arms suddenly. The curse. The curse wasn't on the land at all. It was on Marilyn, and it had been placed there by the damning thoughts of the people of Wilfred. In the same way, it had been lifted. Marilyn's years of giving to the town had dissolved the curse and blessed her. My grandmother's lesson had to do with Marilyn, not with the old mill site at all.

The retreat's land wasn't cursed. An unhappy land spirit inhabited it, and greed was its trigger. The fire and murder when the mill shut down? Sparked by the Wilfreds' greed. Now greed had again enraged the land spirit, and that greed was recent. From what? Fiona was dead now. It couldn't be her greed that had roused the land spirit's ire.

As Mrs. Garlington launched into "Ain't She Sweet" with a particularly lugubrious bass line, the words slipped into my brain: *The man in the picture.*

Fiona wasn't a source of the land spirit's anger. She'd died elsewhere. No, she was a victim of whatever had provoked the land spirit in the first place. She'd seen something, whether she knew it or not. That was why she'd died. It wasn't her own greed that killed her—it was someone else's. It was the man in the picture.

CHAPTER THIRTY-EIGHT

The afternoon she'd disappeared from the mill site, Fiona had seen something that incriminated Lewis Cruikshank's murderer. She'd captured the man in a picture. Earlier, when I'd floated this idea with Sam, he'd dismissed it. At that time, I'd speculated that Fiona had tried to leverage the information for money. Now I realized she had probably not even known what she'd documented. I remembered the pencil I'd found. Had she sketched what she'd seen? No one had mentioned finding a sketch pad.

I skipped down the stairs, switching to the main staircase when I hit the second floor. I paused and scanned the crowd. Where was Sam?

A baby's cry behind me clued me in. I thought it came from the kitchen, but no, Sam was in my office with Nicky in his arms and a bottle on the desk.

"Sam," I said. Another time I would have laid into him for crashing my private office, but I knew why he'd chosen it. With Darla preparing a New Orleans–style feast in the kitchen and dogs yapping in Fiction and Mrs. Garlington on the organ, he needed a peaceful place to feed his son. He wouldn't go to Big House. He'd wanted to be where Marilyn would have been, taking care of Wilfred.

He held the bottle a few inches from Nicky's lips, and the baby batted toward it. "Hi, Josie. I hope you don't mind that I'm here, I—"

"No, that's fine. Listen, when Fiona came home after her disappearance, did she bring her sketch pad? The one she'd used when she was at the mill site?"

He lowered the bottle to the baby's mouth. Nicky closed his eyes and fastened his lips on the nipple as if it were his job. Which, of course, it was.

"No. I have her purse. That's it. We never found her phone, either."

Her phone. Of course. She would have used her phone for photos.

"She didn't leave it in Portland? Brett never mentioned it?"

"No," he said.

At that moment, I knew where the phone was. Where it had to be. The stacking house. The rain filming my office's window reminded me of the surging river outside.

"Any word on the Kirby?"

"You'd have to ask Duke. It doesn't look good, though."

As I rushed through the kitchen to the atrium, I heard Sam's voice calling after me. I didn't have the spare minute to answer.

Duke wasn't in the old sitting room that was now Circulation, nor in old man Thurston's original office, where Lalena gave me the "*don't disturb me now*" look as she laid out tarot cards for a young couple. At last, I found him in the conservatory discussing the finer points of furnace mechanics with Lyndon. The sheriff glanced up from her chair near the tile stove, where she was reading one of Roz's romance novels, a pair of gold reading glasses pushed down her nose. I looked away.

"Duke," I said, nearly out of breath. "How's the river, the levee?"

He shook his head. "The river is at the bursting point. So far, the levee is holding—at least, as far as I can tell from here—but no guarantees. Why?"

I hesitated. I could tell the sheriff about my errand and what I suspected, but what if I was wrong—again? Instead, I smiled in reply and hurried on. Duke's assessment was going to have to be good enough. I circled back to the kitchen and grabbed the jacket I kept just inside my office before dashing out the kitchen door.

"Where are you going?" Darla asked.

"Getting some fresh air."

"Josie, the storm is getting worse," Sam said from my office. "I wouldn't go out there if I were you."

"I'll be back in a minute," I said and grabbed the umbrella behind the door.

Not two yards from the house, my hair was plastered to my skull, and it wouldn't be long before the rain would penetrate my jacket. The umbrella was useless. I tossed it to the side and ran for the cover of the woods.

If I hurried, I could be back within half an hour. I'd be drenched, sure, but it was nothing a good toweling off

and a seat by the fire couldn't cure. Besides, if my con-
clusions were right, I'd have the evidence to pin down
Lewis and Fiona's murderer. If the mill site flooded . . . I
didn't want to think about that. The evidence would be
destroyed.

Dusk was falling, and the storm had darkened the day
enough that I was glad for the flashlight I'd thought to
tuck into my jacket. The Kirby River, normally a lazy
flow of green water with cottonwood fluff waltzing in
slow motion on its surface, now pounded like surf. I
slowed when I reached the woods. Even the trail had become a creek fed by the waterlogged soil.

I continued on, feeling the earth uneasy below me. Un-
like my grandmother, I wasn't usually sensitive to nature.
Books spoke to me, not the landscape. But the energy
here was too strong to ignore. It was angry energy, energy
that had trebled since the last time I'd been here and was
growing stronger every minute.

"Land spirit," I said, my voice barely audible above
the pounding rain and surging river. "I'm here to help.
Whatever—whatever greed angers you, I want to help re-
solve it."

Thunder rumbled through the thickened sky, and the
ground itself seemed to tremble. But no other response.
No snakes this time, no messages.

I'd come to the clearing of the old mill site. Cracks in
the mill's concrete foundation seeped water. The windows on Tommy Daniels's little construction trailer were
boarded over, and a giant "*I see*" still showed in orange
spray paint, with the "*you*" obscured by a blue tarp fastened over the roof. The trailer stood far enough up from
the river to be safe—that is, unless the levee crumbled.
There was no saying what would happen then.

Across the meadow, the Magnolia Rolling Estates' homes perched on cinder-block foundations four feet high, but that would be scant protection if this rain kept up. At least everyone was safe at the library.

As I hurried, I slipped once on the foundation and picked myself up, rubbing the grit off my knees, and ran to the stacking house. Its ground was slick with rainwater, too, and its corners dark and choked with vegetation. I heard the earth chanting in bass tones, a voice more ancient than humankind.

Then, in my periphery, someone ran. I caught only a flash of light blue in the falling darkness. Wasn't that Brett's jacket? I pressed myself against the stacking house's concrete wall and struggled to catch my breath. Whoever it was, I told myself, he was running away. Not toward me. I was safe.

I had no time to dawdle. I hurried to the corner where I'd found Fiona's pencil. It was almost sheltered here. The mossy ground was damp and swollen like a sponge. I looked around once to make sure no one would come up behind me, then reached into a crevice in the wall I'd used so many times. Nothing. I pressed my fingers into its edges, but it was empty.

"No," I said. "It has to be here." I'd been so sure. I dropped to my knees and shined the flashlight over the wall. Could she have stashed her phone somewhere else? The light caught on another recess partially hidden by weeds. I stuck in my whole hand, and my fingers touched cold glass and metal. The missing phone.

As I slid it from its muddy compartment, something else caught my eye. Small, cold, and platinum white with diamonds. Fiona's wedding ring. Understanding enveloped me, and I backed away from the mossy bed. Within seconds, a series of memories flew through my mind. Tommy said Lewis had greeted Fiona like an old friend, and Lewis had told me he'd known a Wilfred. My mistake was in thinking Wilfred was a first name, not a last. The magazine article in the guest trailer about Fiona had been Lewis's, not Russ and Sita's. Fiona's hysterical reaction to Lewis's murder, and her sketch, possibly of one of Lewis's tattoos. And Nicky's cleft chin—just like Lewis's.

Fiona had unexpectedly run into Lewis at the mill site, and, for a moment, they'd resumed their affair. Perhaps they'd arranged to meet back in Portland. They may have even planned to run away together. Fiona had waited for Lewis in the cozy hotel, but he'd never shown up. He couldn't have. He was dead.

This was reason for Brett to have killed both Lewis and Fiona. A crime of passion, as Tommy had implied. But something wasn't right. Something didn't add up. Thunder rumbled, and on its heels, lightning flashed around me, infusing the air with acrid electricity.

Go, the earth whispered. *Leave*.

Chills rippled through my body. You bet I was leaving, and now. It was almost completely dark. No matter. I could find my way home through the woods if I was careful on the slippery trail.

I emerged from the stacking house and had turned to head across the pitted foundation when I heard a deafening roar, a slow-motion explosion of surf.

The levee had broken.

CHAPTER THIRTY-NINE

The river's force pushed forward a wall of water, flattening and spreading around my ankles and surging into the meadow toward the trailer court and town. The entrance to the path back to the library was three feet deep with river and rising. I'd be fine if I could make it as far up the trail as the bluff, but that was no longer possible. What now?

The only way out was to run into the woods west of the mill site—away from town, away from the library—and wait out the storm. Aware all the time that Brett might still be near, I scanned the landscape. My eye caught the construction trailer. It should be high enough to be safe, and it would be more comfortable than passing the night in the forest. As the thought formed in my mind, I was already running through the water toward the trailer.

Breathing so hard I feared my heart would burst, I circled to the back of the trailer. Water lapped at my ankles, but the trailer was sturdily anchored. I prayed it was unlocked, like Russ and Sita's trailer, but knew it wasn't likely. Since it had been vandalized, Tommy would have secured it. But I had to try.

I mounted the three wooden steps to the front door, and before my hand reached the handle, the door opened to Tommy Daniels with a puzzled look on his face. "Red? What are you doing here?"

"The levee broke," I managed to say between gasps. "Can I come in?"

He stepped aside and gestured a welcome. "The levee? No. Can't be." He stepped out and took in the spreading lake around us before shutting the door behind him.

"You didn't know?" The roar, the moans had so crushed me that I was sure everyone north of San Francisco had heard it.

"It's been raining so hard I didn't hear a thing." Tommy had on a baseball cap, brim turned backward, and wore his usual shorts and sandals, although he'd added black cotton socks as a concession to the weather. On a hook on the wall behind him was a black denim jacket, dry. No light blue jacket.

"There's no one else here, is there?" I asked.

He snorted. "Nope. Who'd be out in this weather?"

"Me," I admitted. "I was taking a walk, when, *boom!* I heard the levee give way."

"It likely sounds worse than it is. The millpond probably blew out a section, that's all. We're up high enough to be safe here."

The trailer's windows were boarded over, and an LED lantern lit the papers spread over the built-in table where, if the beer can pushed to the side was evidence, Tommy had been working. Darkness shrouded the rear of the trailer, but I sensed faint book energy. Two books. Some kind of technical manual—for hydraulic pumps, maybe?— and the thriller I'd brought him. I felt its cold mountain weather.

"You were walking in this rain?" he said.

"The library is full of Wilfredians. I had to get some air." He didn't need to know about Fiona's phone. "Night came faster than I'd thought, then the levee." We couldn't see out, and the rain pounded around us as if we were in a tin can under Niagara Falls. "We're safe here, aren't we? The millpond seems to be draining toward town."

He didn't respond at first, and then he smiled, then laughed once. "We'll be safe." He was friendly, even affable, as if he were entertaining a table of cronies at the tavern. "I can't believe it," he said under his breath. "The levee blew out. Now."

"Duke was worried about it. Did he ever catch up with you today?"

"He was looking for me?"

"This morning," I said. "At the café. He had the retreat center plans, and he had questions about stabilizing the levee." I shrugged. "I guess it doesn't matter anymore."

I wondered how long I'd be stranded with Tommy in the trailer. I didn't look forward to a sleeping bag on the floor, and the trailer was cold and damp. I felt another surge of warning from the land spirit. It rose from the earth and vibrated up through the water to send shivers through my bones. Was it my imagination, or did the trailer rock slightly?

Tommy shuffled the construction plans together and set them to the side. "Where is Duke? Maybe I ought to talk with him." His affable tone was gone now.

"Up at the library. Good thing, too." I mentally crossed my fingers that his home's cinder-block foundation was sturdy and tall enough to weather the flood. "I'm surprised he hasn't called."

"He has."

Something in the way he spoke those two words stopped me cold. He didn't want Duke talking about the levee. "It must be expensive to build a levee." Ruff and Sita had committed to the construction—they'd assured me. What if that money was never used as intended—or at all? I watched for Tommy's response.

"Hmm." He stared back at me.

He had gambling debts. It might be easy enough to lay out a plan to appear to strengthen the levee. Cover it with fresh rock, say, but not address its structural integrity. The rest of the money could go in his pocket. Lewis Cruikshank saw the plans. He would have made a fuss about it. Maybe even threatened to go to the Waterses and tell all.

He'd ended up floating in the millpond with his head bashed in.

The stranger Mrs. Garlington had seen. Sam wasn't able to trace the license plate number to an SUV. What if he was a loan shark coming to collect from Tommy? An underworld money lender would take steps to make sure no one could identify him, including using a false license plate. When he'd come up dry with Tommy, he'd returned to vandalize the trailer.

I dropped my hands to my jacket pocket. Fiona's phone was still there. And mine. "I'll call the library and tell them I'm here." I pulled out my phone, and Fiona's slid deeper into my pocket's recesses.

"What's that?" Tommy said.

"What?"

"You have two phones." He leaned across the narrow table, his breath smelling of cheap beer. "I saw you let one slip. One of those was Fiona Wilfred's, wasn't it?" He stepped closer. "What are you really doing here?"

I bolted for the door, only an arm's length away, and pulled it open.

The river swirled dark and vengeful around us. There was no escape.

CHAPTER FORTY

Tommy relaxed into his chair, not even bothering to try to stop me. He didn't have to. The flood lapped at the top step, and the water was too powerful to risk. If I plunged into it, I'd be carried away to my death.

"Shut the door," he said. "And give me the phone."

I closed the door, keeping my back against it. This was as far away from Tommy as I could get, but it was still only a leisurely two steps for him. Now I remembered the detail that had been bothering me. After Fiona disappeared, when I'd asked Tommy if he'd seen Lewis, he said he had, just that morning. That was impossible. By then, Lewis was dead.

"You did it," I said. "You killed Lewis Cruikshank when he figured out you never planned to improve the levee at all. You were going to keep the money."

Tommy didn't reply. He smiled and folded his arms

over his chest. The rain beat against the trailer's metal shell, and the floor beneath us rocked slightly.

"How did Lewis find you out?" I asked.

Tommy shrugged. "He insisted on looking at everything, and when the plans for rebuilding the levee weren't up to his standards, he threatened to tell Ruff and Sita. He wouldn't take my money, either."

Tommy's tone was conversational, as if we were chatting about a basketball game at the tavern. He didn't even bother to deny it. This didn't bode well for me.

"Fiona saw you. Or saw something that could incriminate you. So, you killed her, too."

He didn't move. His smile never even wavered.

"She probably had no idea what she saw. But you killed her anyway."

"Give me the phone," he said. Now his smile vanished.

"Was it gambling debts? That's what got your windows broken, isn't it?"

He stood, and the trailer felt even smaller.

Think, Josie. "You like to gamble, don't you?"

"Why?"

"I have a wager. Or maybe you're not feeling lucky."

Interest flashed in his eyes, and he retook his seat. "I'm listening."

"How about this? I'll put a phone in each hand. Fiona's phone, my phone. You choose one. You choose Fiona's, you keep it. Do what you want. If you choose my phone, I go free."

My phone had a clear, thin case. Fiona's was in a more rugged case, red. Tommy watched me place both phones under sheets from the construction plans. Mimicking Thor, I mixed them up.

"Which one is Fiona's?" Tommy said. "The red or the clear?"

"That's for you to find out." I worked to keep my voice steady. "Do we have a deal?"

I could tell he was tempted. He looked at both sheets of paper, dimly illuminated by the lantern, then at me. He didn't have to take the bet. He could reach over the table and strangle me right now. He didn't need a tire iron or a paper clip to short out the power. As he battled temptation, the seconds seemed to lengthen to hours. The trailer was cold and damp, but I felt perspiration on my forehead.

Books, I willed the two volumes I sensed. *Help me. Anything. Help.*

The books were too slight to be weapons, even if I summoned all my magic to turn them into missiles. What else could they give me?

"That one," Tommy said suddenly, tapping the paper on the left.

Fiona's. He'd chosen Fiona's phone. Channeling Thor and Buffy, I pushed the papers together and slipped out a phone. I wouldn't look at him. "Fine," I said and handed him my phone. "It's Fiona's. There. Take it."

"I won," he said, strangely delighted. "I think I'll take both phones, just to be sure."

I rose and backed toward the front of the trailer. "No. That's not fair. You're a dishonest gambler."

"Ouch, but true."

My breath came quickly. *Help me, books.* I relaxed to let my brain fill with whatever those two books could give me and felt the tingle of magic. An abrupt calm replaced my fear. I gasped as the trailer became a toolshed. I was somewhere else, and, more strangely, I'd become someone else. I was now the wildlife biologist in the thriller. The novel fed me: I knew what I had to do. I grabbed the lantern and switched it off before dropping it behind me. The tiny trailer was now blinding dark.

"You can't get away," he said, raising his voice. For a moment, the trailer came back, and the storm pummeled the tiny trailer. Lightning flashed through the cracks in the boarded-up windows.

He was too right. The trailer was less than twenty feet, front to back, with nowhere to hide. The thriller's prose bored into my brain, and I was once again in a toolshed.

Tommy swung a fist at me—I felt it more than saw it—and I grabbed his hand, using his own momentum to toss him into a wall. The thud shook the trailer and knocked the table's contents to the floor.

What next? I was a librarian, not a prize fighter. Tommy rose and heaved himself at me again. I closed my eyes, seeing the scene from the thriller I needed to play out. I dodged to the side and clung to a wall, letting him stumble and grab the kitchen counter to stabilize himself.

I melded with the novel's heroine and stepped forward, catching Tommy off guard, and smashed my knee into his crotch, following it up with a fist to his solar plexus. As he huffed for air, I drew back and kicked him high. He fell back, and his head cracked against the kitchen counter. My breath came in gasps.

I didn't move. I listened and heard nothing but the pounding rain on the trailer's siding. Tommy was unconscious.

The thriller had saved me so far, but my ordeal wasn't over. The trailer now bobbed, and with a roll, it tipped, boarded windows down. The coatrack toppled, and dishes, tools, and more fell with thuds and clatters. Water seeped up from the cracks in the windows. I fell over, and my head knocked against the wall. Dizzy, I drew myself to standing, a window beneath my feet. The trailer rocked with the flood.

Tommy, still unconscious, slumped sideways. Using a chair for balance, I pulled myself to the edge of the table and opened the door, now directly above me. I grabbed the lantern and clicked it on, praying it would still work. It did. Looping the lantern over an arm, I pulled myself out the door.

Rain surged inside the trailer. The trailer was heavy enough to bob slowly in the current of water, but with the pounding rain, it wouldn't take long before it submerged completely.

I was on the trailer's side, now pointing skyward, the door open next to me. I slammed it shut and grasped its doorknob with one hand and the trailer's slick walls with the other. I didn't know how long I'd be able to hang on. I swiped wet hair from my eyes and couldn't see anything in the night except the jagged bulk of the forest and the deep black river below.

I felt the trailer bump against something hard. We'd floated into the stacking house and were scraping along its side. I grasped the empty frame of a window and swung myself into it, still holding the lantern. The concrete was clammy in my grasp. The trailer bobbed past me, now halfway filled with water and sinking.

All at once, it was strangely quiet. The rain was slowing. Even the earth's growl had softened. I understood. The land spirit had Tommy and was satisfied. I was nearly sacrificed to make it happen, but it had happened. And, against the odds—I choked off a laugh thinking of the bets Tommy might have wagered—I had survived.

From across the old millpond, now absorbed by the ever-widening Kirby River, came the rumble of a diesel engine. It couldn't be a truck, not in this flood. What was it? A hulk boxier than a submarine but too closed off to be a boat chugged toward me.

I waved the lantern and broke into a laugh interspersed with sobs.

It was Duke's M26 Weasel.

CHAPTER FORTY-ONE

Back at the library, Darla pressed a mug of hot tea into my hands and sat me next to the conservatory's tile stove. She'd already made sure I'd changed out of my wet clothes, and she'd toweled down my hair.

Sam took a chair across from me. Roz sat nearby, Nicky sleeping in her lap despite the chaos around us. This was a good baby. I felt the sudden urge to hold something innocent and calm.

"Spill it," Darla said. "I knew something was going on. You should have seen Rodney. He was agitated, kept pacing and pawing at the windows."

"Duke didn't already tell you?" I said. In the hour I'd been home, Duke's voice, louder even than Mrs. Garlington's celebratory rendition of "Anchors Aweigh" regaled Wilfredians with his heroic rescue. I played only a bit role in the story, and it mostly had to do—according to Duke—with flailing and lying limp.

In fact, it had been a heroic rescue, and I didn't begrudge him. Duke had popped up the top of the Weasel and thrown me a musty-smelling rope. Using what strength I had left, I leapt into the water and pulled myself forward, hand over hand, until I was lifted, soaking wet and shivering, into the vehicle by Sam. He tucked a blanket around my shoulders and settled me onto a metal seat naked of any cushioning.

My teeth had chattered. "Tommy Daniels," I'd said. "He's still in there. In the trailer."

"Sit still. Relax. I'm calling the sheriff. She can come get him. He's not going anywhere." He made his call and set down his phone. "How did you get that bump?" He traced a finger over my forehead, sending a combination of thrill and pain through me.

"It has to do with wolverines. Long story," I said.

"Hmm." That was one thing I liked about Sam. He didn't question me. He accepted my crazy statements as a matter of course.

The Weasel putt-putted, spewing diesel fumes, back to the highway, where it crawled up to land and disgorged us. Duke left it in Darla's parking lot, already a few feet deep in water. Poor Darla. The café wouldn't be reopening anytime soon.

Sam and I walked up the hill to the library while Duke fidgeted with the Weasel. The highway was a foot under water, but the Kirby already seemed to be receding. The land spirit had accomplished its goal. I shivered.

"Cold?" Sam said, pulling me near, one arm around me.

"Cold and shaken up." I let myself lean into him. I wanted to cry, but there was no way I would.

Once we'd reached the bridge, we were clear of the flood. I'd arrived at the library as a sodden, wrung-out mess. Darla had instantly taken charge, and now here I was.

"I'll tell you everything," I said to Darla, Roz, and Sam, "but first I want to know how you found me."

"Brett," Sam said. "He burst into the library and demanded to talk to 'whoever was in charge'." Sam's voice was quiet, low.

"Brett? Brett saved me?" I remembered the person I'd seen running from the stacking house. So, it had been him. Maybe he'd been at the mill site remembering Fiona.

"He said he'd seen you at the stacking house, and he'd heard the levee burst. He was afraid you'd be washed away."

I imagined Brett and Sam talking. Their last conversation had ended with Brett accusing him of killing Fiona. Brett had been willing to swallow his pride and make it right.

"Duke was more than happy to press his amphibious military vehicle into service," Sam said.

"Where is Brett?"

"Talking with a sheriff's deputy in the parlor," Sam said.

Rodney strutted in and jumped beside me. I gratefully reached for his purring body. "What's this?" I said, seeing a monstrous blue satin bow on a collar festooned with bells.

"Ruth's work," Darla said. "She won't have him attacking songbirds."

Not that he would. My hand dropped to my pocket to touch Fiona's wedding ring. Then it went to the phone. "Here's Fiona's phone. That's why I went to the mill site, to find it. Tommy killed her because she'd photographed something that incriminated him in Lewis Cruikshank's death."

Sam took the phone and turned it in his hand. He tried to power it up. Dead. "I'll hand this over to the sheriff," he said but didn't move.

"Okay, enough distraction. For us outsiders, tell what happened," Darla said.

I told them how I'd become convinced that Fiona had seen something and maybe unknowingly photographed it. She'd lost her phone. If the phone had still been at the stacking house, where I knew she'd been since I'd found her pencil there, it might have been destroyed in the flood. So, I rushed out to see if my hunch was correct. Then I ended up locked up with Tommy Daniels. And then came Duke and the Weasel.

As I talked, Rodney leapt off my lap and lay by the warm stove. The baby woke up and started to fuss.

"Nicky's hungry. Overdue for bed, too." Sam lifted the baby from Roz's lap. "I'll take him home and drop the phone with the sheriff on the way."

At last, my feet were beginning to warm. My appetite was returning, too. I watched Sam bundle Nicky into his front pack and pull a stocking cap over his black curls, and my heart warmed.

"Josie?" Sam said.

"Hmm?"

"I'm so glad you made it home safely."

Darla tapped me on the shoulder. "Look at Rodney."

He lay on his back, paws up, perfectly relaxed in the warmth of the hearth. On his belly, as carefree as possible, slept a canary, its head tucked under a wing.

"Get that heinous collar off him," I said.

CHAPTER FORTY-TWO

Fiona's funeral was three days later. The church and cemetery lay on the east side of town and had been spared from the flood. Sam had insisted on having her buried in his family's plot.

A nice-sized crowd turned up for the funeral, and if not everyone was a huge fan of Fiona, they respected Sam. Normally after a funeral, people crossed the road to Darla's for an afternoon spread, but the café was still full of silt. Darla said it would be months before she could re-open. The good news was that with the insurance money, she'd be able to build the patio Lewis Cruikshank had sketched for her.

Today, instead of gathering at Darla's, the PO Grocery supplied platters of meat and cheese, and Sam was opening Big House for a post-burial reception.

It was a cool afternoon, but the storm had laundered the sky clean, and sheltered from the wind it was warm enough for me to shrug off my jacket. A dogwood was beginning to leaf out next to one of the stump-shaped Woodmen of the World headstones.

"May we join you?" Ruff said. Sita, swathed in silk shawls, stood at his side.

"Please do." I stood removed from the rest of the mourners. It didn't feel right to be too close. This was an affair for established Wilfredians. I understood why Ruff and Sita might feel the same. "Nice turnout."

"No Brett," Ruff said.

"I'm surprised—yet not," Sita said.

None of us had to respond. Brett hadn't exactly made himself popular in Wilfred, even if he had saved my life.

"There's Sheriff Beattie," Sita said. Meg Beattie, looking like someone's demure aunt in her neat black dress, stood behind Roz. "Darla told me the word was that Sam was on the short list for the open sheriff position."

She and Ruff had caught on quickly to where the grapevine fruited. I'd heard the same, but from Sam. The sheriff was impressed by how he'd mobilized the library during the flood and commandeered the Weasel. He had an interview next week.

"I'm glad you're going on with the retreat center," I said.

"It was funny. During the flood, we spent the evening with everyone at the library and felt so—so part of Wilfred. Then, when we stood above the river and looked down at the mill site, well, it was different somehow."

"Underwater, for one thing," Ruff observed.

"Better energy. In any case, soon that won't be a problem." She looked toward the pastor, who was opening his Bible and pulling out a bookmark. "We'll have a new architect and lead contractor, and this time everything will be checked and double-checked. Wilfred will not flood again."

"Speaking of contractors," Ruff said, "wasn't that strange about Tommy?"

"Really strange," I agreed.

Tommy's body had been pulled from the submerged construction trailer a few hours after my rescue. He was dead. That wasn't the surprise—we didn't expect him to survive the flood. The surprise came when the medical examiner pronounced he'd died not from drowning, but from a snakebite.

Fiona's graveside ceremony was short, and wind blowing hair, people moved toward Big House. I heard Nicky's cry and saw four people instantly surround him, chucking at his chin and offering a bottle. Ruff and Sita joined the mourners, but I held back. I wasn't yet ready to come along. I wandered to the other side of the churchyard to wait until everyone had left.

A scrawny man old enough to be my grandfather but ropy with muscles was resting on his shovel's handle. "Lots of business this week," he said. "The Wilfred lady, and now this."

He pointed a work-gloved hand to a half-dug grave near two others. The Alber plot. I caught my breath and scanned the names.

"Did you know Arlene Alber?" I asked.

"Arlene? Right here. They say the grave's empty,

though. Those are her parents," he said, nodding toward a mossy granite slab for Carl and Zelda Alber. He thrust his shovel into the grave. "This one's for Arlene's daughter. Long story there."

Arlene's body was probably somewhere in Chicago. I hoped she'd lived a full and happy life.

From where we stood, Wilfred probably wasn't all that different from when Marilyn met with Arlene and helped plan her escape. The church would have looked about the same, and the fir trees in the distance would have struck a similar tall green backdrop. The crisp breeze, smelling of conifers and damp, would have been familiar. Family drama was certainly not new.

"Arlene Alber's daughter. She wouldn't be Sarah Free-burger, would she?"

"Yep." He lifted a shovel of black earth and tossed it to the side. "Seraphina Freeburger, the headstone says."

Yes, I thought. Seraphina. "Good luck," I said to him. "And, Sarah, good-bye." Later, I'd bring a plate of brown-ies to set where she rested.

I walked to Fiona's grave. Shortly the gravedigger would return to fill it in. Everyone had left now, and tulips and hothouse gardenias lay on the casket several feet down. A mason jar of daffodils was posed at the grave's edge.

I felt in my pocket for the angular platinum ring I'd picked up at the stacking house. Sam didn't know Fiona had taken it off while she'd held Lewis Cruikshank in the mossy, protected corner.

I dropped the ring in the grave and kicked dirt over it.

I turned to walk home, and movement near the church

caught my eye. Brett stepped forward, his eyes shadowed and his dark hair just beginning to wave where it was long. He'd been here the whole time. We stared at each other a few moments.

In the end, I didn't say a word. I simply waved and made my way up the hill.

Connect with Us

Visit us online at
KensingtonBooks.com
to read more from your favorite authors, see books
by series, view reading group guides, and more.

for sneak peeks, chances to win books and prize packs,
and to share your thoughts with other readers.

facebook.com/kensingtonpublishing
twitter.com/kensingtonbooks

Tell us what you think!

To share your thoughts, submit a review,
or sign up for our eNewsletters, please visit:
KensingtonBooks.com/TellUs.

Grab These Cozy Mysteries
from
Kensington Books

Forget Me Knot Mary Marks	978-0-7582-9205-6	$7.99US/$8.99CAN
Death of a Chocoholic Lee Hollis	978-0-7582-9449-4	$7.99US/$8.99CAN
Green Living Can Be Deadly Staci McLaughlin	978-0-7582-7502-8	$7.99US/$8.99CAN
Death of an Irish Diva Mollie Cox Bryan	978-0-7582-6633-0	$7.99US/$8.99CAN
Board Stiff Annelise Ryan	978-0-7582-7276-8	$7.99US/$8.99CAN
A Biscuit, A Casket Liz Mugavero	978-0-7582-8480-8	$7.99US/$8.99CAN
Boiled Over Barbara Ross	978-0-7582-8687-1	$7.99US/$8.99CAN
Scene of the Climb Kate Dyer-Seeley	978-0-7582-9531-6	$7.99US/$8.99CAN
Deadly Decor Karen Rose Smith	978-0-7582-8486-0	$7.99US/$8.99CAN
To Kill a Matzo Ball Delia Rosen	978-0-7582-8201-9	$7.99US/$8.99CAN

Available Wherever Books Are Sold!

All available as e-books, too!

Visit our website at **www.kensingtonbooks.com**